PRISONER OF THE DALEKS

The Doctor Who *Monster Collection*

Prisoner of the Daleks
Trevor Baxendale

Touched by an Angel
Jonathan Morris

Illegal Alien
Mike Tucker and Robert Perry

Shakedown
Terrance Dicks

The Scales of Injustice
Gary Russell

Sting of the Zygons
Stephen Cole

Corpse Marker
Chris Boucher

The Sands of Time
Justin Richards

THE MONSTER COLLECTION EDITION

PRISONER OF THE DALEKS

TREVOR BAXENDALE

BOOKS

1 3 5 7 9 10 8 6 4 2

First published in 2009 by BBC Books
This edition published in 2014 by BBC Books, an imprint of Ebury Publishing
A Random House Group Company

Doctor Who is a BBC Wales production for BBC One.
Executive producers: Steven Moffat and Brian Minchin

The Random House Group Limited Reg. No. 954009
Addresses for companies within the Random House Group can be found at
www.randomhouse.co.uk

A CIP catalogue record for this book is available from the British Library.

ISBN 978 1 849 90755 2

MIX
Paper from
responsible sources
FSC
www.fsc.org   FSC® C016897

The Random House Group Limited supports the Forest Stewardship Council®
(FSC®), the leading international forest-certification organisation. Our
books carrying the FSC label are printed on FSC®-certified paper. FSC is the
only forest-certification scheme supported by the leading environmental
organisations, including Greenpeace. Our paper procurement policy can be
found at www.randomhouse.co.uk/environment

Editorial director: Albert DePetrillo
Series consultant: Justin Richards
Project editor: Steve Tribe
Cover design: Two Associates © Woodlands Books Ltd, 2014
Production: Alex Goddard

Printed and bound in Great Britain by CPI Group (UK) Ltd, Croydon, CR0 4YY

To buy books by your favourite authors and register for offers,
visit www.randomhouse.co.uk

INTRODUCTION

I loved writing *Prisoner of the Daleks*. It some ways it was the easiest *Doctor Who* book I have ever written.

I didn't think it would be, not at first. When I was asked to do it, the responsibility seemed very great. Daleks! With David Tennant as the Doctor! On his own, with no companions, no reference to the Time War or the ongoing series... Oh, there was so much that could go wrong. I felt flattered – honoured, really – to be asked, because this was the first full-length original *Doctor Who* book to feature the Daleks for a long, long time. But I was being put in a position of trust. I had to get it right.

A bit of background: the book I had to write was to be one of a series of original novels to celebrate and showcase the most famous monsters of *Doctor Who*, to be published in the year of the TV 'specials' – in the fabulously popular Tenth Doctor's final, bravura year.

There were other monsters, of course. But this one was to feature the Daleks, the Doctor's all-time greatest enemy, *Doctor Who*'s premier monster, the one thing besides the Doctor and the TARDIS that *everyone* knows about.

I fully expected to be paralysed with anxiety. Could I think of a good enough story? A killer story that would do the Daleks and the Doctor justice in print? A story that would satisfy both the new fans of the show, and older fans too. Casual readers and loyal readers. It sounded difficult, to say the least.

But it wasn't all that difficult in the end, because the story I'd been waiting to write since I was – ooh, well, since Jon Pertwee was the Doctor – just burst straight out. It was a story that practically wrote itself, with characters I'd never thought of yet but I knew already.

And the Daleks – well, they were a joy to write! They have no redeeming qualities whatsoever. They are pure, they are unrelenting, they are merciless. They are Daleks. Everyone knows what they're like.

I mentioned Jon Pertwee (all right, no one just *mentions* Jon Pertwee – you say the name with reverence). He was the first Doctor I watched as a spindly, impressionable child. Now, as a spindly, impressionable adult, some of his TV stories still loom large in my subconscious. One of them was *Planet of the Daleks* (that was 1973 for those who remember or care). I watched, breathless with fear and apprehension as the Doctor (or 'Doctor Who' as we all thought of him then) was captured and imprisoned in the depths of a Dalek base on the remarkably inhospitable planet of Spiridon. I simply couldn't think of greater danger for the Doctor to be in. He'd been captured! By the Daleks! He was doomed! (I said I was impressionable.)

And then there were the other details from that story – the effect sub-zero temperatures had on the Dalek machines, the band of plucky men and women that helped, or hindered, the Doctor. The incredibly brave companion. All these things had been injected deep into my consciousness and I knew I had to honour them in my Dalek story. At the very least I owed it to my 8-year-old self.

The Dalek interrogation scene from *Day of the Daleks* also took its toll on my young psyche. (It was 1972 – I was even *more* impressionable then.) The Doctor, once again at the total mercy of his arch enemies, strapped to a table, uncharacteristically supine, subjected to his tormentors' worst compulsions. And no one's compulsions are worse than the Daleks'.

Oh yes, I had to have an interrogation scene.

Over the years, other things had also fed into my idea of the perfect Dalek story: I wanted to get *inside* a Dalek, literally and figuratively. There's no better *frisson* of fear, of the abominable, than looking inside a Dalek casing and finding the terrible creature that lives there. It's so deliciously reminiscent of looking for the sort of things that might live under a damp rock. But I didn't want to just *see* it – we all know what the mutant inside looks like now – I wanted to *meet* it. I wanted the Doctor to sit down and talk to a Dalek in its purest form, one to one, undisturbed.

Surprisingly, the Doctor rarely gets to speak with Daleks – he has conversations and arguments with Davros, occasionally, but never with an actual Dalek. They shout at him and try to kill him and he defies them and beats them – but they never stop for a chat. Of course that's largely because Daleks are not great conversationalists in the normal sense. But for my book I needed a Dalek that could hold its own against the Last of the Time Lords, a singular being that had to be a character in its own right. Not the pathetic, dying remnant torn from its casing, but the top dog, the Dalek that *other* Daleks feared.

I had that character in mind – a notorious Dalek inquisitor, called in to interrogate the captured Doctor. It was to be brilliant, malevolent, and very much the Alpha-Dalek. But what could I call it? It needed a name, and Daleks don't really have names (unless they happen to be a member of the exclusive and as-yet-unformed Cult of

Skaro). I didn't want any old name though. It had to mean something. For a long time I referred to this Dalek in my notes as 'Dalek X', hoping I would think of a suitable name later. It took a lot of rumination and staring at those handwritten notes before I realised that the perfect name, the obvious name, was staring me in the face.

You'll meet him in this book and I hope you like him.

I hope you like the other characters too – the rough, tough, space captain Jon Bowman (originally called Archer until I found out that there was another Captain Archer in space…), his crew of misfits and ne'er-do-wells, and the lovely, lively Stella. She was to be the 'guest' assistant for the Doctor, the stand-in for his usual companion while he travelled alone. The Doctor liked her. I liked her. I hope you like her, too. You'll see how she gets on when you read the book.

I'm extremely grateful I had the chance to write this book. I hope I did the Doctor and the Daleks justice in the end.

Trevor Baxendale
October 2013

For Martine, Luke and Konnie – for ever

PROLOGUE

It was a forgotten world.

On the very edge of explored space, the planet resembled little more than a speck of dirt floating between the stars. From the surface of this world, the nearest sun was visible only as a distant blue glow on the horizon. The planet existed in perpetual dusk.

It had once been inhabited by men intent on pushing back the dark boundaries of the universe. The planet had been a useful staging post between the old worlds and the distant, uncharted stars beyond.

The debris of men impatient to be gone littered the dusty surface: empty, prefabricated buildings, corroded machinery, plastic components brittle with neglect. The computers lay dormant, their purpose lost in shadowy, offline sleep.

But even a remote and unremembered place can become important – if only to those who visit.

There was no wind to trouble the dust that had settled over the ages, but, at a secluded point in the middle of the abandoned central structure, a breeze appeared from nowhere. Scrubby little weeds, struggling through the cracks in the paving stones, shivered and withdrew. A sudden, wild noise reverberated from the walls of the surrounding buildings, reaching a crescendo of wheezing and groaning as a tall blue box surged into existence from nowhere.

The TARDIS doors sprang open and the Doctor leapt out, thoroughly annoyed.

'All right! That's it!' he yelled. 'I've had enough. What's got into you?'

The TARDIS made no reply.

The Doctor shoved his hands into his pockets and thrust out his bottom lip. 'You've been acting all funny since we left Earth. What's the matter? Bit of grit in the old dimensional stabilisers? Broken sprocket on the relative time filter?'

Still no reply.

The Doctor sighed. 'You're costing me a fortune in repairs, you are. How can I be expected to run a classic TARDIS if it keeps jumping time tracks every time it lands?'

Gradually, the Doctor seemed to become aware of his surroundings, as if the silence had politely, and impossibly, cleared its throat.

He turned on his heel. His canvas trainers were already covered in dust. He let his gaze wander around the empty buildings and crumbling machinery and then sniffed. 'So where are we?' he wondered aloud. 'And is there really any point in talking to myself?'

He shot a black look at the TARDIS and then closed and locked the door. 'You can't even bring me anywhere interesting any more,' he grumbled. Then he relaxed a little and smiled, giving the police box an affectionate pat. 'Who am I trying to kid? There's always *something* interesting…'

He wandered down a path between two prefabs and called out 'Hello!' a few times. 'Anyone home?'

There was no reply.

'Hello!' he called again. His voice came back to him in a

mocking echo. Above him, beyond a thin grey mist, was nothing but deep space and a distant neutron star.

'Brrr,' he said, wishing he had stopped to collect his coat before leaving the TARDIS. He trudged on until he found a steel podium, pitted with corrosion, supporting an old, scratched monitor screen. He pressed a few buttons on the keyboard but nothing happened. He tried giving it a whack with the flat of his hand, but it still wouldn't respond.

The sonic screwdriver broke through the computer terminal's dormant status in seconds. A minute later, the Doctor's face was bathed in a cool light as the screen activated. A rather fuzzy graphic swirled into focus:

WELCOME TO LODESTAR STATION 479.

'Well, thank you very much,' replied the Doctor. 'Lovely to be here. Not.'

He put on his glasses and started scrolling through the data.

'Ah, now that's interesting,' he said, smiling and nodding. 'No wonder this place is deserted. No one's been here for, ooh, absolutely *yonks*. No need for a refuelling station in this part of space any more, is there? And here's poor little you, the computer interface, all forgotten and alone.'

He used the sonic screwdriver to delve a little deeper into the computer's databanks. 'Blimey, what's been going on in here, then? Your independent sub-routines have been messed around a bit, haven't they?'

Frowning, the Doctor glanced around for the nearest doorway. 'I'd better check your operational hard drive's not corrupted,' he muttered. 'Wouldn't do for a place like this to go haywire. You'd have the Health and Safety department of the Shadow Proclamation down on you like a ton of bricks.'

The screwdriver made short work of the door and the Doctor went inside. It was cold and smelled of metal and oil. He was reminded of old, forgotten refineries on Earth; places full of the hard edges and unforgiving angles of brutal practicality. He found a stairwell and trotted down the steps, the metalwork rattling under his plimsolls.

He hooked out a pencil torch from his pocket and switched it on. The beam found walls studded with rivets and disused electrical cable. It was colder down here and there were cobwebs hanging thickly in the shadows. The Doctor brushed some aside, surprising a number of arachnid life forms that immediately ran for cover, their spindly legs skittering across the ceiling. He avoided some of the larger webs; he'd got on the wrong side of enough spiders in his life to know when to keep clear.

Further down, he reached a bare corridor with a concrete floor covered in debris and grime. His torchlight roved the area until it found a sign saying:

COMPUTER DATA CORE
NO UNAUTHORISED ACCESS

The access door was locked but it didn't take long to pick it. The sonic screwdriver proved to be all the authorisation he needed.

'That's odd,' the Doctor said aloud. His voice sounded flat in the confined space beyond. There didn't appear to be any computer terminals in here, and certainly no sign of any data core.

Something lying on the floor caught his attention. It was white and smooth; half-hidden in what looked like a pile of laundry. The torchlight gleamed on bone and in that instant the Doctor recognised the shape as a human body, curled up against the opposite wall. It was a complete skeleton, held together by the last remnants of dried skin. It was wearing the remains of a one-piece overall, the decaying fabric tucked into cracked plastic boots.

The Doctor knelt down and inspected the body but there was no way of identifying it. 'What were you doing here, then?' he wondered grimly. 'Same as me, probably. Sticking your nose in where it doesn't belong…'

The door shut behind him with a loud clang.

The Doctor jumped up and tried to open it, but it was locked. He tried the sonic screwdriver again but it was no use. 'Deadlock sealed *and* rusted,' he muttered ruefully. 'It's just not my lucky day, is it?'

He stepped away from the door and checked the cell – because that's what it had suddenly become – for any other way out. Of course there was none. He was trapped in here, alone but for the emaciated corpse on the floor. No way out and no one to know, or care, that he was here.

'Nice one, Doctor,' he congratulated himself. 'Now all you can do is sit and wait. Someone must have programmed the door to shut like that. They'll have to come and inspect their trap sometime, see if they've caught anything.'

He stared mournfully at the skeleton. 'Any time soon…'

CHAPTER
ONE

'Don't be such a baby,' said Stella.

Scrum tried to pull his arm away, but Stella had a good grip on it. 'Ow! I'm not a baby! Ow! Ow! Ow!'

She dabbed the antiseptic wipe against the wound and then smiled brightly at him. 'There you are – all done.'

Scrum withdrew his hand slowly, almost disbelievingly. The gash on his forearm looked sore but clean. 'Isn't there anything else you can do?'

'Amputation?' Stella suggested archly.

'I mean *really*. It hurts, you know…'

Stella rolled her eyes. 'How about a cryo-charge?'

'What does that do?'

'Lowers your body temperature to absolute zero in about half a second. Literally freezes you on the spot. We take you back to a planet where there are proper hospital facilities and they thaw you out and treat you.' She smiled. 'Don't look so worried, Scrum, I'm only kidding. I wouldn't waste a cryo-charge on a great oaf like you. They're for emergencies only.'

'OK. You win.'

'Here.' Stella tossed a plastic-wrapped bandage at him and it bounced off his head. 'Last of the field dressings. All yours, big boy.'

'Don't make fun of me,' Scrum said. 'I'm not combat trained. I don't even like fighting. I'm a computer technician, not a soldier.'

They were sitting in the tiny medical compartment of the ship – it was too small to call it a sickbay. It was just big enough to hold a narrow bunk, some computers, stores, and a swivel chair for Stella. She spun round and picked up her bottle of water. 'You were lucky not to lose your arm,' she told him, taking a drink. 'A couple of centimetres either way and you'd be doing your computer programming one-handed.'

Scrum looked forlornly at his arm and then tore open the field dressing with his teeth. He seemed to have shrunk even more than usual. He was short, a bit overweight, with sad eyes and lank, prematurely grey hair tied back in a stubby ponytail. The tip was dyed green, the only remnant of an effort, long ago, to make himself look more 'interesting' to women.

Stella put her water down. 'What's up? C'mon, you can tell me.'

'I nearly got us all killed back there,' he said quietly. He looked up at her. 'It wasn't even a proper mission. It was just a stupid bandit trap and I nearly got us all killed.'

'Forget it. You're alive and we're alive and that's all that counts. Like I said, you were lucky. We're always lucky.'

He sighed. 'Some day our luck will run out.'

'We can make our own luck. Come on, let's get something to eat.' She led the way down the narrow passageway to the galley.

Scrum followed, pressing the bandage into position. 'Bowman doesn't believe in luck. He won't see it that way.'

'Leave Bowman to me,' Stella advised.

A tall, dark, muscular man in combat fatigues was doing pull-ups in the galley, hanging from a duct running across the ceiling that bent and creaked under his weight. He broke into a wide grin when he saw Stella and Scrum.

'Hey! How goes it, my friends? How's the walkin' wounded?'

'I'll live,' said Scrum, forcing a smile. 'Apparently.'

Stella slumped into another chair and scooped her black hair up into a scruffy topknot, tying it off with a rubber band. 'We're seriously low on stores, Cuttin' Edge. I'm down to using some old antiseptic wipes because I haven't even got any bactoray. We're going to have to stop soon and pick up some provisions.'

Cuttin' Edge dropped lightly to the deck. 'Man, that ain't gonna be easy. We're in deep space, right near the border.'

'I'm going to have to put it to the captain.'

Cuttin' Edge wiped his neck with a towel and grinned. 'Hey, rather you than me, babe.'

Stella paused outside the entrance to Bowman's cabin. It wasn't very often the crew called on the captain. She took a deep breath and opened the door. 'Sorry to disturb you, skipper...'

Jon Bowman dismissed the apology with a single movement of one finger. He was a big man in every sense of the word: tall, broad shouldered, a body toned and hardened by decades of combat. His face looked as though it had been hewn from a single piece of granite, deep-set eyes burning beneath a jutting brow, a slightly broken nose above thin, straight lips. His dark hair was unkempt, streaked with grey now, tied back with an old, blood-red bandana.

'Ship's damaged,' he said without preamble. His voice was a deep, masculine growl. He never had to raise it to be heard and he never wasted a word. 'Pirates blew a hole in one of the aft fuel tanks. We're going to have to stop for repairs.'

Stella breathed a quiet sigh of relief. What was it she had told Scrum about being lucky? 'Any suggestions on where?' she asked.

Bowman sat forward in his chair. He had a small desk, cluttered with old pieces of equipment, weapons, monitors, charts. There was a small 3D holopicture of a young man and a woman, grinning at the camera, their arms wrapped around a lanky, dark-haired teenager with a broken nose. He was smiling too. Stella liked to think this was the young Jon Bowman, a lifetime ago, with his parents. But had he ever smiled? Stella never dared to ask.

Bowman tapped one of the chart screens on his desk. He moved the holopicture aside to give him more room. 'We're in the Kappa Galanga sector. There's nothing here – except pirates – and the very edge of Earth space. We're twenty light years from the nearest habitable star system, forty from what you might call civilisation. We don't have enough fuel left for either.'

Stella frowned, peering at the charts. 'So…?'

Bowman pointed to a single point of light on the map with one thick finger. 'There's only one option. This place. Small, forgotten, not even listed on some recent charts, but it's within range. Used to be a frontier staging world, so it's probably got what we need.'

'It's right on the border,' noted Stella cautiously.

Bowman looked up at her. His grey eyes were as cold as steel. 'I didn't say it wasn't risky.'

'But you did say it's our only option.'

'That's right.'

Stella looked closer, reading the name attached to the tiny planet. 'Hurala. Sounds lovely.'

'It won't be.'

*

10

The *Wayfarer* was a converted naval patrol ship that had been rescued from scrap twenty years before Bowman got hold of it. It had been refitted more times than any one of its current crew could guess, and certainly more times than the entries in its log book showed. The interior of the ship had evolved in accordance with the needs of its various crews over the years, but it remained cramped and claustrophobic. As the *Wayfarer* came in to land on the planet Hurala, Stella grew ever more desperate to get out and get some fresh air. She was starting to feel trapped. She leant over the back of the pilot's seat, peering over Cuttin' Edge's shoulder at the craggy, brown surface of the planet as it sped beneath.

'Spaceport,' said Scrum, tapping one of the displays on the flight console. 'Twenty kliks north-west.'

Cuttin' Edge brought the ship down on one of the small landing pads situated on the perimeter. The buildings were little more than rusting hulks, and there were no other ships in sight.

'It's actually an old refuelling station,' Scrum explained. 'This kind of place was fully automated anyway. As long as there's still some juice in the tanks we can fill up and be on our way.'

'OK,' said Bowman. His voice rumbled quietly from the rear of the flight cabin. 'Let's get this done. I don't have to remind you guys that we're right on the edge of human space. There's nothing and no one here, but I don't want to hang around and risk attracting any unnecessary attention. One hour's shore leave and then we go.'

They filed out of the ship, stretching and yawning.

Scrum was holding a portable scanner. 'Let's see if this thing can find the nearest astronic fuel terminal.'

'Oh, man,' said Cuttin' Edge. 'It feels good to just *walk*.' He strode purposefully to the rim of the landing pad. 'Reckon we can get anything to eat around here?'

'Depends on whether they left food behind when they abandoned the place,' said Scrum, concentrating on his scanner. 'And whether they left it in a stasis field. They probably switched them all off, and that accounts for the pong.'

'Nuts,' said Cuttin' Edge. 'I'm gonna take a look. Comin', bro?'

Scrum nodded, still looking down at the scanner display, and set off after his friend.

Stella watched them go with a smile. They made an unusual pair, complete opposites but the best of mates. Stella wondered what it must be like to have a good friend, someone you could rely on, share secrets with, even share a life with. The crew of the *Wayfarer* were her friends, but they were also colleagues. Something inside her longed for more, for a better life. She just didn't know how to find it.

'Doesn't do to think,' growled Bowman.

'It's this place,' Stella said. 'So silent and forgotten. It reeks of death.'

'What put you in such a good mood?'

She sighed. 'Maybe I need a break.'

'You sure that's all you need?' Bowman asked. 'I know you only joined up short term. If you want to go, then go.'

'Why, captain, I do believe you have a heart after all.'

'Who, me? Forget it.'

Someone moved into view behind Bowman, stalking across the concrete from the *Wayfarer* like a panther. Koral was tall, tawny like a lioness with bright, burning eyes. She wore supple, natural buckskins and leather boots.

She was humanoid, but sometimes seemed more like an animal – powerful, predatory, slightly aloof. Stella still wasn't certain exactly what Koral's relationship was with Bowman, but she seemed to act like some sort of personal bodyguard.

Koral whispered something to Bowman. When she spoke, Stella glimpsed sharp, white fangs.

'It's OK,' Bowman said quietly. He always spoke softly to Koral. 'We're only staying for a short time.'

Koral nodded and moved away, as indifferent to Stella and the rest of her surroundings as a cat.

'What's up with her?' Stella asked.

'She wants to know why everyone's so nervous,' Bowman said. 'Says she can smell the sweat.'

'It's the life we lead, I suppose.'

'That, and the fact that this place is so … wrong.'

'Wrong?'

Bowman nodded. 'It's empty. Abandoned. A corpse of a world. Like you said, it reeks of death.'

Stella shivered. And then they both heard a cry – Cuttin' Edge's voice, calling them from some way off. 'Hey! Dudes, over here. You gotta see this!'

They found Cuttin' Edge at a small intersection between the old prefab buildings. Scrum was standing to one side, busy taking readings with his scanner, moving the device around for a better signal. Koral paced the area, looking this way and that for any sign of danger.

Cuttin' Edge was excited. 'Well? What do ya think?'

He gestured theatrically at a tall blue box with panelled sides and small, frosted windows set high up on a pair of double doors. A sign across the top read:

POLICE PUBLIC CALL BOX

'What is it?' asked Stella, unimpressed. It was odd, but not spectacular.

'My guess is it's a police public call box,' said Scrum drily.

'Police?' echoed Cuttin' Edge. 'What the hell is "police"?'

'Old-fashioned word for law enforcement,' said Bowman.

'Then what's it doin' out here?' Cuttin' Edge wondered. 'Ain't no law around these parts, and that's for sure.'

'Maybe it was put here years ago,' suggested Stella.

'And they left the lights on?' Cuttin' Edge rested the palm of one hand against the side of the object. 'Hey – it's hummin'.'

Stella had walked right around the box. She tried the door but it was locked.

'Well, it's weird,' said Bowman, 'but it isn't what we're here for. Scrum, have you found anything we can use yet? There must be some fuel left in the tanks somewhere.'

'Oh, there is,' Scrum confirmed. 'But I'm picking up other readings too. The scanner shows that the automated computer system is still running. Refuelling shouldn't be a problem. But the computers are using a strange signal code, one I can't properly identify.'

'Does it matter?'

'Well, no, not really. Except for one thing: I'm picking up another, equally unusual signal from deep underground. Almost directly beneath us, in fact…'

Bowman frowned. 'What kind of signal?'

'It's some kind of reverberation. A knock, or a tap, only it isn't mechanical. We can't hear it, of course, but if I isolate the vibrations and enhance the audio signal…' Scrum fiddled with the controls on his scanner, and suddenly the air was full of a hiss of white noise and a strange, rhythmic tap of metal on metal. And it kept repeating itself:

Tap. Tap. Tap. Tap-tap-tap. Tap. Tap. Tap.

'Unbelievable,' whispered Scrum after they had all listened to it several times. 'It can't be...'

'Can't be what?' asked Bowman.

Scrum seemed awestruck. 'Well, it barely seems possible...'

'Spit it out, dude,' said Cuttin' Edge.

Scrum licked his dry lips. 'Thousands of years ago, way back on Earth, long before there was any space travel, a man called Morse invented a code that could be signalled by short and long sounds – dots and dashes – to represent every letter of the alphabet. Three dots and three dashes, followed by another three dots, spells SOS.'

'It's a cry for help,' said Stella.

They traced the signal quickly enough. Koral was left guarding the entrance while the others descended several levels beneath the spaceport via a series of rattling metal staircases.

'This whole complex extends far underground,' explained Scrum as they went. 'The refuelling silos must have been *huge*.'

'They needed them in those days,' said Bowman.

Eventually they reached a small corridor lined with doors and a number of computer terminals. Scrum traced the SOS signal to a heavy-looking door marked with warning signs.

'Shh,' ordered Bowman. 'Listen.'

They could all hear the tapping now – faint but distinct – through the metal door.

'I wonder how long they've been stuck down here?' Stella said.

'Wait a sec,' said Cuttin' Edge. He had stepped back a little, to give him room to unsling his gun. All of them were armed, but only Cuttin' Edge had brought an assault rifle.

'Do you think that's necessary?' asked Stella.

'Hell, we don't know anythin'. We don't know what's behind that door. But we do know this is pirate country.'

'You think it's a pirate in there?'

'Or something worse. A mutant, maybe. Or a plague victim. Could be the "police" locked up whatever it is in there for a good reason.'

'And it knows Morse code?' queried Stella.

The tapping had continued all the while, completely oblivious to the discussion.

'Could be a trick.' Cuttin' Edge cocked his gun and took aim at the door. 'We just gotta be careful, that's all I'm sayin'.'

Bowman drew his own blaster pistol. 'Only one way to find out. Get that door open, Scrum.'

Scrum started work on the small control panel next to the door.

'Here's that other strange signal again,' he said, frowning. 'Like the computer's working on a different system to the original design. The door's been deadlock sealed. But I should be able to override it... aha!'

The control panel bleeped and, somewhere deep inside the door, heavy metal bolts slowly withdrew.

They all moved back to allow a clear field of fire as the door slid open.

Sitting on the opposite side of the tiny cell behind was a man in a brown pinstriped suit. He was holding a teaspoon. He looked up at the people gathered in the doorway and, despite the guns trained directly on him, broke into a huge grin that lit up his face.

'Hello!' he said cheerfully.

CHAPTER
TWO

'Who the hell are you?' Bowman's voice sounded like the distant thunder of an approaching storm, but the man in the cell didn't seem bothered.

'I'm the Doctor!' he announced, standing up. He was remarkably tall and thin, with dark, spiky hair and darting eyes.

There was a loud click as Bowman cocked his blaster pistol. The muzzle was trained on a spot right between the Doctor's eyes. 'What are you doing in here?'

The Doctor looked quickly around the bare cell, almost as if he was a child caught pilfering from the larder. 'Nothing!' he said. 'Well, I *say* nothing. I've been sitting on my backside tapping out an SOS and waiting for someone to turn up. But apart from that, nothing.'

'How long have you been here?' asked Stella.

'Oh, ages. Absolutely ages. Well, five days, fourteen hours and twenty-seven minutes, actually, but who's counting?'

Stella gazed around the cell, utterly confused. '*Five days...?*'

'Yeah, I'm starving. You haven't got anything to eat, have you? And a cup of tea would go down an absolute treat.' He beamed and winked at her.

'Stop talking!' ordered Bowman. 'Cuttin' Edge – search him.'

Cuttin' Edge slung his rifle and moved in, knocking the

19

Doctor's arms up out of the way and expertly frisking him. His suit was pretty tight fitting, Stella couldn't help but notice, and it would be difficult to conceal any fancy weaponry. In fact, he didn't seem to have anything on him except the teaspoon, a pencil torch, a pair of old-fashioned thick-rimmed spectacles, a wallet and some kind of cylindrical device with a blue light at one end.

'What's this?' asked Bowman, holding up the device.

'Sonic screwdriver.'

'Huh.' Bowman tossed the screwdriver back and the Doctor returned it to his pockets, along with all the other items except for the wallet.

'Here's his ID,' said Cuttin' Edge, flicking open the wallet. He paused and frowned. 'Says he's a *pirate*.'

'What? Give me that,' said Bowman, taking the wallet. He flipped it open and looked. 'Don't be an idiot. It says he's a…' The captain hesitated, squinting, turning the wallet around so that he could hold it up the light better. 'He's a… What does it say? I can't make it out.'

He gave the wallet to Stella. She opened it, looked up at the Doctor, then looked at the wallet again. 'It doesn't say anything. It's blank.'

The Doctor gently took the wallet from her and slipped it into a pocket. He was smiling at her, almost admiringly.

Stella felt herself start to redden and said, 'You can't have been down here that long. You're still clean shaven.'

The Doctor rubbed his chin experimentally. 'Well, yeah… but you wouldn't believe the concentration it takes not to grow a beard for that long. It's going to itch like mad later on.'

'OK, that's enough,' said Bowman. 'I don't know what the hell you're doing here, Doctor whoever you are, but

I can't afford to hang around on this dump any longer.' He turned away, losing interest, and spoke to Scrum. 'Get back to the ship and start refuelling. I want us off this rock PDQ.'

Scrum nodded and turned to leave. Then he said, 'What about the signal, skipper?'

'What signal?'

'The extra signal the computer's using.'

'Not interested. It's nothing to do with us. Now get going.'

Scrum left, and Stella saw the Doctor watch him go with a sharply quizzical look in his eyes. Bowman ordered Cuttin' Edge to check the area for provisions and, glaring sullenly at the Doctor, he left as well.

'Scrum has a point, you know,' Stella said to Bowman. 'None of this makes sense. Why's this guy been locked up down here? Who locked him up?'

'You know, that's the first intelligent question anyone has asked,' said the Doctor brightly. 'What's your name?'

'Stella.'

'Well, you know what, Stella? I'd quite like to know who locked me up as well. Because until you lot arrived, I thought I was the only person on this planet.'

'What brought you here?' asked Bowman. He was watching the Doctor suspiciously all the time.

'I'm not sure. My ship got dragged off course.' The Doctor's cheery demeanour had suddenly been replaced by a thoughtful frown. 'There's something going on here that really isn't right.'

'Could it be something to do with that rogue computer signal Scrum was talking about?' wondered Stella.

'Let's have a look, shall we?' The Doctor stepped past her to get to the computer terminal, pulling out his spectacles. He switched the machine on and the display screen lit up:

WELCOME TO LODESTAR STATION 479

'Yeah, yeah, done all that.' He flicked through to another screen:

HURALA – GATEWAY TO THE STARS

'What does that mean?' Stella asked.

The Doctor pulled a face. 'Not much. These places were just stopping-off points for people on their way to more interesting places. Look, here's a list of the nearest planets: Klechton – pretty dull, that one, to be honest. Jalian 17 – all right for a party if that's your thing. Tenten 10 – the Decimal Planet. Blenhorm Ogin – never heard of it…'

'Oh!' exclaimed Stella, pointing. 'Look! Arkheon! I've heard of that! They used to call it the Planet of Ghosts.'

'Oh yeah,' said the Doctor, nodding enthusiastically. 'Always wanted to go there, never did get round to it. Think I did the London Dungeon instead. Or was it Madame Tussauds?'

'Can we get a move on?' snapped Bowman impatiently.

'Nearly there,' said the Doctor. Soon the little screen was filling up with more technical information. 'Now then… This is the baseline program for the refuelling station. It's fairly standard, but it's been dormant for years. It's activated again now, though – has been since I arrived. And *that* seems to have kicked off another program, something buried deep in the main server. Let's see if I can drill down…' He took out his sonic screwdriver and aimed it at the computer. '*Bingo!*' he suddenly yelled, making Stella jump and Bowman glare murderously at him.

'What is it?' asked Stella.

The Doctor tapped the screen. 'Oh, that's good, that is. Look – an override system. It's a new program, bolted on. When it's activated – like now – it assumes total control of the entire base. No one locked me in that cell. It did it automatically. The base sensed I was in there and sprang the trap. Bang! Clever!'

Stella frowned. 'But why? What for?'

The Doctor grinned. 'Aww, you ask all the right questions, don't you?'

'Well, here's another good question for you,' growled Bowman. 'What about that other poor guy in the cell?'

The Doctor looked sadly at the skeleton lying on the floor. 'I'm not sure. Possibly the same thing happened to him, but he wasn't as lucky as me.'

'You can say that again.'

'Or,' suggested Stella, 'perhaps he was one of the people who installed the override system. Well, someone must have done it. Maybe he got caught in his own trap.'

The Doctor's face darkened. 'Or maybe he was expendable.'

'Dead men tell no tales,' said Bowman grimly.

'Exactly.'

Stella shivered. 'But why? What's it for?'

'There you go again,' said the Doctor. 'Asking all the right questions at all the right times. Keep 'em coming.'

'You like questions?'

'Love 'em! But you know what I like more than a good question? A good answer.' The Doctor looked expectantly at her and Bowman. 'Got any?'

They both shook their heads.

'Ah well, can't have everything I s'pose.' The Doctor turned back to the computer terminal and went to work again. 'Maybe I can isolate the new program from here.'

'Do you need to?' asked Bowman.

'The trap was sprung when I went in that cell, and the computer's sending a signal to alert someone. Your pal Scrum found it – but I wonder who it's meant for?'

'You mean whoever set the trap?' asked Stella.

'Got it in one.' The Doctor adjusted a control and they heard a strange, crackling signal repeating over and over.

'Not Morse code again,' said Bowman.

'No, far too complex.' The Doctor screwed up his face in concentration, as if trying to decipher the strange noise. 'It does sound familiar, though…'

'The thing is,' said Stella, 'that must have been transmitting ever since you arrived here. Five days, fourteen hours…'

'And… oh, thirty-one minutes, now. Yes. Good point. Whoever's supposed to receive that signal will have already done so.' The Doctor's face dropped. 'Which means they could be here any minute to collect their prize.'

Bowman grabbed his communicator. 'Scrum – get that ship ready to go double quick. We're expecting company.'

There was no reply.

'Scrum? Do you copy?'

A loud squawk of static burst from the communicator. They could hear Scrum's voice saying something but it was impossible to tell what.

'Something's interfering with the communications field,' realised the Doctor. Suddenly he was very serious. 'Whoever they are, they're already here.'

Stella swallowed. There was a rising tension in the air, as if everything around them was becoming charged with static electricity.

The Doctor was working at the computer again, rattling

the keys with frantic speed. 'If I can isolate the signal and jam it from here…' Suddenly he stopped dead, fingers curved over the keyboard. 'Oh no. No no no. Listen to that.'

Stella and Bowman listened to the sound emanating from the computer speakers. It was a slow, heavy throb, like an electronic heartbeat.

The Doctor's face was ashen. 'It can't be…' he said. 'It just *can't* be.'

Bowman had drawn his blaster again. 'You'd better believe it,' he said.

And then, with a terrible screech of rending metal, the doorway at the end of the corridor exploded open. Shrapnel sliced through the air and the three of them were already crouching, turning away, as something large and metallic swept through the wreckage.

Stella gaped in shock. There were three of them, filing through the remains of the door, their burnished bronze armour glinting dully, weapons swivelling in their sockets, eyestalks turning to stare at them with glowing blue lenses.

'Daleks!' said the Doctor, horrified.

'EXTERMINATE! EXTERMINATE! EXTERMINATE!'

CHAPTER
THREE

Stella cringed as the first Dalek screamed '𐤄𐤗𐤕𐤄𐤓𐤌𐤉𐤍𐤀𐤕𐤄', knowing the end was about to come.

But just as the Dalek's gun blazed, a hail of automatic gunfire crashed into its head and neck section. The bullets had little effect, intercepted by the Dalek's protective force field before they could strike home, but it was just enough of a distraction to allow the Doctor to shove Stella and Bowman out of the way.

The Dalek blaster beam illuminated the corridor with a terrible blue glare. 'Acquiring secondary target!' grated the Dalek, its eyestalk swivelling. 'Exterminate!'

On the stairs above them, Cuttin' Edge was taking aim with his assault rifle. He squeezed off another shot, the gun recoiling heavily, and this time the effect was rather different. The force field sizzled and there was a brilliant explosion.

When the smoke cleared, the Dalek was relatively unharmed, apart from a burning dent in its armour, but even the slightest delay was just enough for the humans to escape, running for their lives up the stairs. Fear is a great motivator.

Cuttin' Edge sprayed the corridor with bullets and then sprinted after his friends. Directly in front of him was the Doctor, urging them all to greater speed as they clattered up the stairs.

'How did you do that?' he demanded. 'Guns don't work

on Daleks.'

'This one does,' said Cuttin' Edge with a savage grin. 'We're Dalek bounty hunters.'

Stella caught a sudden glimmer of hope in the Doctor's wide-eyed stare. 'Is that right?'

'ELEVATE!' They all heard the harsh command echoing up from below. They didn't need to look down to know that the Daleks were rising up the stairwell behind them.

'Hurry up!' yelled the Doctor, pushing them all forward. Stella stumbled and he caught her, lifting her, propelling her up the last few steps with remarkable strength. Bowman kicked open the door and they piled out into the dusty street outside. Cuttin' Edge slammed the door shut and spun the lock. Then he aimed his rifle at the mechanism and blasted it into molten slag.

'That won't stop them,' said the Doctor.

'I know, but it makes me feel better.'

'Stop talking and *move*,' ordered Bowman, leading the way along the passageway at a run. He already had his communicator out again and was calling for Scrum to get the *Wayfarer* ready to leave.

Stella saw the Doctor turn back as the Daleks blasted their way out of the stairwell building. The first Dalek emerged, the glowing blue eye roving around until it fixed on them. Its body swivelled around and it started to glide after them.

And then stopped.

'WARNING!' grated the Dalek. 'WARNING! OUTER CASING UNDER ATTACK!'

A patch of black was spreading over the bronze dome of the Dalek's head section. Where Cuttin' Edge's last shot had struck, the metal was beginning to dissolve.

'EMERGENCY!' cried the Dalek. 'PROTECTIVE ARMOUR

COMPROMISED!'

The other two Daleks examined the damage. 'MOLECULAR DISSOLUTION VIRUS. RETURN TO THE SHIP FOR REPAIRS!'

'I OBEY!' The Dalek rose into the air, its dome fizzing as the virus spread remorselessly, and flew away.

The remaining Daleks turned and glided after their prey.

Stella, Bowman, Cuttin' Edge and the Doctor hared through the base, dodging from building to building and alley to alley.

The Doctor skidded to a halt at one junction, grabbing Stella by the arm. 'This way! I've got my own transport.'

'Where?'

'Follow me! Come on, you lot – *allons-y!*'

'Let him go, Stella,' said Bowman. 'We're heading for the *Wayfarer*.'

Stella hesitated. Behind her, Bowman and Cuttin' Edge were glaring at her, urging her to follow them.

'We don't have much time,' Bowman insisted. 'What's the problem?'

The Doctor had stopped and was looking back at her. And there was something in his eyes, a kind of longing, or a bitter hope. He held out his hand. 'You'll be safe in the TARDIS. Come with me!'

In the end the decision was made for her. A Dalek slid into view at the end of the passageway, blocking off the Doctor's retreat.

'HALT – OR YOU WILL BE EXTERMINATED!'

Cuttin' Edge opened up with his rifle. Gunfire filled the alley with crackling thunder.

The Dalek blasted at them, but the shots went wild and

suddenly they were all running again, tripping over each other, yelling at each other to move *faster*.

They reached the edge of the spaceport landing bays. And there, right in front of them, was the *Wayfarer*. Stella had never been so glad to see the old crate.

'That's your ship?' asked the Doctor, surprised.

'Yeah,' growled Bowman. 'Why? Don't you like it?'

'I know it doesn't look like much—' began Stella.

'But it's got it where it counts,' finished the Doctor. 'Don't worry, my ship's just the same.'

Scrum was unhooking a series of heavy cables from the spacecraft's underside. They were connected to a number of squat machines placed around the perimeter of the landing pad.

'She's not full yet, but we're good to go,' he called. 'Koral's already onboard.'

'Get her started!' roared Bowman.

Daleks were gliding into view from the edge of the spaceport. The blue lights of their eyes all turned to face the *Wayfarer* crew as they ran the last few metres to the ship.

'HALT!'

None of them did. Scrum was already inside the ship and the engines were whining into life, the whole vessel shuddering with compressed power.

Bowman sprinted to the foot of the ramp and turned to give the Doctor and Cuttin' Edge covering fire as they helped Stella onboard. The smell of energy-weapon discharges filled the air.

And then suddenly the ship began to lift off, the landing ramp still extended. Bowman grabbed hold of one of the hydraulic supports, raising a leg to plant his foot firmly on the Doctor's backside, propelling him into the ship.

Dalek gunfire screamed all around them, lighting the ramp with electric blue flashes.

The Doctor scrambled to his feet. Ahead of him, Cuttin' Edge was helping Stella as the ship swayed. She was grinning, overjoyed to have made it, giving the Doctor a happy and relieved thumbs up as he came towards her.

'Scrum!' yelled Bowman. 'Get us the hell out of here!'

'Aye aye, captain!' Scrum called back from the flight cabin. 'We're on our way...'

Something exploded behind them, outside the ship, probably one of the refuelling pumps at the side of the landing apron caught in a Dalek blast. The fireball ripped through the air, causing the *Wayfarer* to stagger slightly, and debris filled the open landing ramp area just before the interior hatch finally hissed shut. The shockwave had already blown Stella backwards and sent the Doctor, Bowman and Cuttin' Edge sprawling.

'Stella!' The Doctor saw immediately that she was injured. There was a lump of metal, part of a fuel tank, sticking out of her thigh.

The Doctor crawled towards her. She was leaning against the bulkhead wall, her face pale, staring at him. The leg wound was deep and serious, with dark arterial blood spreading across her trousers.

'Oh, but that *hurts*,' she croaked.

'It's all right,' he said hurriedly. 'It's just a flesh wound. You'll be OK.'

'Hey,' she said, smiling weakly. 'I cross-trained as a medic, y'know. I can tell how bad it is.'

The Doctor squeezed her hand. 'You'll be fine.'

'We've got no more medical supplies onboard. Used the last of them on Scrum.'

Bowman stepped forward. 'Stop talking. You need to get into the med room.'

'Yeah,' agreed Cuttin' Edge. 'Man, that was close, but we're OK. Everything's gonna be fine, babe. We're outta here.'

The *Wayfarer* had swung away from the spaceport and was climbing, Scrum easing the ship up through the atmosphere as quickly as he could.

Bowman said, 'I'll get the medical computers fired up. Bring her through.'

'Don't waste your time,' said Stella as he left. She was pale and clearly in pain, but she kept on smiling. 'You'll be putting me back together with packing tape.'

'Try not to talk,' advised the Doctor.

'Hey, give a girl a break, I'm pleading for my life here...' Stella smiled grimly, tears filling her eyes. 'And don't let Cuttin' Edge operate, do you hear? He can't even use a knife and fork properly.'

'Are you kidding?' said Cuttin' Edge. 'I ain't goin' near that medical stuff. Never do. Anyway, *he's* the only doctor around here.' He jerked a thumb at the Doctor.

'I thought you said he was a pirate.' Stella laughed and turned to the Doctor. 'Want my advice? Try one of those emergency cryo-charges. Freeze me and get me somewhere they can operate properly.'

'Good idea,' said the Doctor. 'You keep on coming up with them.'

There was a loud screech of metal from behind them. The interior airlock door buckled and then jerked in its housing, sliding away with a grinding protest. Beyond the door was the studded shape of a Dalek.

'What the hell!' yelled Cuttin' Edge, diving for his rifle.

The Dalek's sucker arm pushed the remains of the

airlock door to one side, the metal and plastic crumpling in its grip. Its single blue eye blazed at them and its head lights flashed.

'EXTERMINATE!'

The Doctor had tried to pull Stella away, but it was too late.

The extermination beam struck her full in the small of the back, illuminating her with such powerful radiance that her skeleton and internal organs were clearly visible. The beam was kept trained on her, pinning her against the wall, its shrill whine merging with the horrendous scream of agony that seemed to fill the ship.

Eventually, after what seemed like an age, the beam ceased and her corpse slid to the floor.

Chapter
Four

Cuttin' Edge opened fire at the Dalek with a scream of rage. The shots ricocheted around the airlock passage, sparking off the force field, filling the air with a storm of ammunition. The Dalek's eye turned implacably towards Cuttin' Edge as he stepped forward, rifle jammed against his shoulder, emptying the magazine into its head and neck. The Dalek remained impervious. It waited a second for the rifle to empty and then brought its own gun to bear on the human.

The Doctor lunged forward, hurling something at the Dalek. For the briefest of moments there was a clang as it struck the metal casing and a brilliant blue-white glare filled the airlock. Cuttin' Edge staggered backwards, caught in a sudden blast of incredibly cold air that took his breath away. He fell on top of the Doctor and they collapsed together in a heap of arms and legs.

Silence.

Cautiously, they sat up on the floor and looked at the Dalek. It was frozen – literally. A chill white mist floated around the familiar domed shape, and the metal casing was covered from top to bottom in a thick white frost. Behind the lens of its eye, the blue light slowly faded, replaced by an icy darkness.

'What…what was that?' gasped Cuttin' Edge. 'What did you do?'

'I used one of the emergency cryo-charges.' The Doctor

got up and looked around the airlock, where the Dalek stood in a small blast area covered with ice.

Cuttin' Edge, satisfied that the Dalek was immobilised, ran over to where Stella lay. At that moment Bowman came running too, his boots pounding on the metal floor. He glanced uncertainly at the frozen Dalek and then knelt down by Stella. 'What happened?'

'Dalek chased us, must've got inside the airlock somehow,' Cuttin' Edge said quietly. He didn't need to say any more.

Bowman stared in disbelief at Stella's smoking body, his lips tightening and a muscle trembling in his jaw.

'I'm sorry,' said the Doctor behind him. 'I'm so sorry.'

Bowman took a long, shuddering breath, and then stood up. He straightened his shoulders and lifted his head. His face was an expressionless mask, but the deep-set eyes were smouldering with fury as he turned to look at the Doctor. 'Get that *thing* off my ship.'

He didn't need to point at the Dalek. Everyone knew what he meant.

'I'm sorry, I can't,' said the Doctor. His voice was barely a whisper. 'The outer airlock door's been damaged – probably in the explosion as we took off. It's jammed. We might be able to—'

Bowman ignored him, turning back to Cuttin' Edge. 'Get it fixed. Get rid of it.'

'Yes, sir.'

The Doctor said nothing. Bowman looked back at the immobile Dalek for a second and then asked, 'Is it dead?'

The Doctor approached the Dalek cautiously. He waved a hand in front of the frost-covered eyestalk, but there was no response. Very carefully, he walked right around the Dalek, inspecting it from every angle. Finally he poked the gun-stick. There was no reaction. 'No vision, no motive power, weaponry offline. I'd say it's as good as dead.'

'As good as?'

'You never can tell with a Dalek. But it's cryogenically frozen – they are sometimes susceptible to a sudden reduction in temperature, particularly if caught off guard. Cuttin' Edge was shooting at it from close range, so there would have been quite a bit of power diverted to the defensive force field. Enough to allow the cryo-charge to do its stuff, at least.'

'That was quick thinking.'

The Doctor shook his head. 'Not quick enough. And anyway, it was Stella's idea.'

They should have been celebrating, thrilled and excited by the fact that they had defeated an unstoppable foe – but instead, all they felt was a sense of utter failure. None of them could bear to look at Stella's body.

'I should have acted faster,' insisted the Doctor. 'She didn't deserve to die like that. No one does.'

'I don't know what the hell you were doing on that planet,' Bowman growled, 'but everything went wrong the moment we found you.'

'It's not my fault,' said the Doctor.

'Just keep telling yourself that.'

Cuttin' Edge stepped up. 'Easy, skip. We need to move Stella.'

'Looks like we're stuck with you,' grumbled Bowman menacingly at the Doctor. 'At least until we get that airlock fixed. Until then, keep out of my way.'

Once the *Wayfarer* was in deep space and travelling at top speed, Bowman went to his cabin and ordered that no one should disturb him. Scrum was left at the helm while Cuttin' Edge, having helped move Stella's body, went to fix the airlock.

He found the Doctor there, examining the Dalek with his sonic screwdriver. 'The cryo-charge worked better than I thought,' he said. 'This thing seems to be completely defunct. It acts as a life-support system for the creature inside, so I imagine it's dead.'

'You know a bit about the Daleks, then?' asked Cuttin' Edge warily.

'A bit.'

Cuttin' Edge peered at the Dalek, which was still wreathed in a freezing mist and caked with frost. 'Man, we were lucky. I really thought my time was up.'

'It wouldn't have worked if you hadn't been shooting at it.' The Doctor glanced at the rifle slung over Cuttin' Edge's shoulder. 'What kind of ammunition does that thing take? You damaged that Dalek on Hurala – I've never seen that done before with a conventional firearm. Lucky shot at the eye, maybe, but that was something special.'

'MDV,' said Cuttin' Edge. 'Molecular Dissolution Virus. It's something Scrum developed. Bastic-headed bullet to penetrate the force field. Then it infects the armour plating and just eats its way through.'

The Doctor raised his eyebrows. 'Ingenious. It'd have to act fast, though. It would take an extremely aggressive MDV to beat the automatic self-repair molecules that make up the bonded polycarbide.'

Cuttin' Edge was peering carefully at the head and neck section of the Dalek. 'What I don't understand is why the thing didn't work this time. I had it point-blank. Should've rusted its damn head clean off.'

'Well, your weapons are smart all right,' said the Doctor, 'but the Daleks are smarter. Their armour learns and adapts. By the time your metal-eating virus was chewing its way through that first Dalek, it was already analysing the damage and transmitting emergency defence protocols so its mates wouldn't get caught out in the same way.'

'Now you're sounding just like Scrum,' Cuttin' Edge muttered. 'He's usually the brains of this operation.'

'Operation?'

'We're bounty hunters employed by Earth Command to kill Daleks. We get a fixed bonus for every eyestalk we collect. Which reminds me…' Cuttin' Edge reached for his belt, unhooking a laser tool.

He moved to grab the Dalek's eyestalk but the Doctor batted his hand away. 'Don't touch it! These things can absorb genetic data from your DNA – all it takes is one touch, and it might be enough for it to start regenerating.'

'I thought you said it was dead.'

'You can never be too careful where Daleks are concerned, believe me.'

Slowly, reluctantly, Cuttin' Edge returned the laser to his belt. 'So what's your story? How come you know so much about the Daleks? You don't look like a soldier.'

'Nor did Stella.'

Cuttin' Edge stiffened. 'She was different.'

'So am I.'

'If you say so.' Cuttin' Edge didn't sound convinced. 'Just what *were* you doin' on Hurala, anyway?'

The Doctor sighed and scratched the back of his neck. 'I'm not sure, to be honest. My ship was acting up a bit – guidance systems all gone to pot.'

'You're a long way lost to be out here, dude.'

The Doctor looked up with a smile. 'You know, I think that's the first time anyone's ever called me "dude".'

'Don't get carried away. Captain Bowman wants you off the ship, an' I ain't arguin' with him. And besides, it don't alter what I said: your ship must be *way* off course for you to end up this far from Earth space.'

'Oh, it's not space I'm worried about,' said the Doctor, lost in thought. 'The TARDIS seems to have slipped a time track... I've travelled back in the Daleks' own time line to way back when.'

'I thought Scrum talked funny, but you beat him hands down, dude.'

'I *really* shouldn't be here,' said the Doctor seriously. He almost seemed to be talking to himself. 'I mean, this is wrong in so many ways. I've gone back to a point before the Time War even started, and that's impossible. Well, I say impossible. Clearly it's *not* impossible. I'm here and so are the Daleks, right in the middle of the great conflict with Earth's first Empire.'

'You ain't making any sense *at all*.'

'What year is it, Cuttin' Edge?'

'You were only in that cell for five days. Get a grip.'

'Just answer the question.'

Such was the severity in the Doctor's voice that Cuttin' Edge answered automatically.

'Ahh,' said the Doctor, nodding slowly as realisation dawned. 'Let me guess: the Daleks are rampaging through the galaxy. The Earth Empire is resisting them in every way it can, but the battles rage on year after year across all the solar systems. Some humans have never known a time when they've not been at war with the Daleks.'

'Guess so.'

'The Dalek Generation. But you've reached the tipping point, haven't you? Two mighty galactic powers, facing off across the stars. Two giant superpowers vying for supremacy, slugging it out planet by planet. It could go either way.'

'That's about the size of it. We're doin' what we can out here on the edge, raiding Dalek space, messin' with their supply lines. Earning a living.'

'You've chosen a harsh life.'

'Never known any other kind. I was brought up on Gauda Prime and we're born fightin' there. Regular army couldn't stomach me – said I was too much of a loose cannon, an' I wouldn't let them recondition me.'

'Good for you. It's always best to just say no.'

'Ended up on the *Wayfarer* with Captain Bowman. There ain't nothin' he don't know about killin' Daleks.'

'Then we've more in common than I thought,' the Doctor commented drily.

'Hey, Bowman's all right. He's a soldier's soldier, if you know what I mean. They don't come any tougher than Jon Bowman. He was a trooper in Earth Force One, back in the day. A veteran of the Draconian Conflicts too. They say he was on the front line at Tartarus. He's an expert in weapons an' tactics and he was stickin' it to Skaro's finest before I was out of short pants.'

'I'm glad to hear it. Don't think he likes me much.'

Cuttin' Edge looked away. 'We all liked Stella. She was one of the good guys. Captain Bowman was like a father to her.'

'I'm sorry.'

The door hissed open and Scrum came in. He nodded at Cuttin' Edge but avoided looking at the Doctor. 'Skipper says we're going back to Auros.'

'Auros?' repeated the Doctor.

'Stella's planet,' explained Scrum bleakly. 'We're taking her home.'

CHAPTER
FIVE

Auros was one of the colony worlds that formed the backbone of the Human Empire. Even at the *Wayfarer*'s top speed, it would take the best part of a day to get there. Bowman remained in his cabin, while Stella's body was stowed in the medical bay, cryogenically frozen in the same way as the Dalek. No one appreciated the irony, least of all the Doctor.

He paid his respects. She was lying peacefully on the narrow examination couch, arms folded across her chest, looking like a marble effigy on a tomb. Her skin was as white and perfect as alabaster, covered by a thin veil of freezing mist.

He wanted to say he was sorry, but what would be the point? She was gone. Whatever had made Stella unique was no longer here. Her body remained, but the person – the intelligence, the good humour, the courage that he had glimpsed so briefly – they were gone from the universe for ever. It was something the Doctor would never truly understand.

'You really liked her, didn't you?' Scrum asked from the passageway. There wasn't room for more than two people at a time in the medical cabin.

'Yes,' replied the Doctor. 'I did. She reminded me of someone… something… I miss.'

'She was good company.'

The Doctor bit his lip and nodded. 'Yeah, I bet she was.'

'Doesn't do to dwell,' Scrum said. 'She's going home, that's all we need to know.'

'Does she have any family?'

'No, I don't think so.'

'That's good.'

Scrum shrugged. 'Never really thought about it. So many people are orphans now.'

'Because of the Daleks?'

'Yes. They call it the Dalek Generation.'

'I know.'

Scrum cleared his throat, clearly wishing to change the subject.

The Doctor looked up and forced a smile. 'Has Cuttin' Edge managed to fix that airlock door yet?'

'He's working on it.'

'Not too hard I hope.'

'He'll have it fixed in time for us to land on Auros. You can get off there.'

The Doctor nodded. 'I'll need to get back to Hurala. My ship is still there.'

'Hurala will be crawling with Daleks.'

'That's what worries me.'

The Doctor followed Scrum down the narrow passageway to the galley area. He could hear the sound of Cuttin' Edge's tools further down the corridor by the airlock. Glancing along the passage, the Doctor was surprised to see that the Dalek had gone.

'We had to move it,' Scrum explained. 'Cuttin' Edge didn't have any room to work.'

'That was risky,' said the Doctor. 'Even a dead Dalek is dangerous. They've got a hundred different automatic defences.'

'It's all right, we didn't even touch it. I used a couple

of cargo grapplers to shift it down to the hold. Besides which I think that cryo-charge has completely disabled the thing. It didn't even twitch when Cuttin' Edge took its eyestalk off.'

The Doctor stopped in his tracks. 'He did what?'

'Cut off the eyestalk. You know, for the bounty.'

'I told him not to do that.'

Scrum looked at the Doctor, a little bemused. 'Doctor, he doesn't take his orders from you. Captain Bowman is in charge here, in case you hadn't noticed. And the bounty on those things is what keeps us alive. It's a confirmed kill, and that's what Earth Command pays us for. We deliver that eyestalk to the authorities on Auros and we can afford to eat again.'

The Doctor said nothing. He sat down in the galley, tight-lipped.

Scrum sat down opposite him. 'I've been thinking about that Dalek, actually. It's not often I get the chance to look at one up close – at least, not for long. There must be a lot of stuff I could learn from it, if I could take it apart.'

'Don't even think about it,' warned the Doctor darkly.

'It's dead. I could crack it open with the right tools.'

The Doctor stared at him. 'Believe me, you really don't want to do that. Every Dalek has defences against that sort of thing. It would be like playing with a live hand grenade. The creature inside may be dead, but that casing is chock full of anti-handling devices and booby traps that would make your hair curl. There are enough self-destruct mechanisms packed inside one of those things to keep a team of bomb-disposal experts happy for a month.'

'But while it's here—'

'Forget it. As soon as that airlock door is fixed, dump

it in deep space and forget it about. Consider yourselves lucky that we didn't all end up like Stella.'

The Doctor regretted the outburst straightaway, but it was too late. Scrum stared coldly at him for a minute or two and then got up to leave.

'If Bowman has his way, you'll follow that Dalek straight out of the airlock.'

The Doctor raised an eyebrow. 'I thought only pirates made people walk the plank.'

'Just remember, Doctor – Stella was our mate. She was one of us. You aren't.'

Scrum went out, leaving the Doctor sitting in the galley alone.

Cuttin' Edge was working on the door. The outer bulkhead had been slightly distorted, causing the running tracks for the main airlock to jam. He had the tools to fix it, but the truth was, he just couldn't concentrate.

All he could think about was Stella. All he could hear was the shrill scream of the Dalek's death ray, and the equally shrill scream of his friend as she died, spread-eagled against the wall by the sheer force of the energy blast. All he could see when he closed his eyes was the brilliant blue flare, and Stella's skull, thrown back with its jaws wide open.

His hand slipped and he barked his knuckles on the metal grating of the deck. He swore and then threw the gravity spanner across the passageway, where it hit the floor with a heavy clang.

'You'll get me next time,' said Scrum. The spanner had just missed his foot as he came round the corner.

Cuttin' Edge shook his head. 'I can't do this.'

'Course you can. You've been taking this old crate apart

and putting it back together for years. We both have.'

'I don't mean that. I can fix this thing in my sleep.' Cuttin' Edge heaved a sigh and sat back on his haunches, resting his muscular arms on his knees. 'I mean… Hell, I don't know what I mean.'

'We fight Daleks for a living,' said Scrum quietly. 'We could be killed any day, any one of us. You know that. We all know that – Stella did too.'

'That don't make it any easier. She never wanted to be part of this, not like us. Her dyin' like that – it just feels wrong, bro.'

'I know what you mean.' Scrum sat down on the deck opposite him and reached into a belt pouch. He produced a small metal flask, unscrewed the lid, and took a sip. 'Here.' He passed it to Cuttin' Edge.

'What is it?'

'It's an old Earth drink. Very old. It's expensive, because it's so rare.'

Cuttin' Edge raised the flask, swallowed, and almost choked. 'Hey – what the hell is that stuff? Damn' near killed me!'

'Consider it medicinal.'

Cuttin' Edge took another sip and then gagged and blinked. 'What's it called?'

'Ginger beer.'

'Sure has a kick.'

'I only use it for special occasions.' Scrum took the flask back and drank again. 'To Stella – one of the good guys.'

'Amen to that.'

They sat in companionable silence for a few minutes, passing the flask back and forth. Eventually Scrum put the lid back on and stowed it away. 'What do you make of that Doctor?' he asked.

'Well, he sure ain't no pirate,' said Cuttin' Edge. 'But other than that – I don't know. I don't understand half of what he says. He's a bit like you, in that respect, only better lookin'.'

Scrum sniffed. 'He knows things.'

'Like what?'

'About the Daleks – stuff he isn't telling us.'

'Maybe. It don't really matter, though – either way, Bowman's gonna kick his bony butt off the ship as soon as, and a good thing too.'

'Why do you say that?'

Cuttin' Edge leant forward. 'Because whatever, or whoever, he is – he's brought us nothin' but bad luck.'

The Doctor had decided that there was no point in sitting in the galley doing nothing but look morose. He was stuck on the *Wayfarer* at least until it reached Auros, and so he might as well get his bearings. Besides, he couldn't resist having a little look around. Which, he reflected, was what had got him into this mess in the first place.

The first thing he decided to do was check out the engine room. It was a small ship, but powerful, and he wondered what kind of propulsion system it used. Not many spacecraft of this era relied on antiquated fuel systems like astronic recharge.

On the way to the engine room he passed by the hold, and the Doctor couldn't help but pause to look in through the plastic window in the door.

There was the Dalek, like some terrifying ice sculpture, glistening in the cargo bay lights. Where the eyestalk should have been attached to the dome, there was only the stub of the pivot nestling in its metal cowl. A couple of wires and fibre-optic filaments dangled from the hole.

Even robbed of its eye, the Dalek looked dangerous. The very shape of it chilled the Doctor to the bone. He had too many bad memories, too many nightmares, to feel anything but revulsion.

And fear.

He took a deep breath and the little window clouded over slightly, obscuring the frost-whitened demon within. It was only that which prevented the Doctor from spotting the single drop of water that fell from the rim of the Dalek's sucker arm.

The engine room was a little further on, to the rear, or aft, section of the vessel. The closer the Doctor got to the heavy astronic motors, the more he could feel the vibration through the soles of his trainers. The noise level increased too. He thought he could detect a slightly irregular beat coming from the coolant pumps, and felt a flicker of interest – it almost certainly meant a problem with the regulator valves, and perhaps he could fix them, or improve them, and thus gain some points with the rest of the *Wayfarer* crew.

But something caught his eye as he approached the engine room. Further down the corridor, there was a movement in the shadows.

'Hello?' he said, trying to see what it was. It was dark down here, the passageways lit only by a series of small amber lights running at shoulder height along the walls. Thick cables and pipes ran the length of the ceiling and steam from the coolant pumps floated up through the deck plates, a sure sign that the regulator valves were worn.

'Anyone there?'

The Doctor caught a brief glimpse of something lithe

and dark, with bared fangs glinting in the lights – and
then it was on top of him, bearing him to the ground with
an angry snarl.

CHAPTER
SIX

'Captain wants to see you,' it said in a sibilant whisper, completely at odds with the ferocious beast the Doctor had been expecting.

He frowned. 'What?'

'I said, the captain wants to see you,' repeated the alien sitting on his chest.

He lay there for another moment, unable to think of a suitable reply.

'*What?*' he said again, eventually.

She jumped off his chest. When the steam from the coolant pumps had drifted away, the Doctor saw a tawny, humanoid figure with a pair of luminous eyes. He scrambled to his feet, straightening his jacket in an attempt to regain some of his dignity, and peered at the strange, leonine face.

'Do you attack all your guests like that?'

'It depends.' Again, the reply was barely more than a whisper.

'Depends on what?'

'On whether I like them or not.'

'I see,' said the Doctor, rubbing his throat. Only seconds before, he'd been convinced this creature was going to rip it out with her bare teeth. 'I take it you don't like me much, then.'

'If I didn't like you, you'd be dead already.'

She turned and led the way down the passageway,

disappearing into the shadows.

'Right,' said the Doctor. 'That's that clear, then.'

Bowman was sitting at his desk, cleaning a large automatic blaster. He didn't look up at the Doctor until the door hissed shut behind him.

'Doctor,' said Bowman eventually. He said the word as if it tasted bad.

'Captain.'

'It's been a long time since I was entitled to any kind of rank,' he said. 'I'm captain here only because the *Wayfarer*'s my ship – and this is my crew. Officially, we don't exist.'

'You're mercenaries.'

'Bounty hunters.' Bowman sat back and folded his arms, the muscles rippling beneath skin tanned by the suns of a hundred different worlds. There were signs of many old wounds, and one livid white scar on his forearm. 'Mercenaries will work for whoever pays them the most. We hunt Daleks, and Earth rewards us for every kill. There's a difference.'

'If you say so.'

'I do. We work for Earth Command and no one else.'

'I know Earth Command. They're running scared. The Daleks are engaging them on every front, pushing back the boundaries of Earth control. And now Earth's prepared to use any and every method to stop the Daleks in their tracks – even mercenaries. Or bounty hunters.'

'You say that like it's a bad thing.'

'The problem is escalation. Tit-for-tat raids in the border regions, no one really cares. But then a planet gets wiped out and suddenly it's all over the news. But it's no use trying to hold back the Daleks with a bunch of willing cut-throats on the front line. Earth will have to send in troops – thousands of 'em. Half of them will be no more than kids themselves, joining up because they think it's the right thing to do.'

'And you don't think it is?'

'I don't believe in innocent people getting slaughtered.'

'The Daleks want to conquer our entire galaxy. We have to fight them.'

'Of course you do. But it's the way you fight them that matters. They *want* to drag you into a long, drawn-out war because that's what they like. Destruction, killing, slaughter – *extermination*. It's what they do. You're playing right into their hands. Suckers. Whatever.'

'You seem to know a lot about them.'

'Enough to know that, eventually, if you're not careful, the Daleks will drag you all down fighting. Every single human being. It's what they want.'

Bowman watched the Doctor carefully, as if weighing up his words and trying to decide whether to question him further or just shoot him on the spot. There was an unreadable, stony look in the captain's eyes that told the Doctor it could easily go either way. But at that moment there was a distinct change in the background rumble of the *Wayfarer*'s engines as the ship altered course. The intercom on Bowman's desk bleeped and Scrum's voice said, 'Just entering the Auros system, skipper.'

'OK,' Bowman replied. 'Let me know when we're coming into orbit.' Then he turned back to the Doctor and said, 'Sit down.'

There was a seat in front of Bowman's desk and the Doctor sat, lifting his feet and resting his trainers casually on the edge of the desk. Something caught his eye immediately, and he reached out to pick up the holopicture. 'Aww, is this your mum and dad? That's so sweet! You've got your mum's eyes, you know. Only she doesn't seem to be frowning so much in that picture. Bet she doesn't even know what you do for a living. Bounty hunter, eh?'

'Put that down,' growled Bowman.

The Doctor tossed the holopicture across the desk and Bowman caught it with a snap of his hand. 'Now – what did you want to see me about? And who's that charming creature who fetched me here – your bodyguard? Hired muscle? Ship's cat? You don't look like you need any of them, to be honest.'

'I don't. But Koral is unique. She is fast, strong and very loyal. She also has claws that can rip through sheet metal.'

'Really? I don't think I've seen her kind before.'

'Her planet was destroyed by the Daleks – she's the last of her kind.'

'I know the feeling.'

'I saved her life,' Bowman said simply. 'She was dying, suffocating in the smoking ruins of her own world. I took her onboard the *Wayfarer* and nursed her back to life. Now she believes she owes me that life, quite literally. She has sworn to protect me.'

'It's an old story,' the Doctor remarked, 'but I still don't think you need it.' He nodded at the heavy blaster pistol resting on the desk.

'True, but what else is there for her to do? Life with me gives her the one thing she craves – the chance to destroy Daleks. Something I have seen her do with her bare hands, incidentally. In a recent encounter with some space pirates, one of my crew was slightly injured in the altercation. Koral leapt on the bandit who fired the shot and ripped his head clean off with one stroke of her claws. Her loyalty extends through me to the rest of the crew.'

The Doctor whistled. 'And the rest of your crew… what kind of tricks can they do?'

'Scrum is a brilliant computer technician and theoretical scientist – or so he tells me. He's also a wanted criminal throughout Earth space, so it's difficult to substantiate his claims. But as he invented most of our anti-Dalek weaponry and defence systems, I'm willing to give him the benefit of the doubt.'

'And what about Cuttin' Edge?'

'Used to be a Space Marine, one of the best – except that he couldn't handle military discipline and ended up on the wrong end of a dishonourable discharge. Something to do with murdering his commanding officer, I believe.'

'And what about Stella?' The Doctor spoke softly, cautiously, but he had to ask. 'She didn't exactly fit in with you lot – criminals, killers, people who can tear through sheet metal.'

Bowman stared at the Doctor. 'Stella was a good kid. That's all you need to know.'

The Doctor nodded. 'I liked her.'

'You hardly knew her.'

'I'm a good judge of character.'

'Is that so?'

'Yeah, so look: I really don't want to hang around here any longer than I have to, and I know you certainly don't want me here, so how about we forget all this chit-chat and go our separate ways? You needn't bother throwing me overboard, either. Just drop me off when we get to Auros and we'll call it quits.'

Bowman didn't reply straight away. He simply continued to work on the blaster pistol, clicking each component into place without even looking.

Eventually, he said, 'Not so fast, Doctor.'

The Doctor watched as Bowman finished reassembling the gun.

'You see,' Bowman said, 'I've been thinking about you, Doctor. It's been preying on my mind ever since we left Hurala. That planet's nothing but a forgotten piece of grit on the edge of space. So what were you really doing there? And, more importantly, what were the Daleks doing there? They don't do anything – or go anywhere – without a reason.'

'I've no idea,' replied the Doctor. 'I shouldn't really have been there myself. I can hardly speak for the Daleks.'

'Is that so?' Bowman made no attempt to hide his scepticism. 'Come on, Doctor. I know you're a spook.'

'Spook?'

'Earth agent. Military intelligence. Why else would you be stuck on Hurala just when the Daleks turn up? You couldn't even provide any proper ID. You've got "secrets" written all over you. There wasn't any other spacecraft there when the *Wayfarer* touched down. I bet if I asked you straight how you got to Hurala you wouldn't be able to answer.'

'It's difficult to explain, it really is.'

Bowman curled his lip. 'Let me guess – if you told me, you'd have to kill me?'

'I'd probably have to stop you laughing first.'

'Want to bet?' Bowman aimed the blaster casually at the Doctor's head. 'Let's get one thing straight. I don't like spooks and I don't like you. But one way or another I'm going to find out what you were doing on Hurala, and why the Daleks were there.'

The intercom on Bowman's desk bleeped again and Scrum's voice crackled through: 'Skipper! We're just coming into orbit around Auros…'

Both Bowman and the Doctor heard the strange, anxious tone. 'What's up?' asked Bowman.

'Something's wrong,' Scrum replied, his voice trembling. 'Badly wrong. You'd better come and take a look, skip. Auros is burning.'

CHAPTER
SEVEN

The planet was on fire. From the large portside viewing window, the crew of the *Wayfarer* looked down in disbelieving horror as the surface of the planet churned and broke apart, molten lava erupting from beneath the shattered crust, incinerating everything in its path and filling the atmosphere with toxic gas.

Auros had been a typical human colony world – naturally located in a temperate biosphere around its parent sun, with one small moon. It was a beautiful planet, with equatorial rainforests, mountains, deserts, grassland and oceans, and men had come here in their droves, keen to escape the overcrowded Earth.

The Doctor looked up from the unfolding devastation. Scrum was white-faced, and there were tears running down his cheeks. 'Any communications?'

Scrum shook his head. 'We didn't establish contact beforehand. We're not always welcome.'

'There were some ships flying away when we got here,' said Cuttin' Edge slowly. 'Looks like they were evacuatin'. A couple of them said we should clear out too. Auros is goin' down.'

'The last ship to leave told us to cut and run,' Scrum added quietly. 'They said the Daleks were coming.'

A chill spread through the *Wayfarer*, and even Koral – watching from the shadows through narrowed, smouldering eyes – moved closer to the others.

Jon Bowman stood behind all of them, like the statue of an ancient god overlooking Hell. His hard, rock-like face reflected the orange and red glow of the dying planet. 'I've seen this before,' he growled. 'It's the Osterhagen Principle.'

'They've scuttled the planet,' explained the Doctor in response to Scrum's questioning look. 'There's a network of nuclear devices across the planet, buried deep below ground. It's a self-destruct mechanism.'

'It's designed to prevent the enemy getting hold of the planet,' said Bowman. 'When all else fails.'

'I know what it's for,' said the Doctor bleakly. 'It was invented on Earth over five hundred years ago. It was a bad idea then and it's a bad idea now.'

Cuttin' Edge stepped back from the window, rubbing a hand over his shaven head in confusion. At first he seemed almost lost for words, but then he said, 'Hey, they must have done it for a reason, man.'

'You heard what they said,' Scrum argued. 'The Daleks are coming. Maybe this way the population will have time to escape.'

'Yeah,' Cuttin' Edge nodded. 'Yeah. At least this way the Daleks don't get the planet.'

Cuttin' Edge was desperate to make sense of what he was seeing, to find a way to come to terms with the terrible destruction consuming the charred surface of the world below. But all the Doctor could feel was the bile rising in his throat, a stark revulsion that he couldn't contain. 'It's a stupid, stupid waste,' he said. 'All they've done is save the Daleks a job. They'd have destroyed a planet like that anyway. Now they don't even have to bother.'

Scrum glared at the Doctor, and there was hate in his tearful eyes now. 'Don't say that,' he moaned.

'I'm sorry,' said the Doctor quietly. 'But it's what the Daleks do.'

'I can't watch it any more,' said Scrum. He turned away from the window and leant his head against the wall. His whole body was shaking.

'Take it easy, bro,' said Cuttin' Edge. He rested a hand on his friend's shoulder and shot the Doctor a venomous look.

'Satisfied?' Bowman growled at the Doctor. 'First Stella, now her homeworld. What's going on?'

'I don't know,' the Doctor said. He looked out of the window again, keen to avoid their accusing stares. On the surface of the planet below, vast chunks of charred land broke away into seas of boiling lava. 'But it wasn't the Daleks who did that.'

'What do you mean?'

'Human beings did that,' the Doctor said in a funereal tone. His big, dark eyes never left the planet. 'All those cities and homes and farms and fields... the sum of human endeavour on a beautiful new world. All gone – deliberately wrecked. A self-inflicted wound.'

Bowman's temper flared. 'What choice did they have? Auros is too far from Earth Command for them to protect it against a fleet of Dalek destructor ships. *This* was the only way to protect them. The only way. Don't you see that?'

'All I see is a planet in flames and not a Dalek in sight.'

'Then the survivors should count themselves lucky.'

The Doctor tore his gaze from the planet's death throes. He stared at nothing, thinking furiously. Then he clapped a hand against his head and yelled, 'Of course!'

The others stared at him.

He looked up, his eyes wide with a sudden, horrific realisation. 'Oh no. Oh no, no, no...!'

And then he pushed straight past Bowman and ran towards the flight cabin. 'We need to contact them – warn them! Hurry!'

Bowman jerked his head, and Cuttin' Edge and Scrum obediently set off after the Doctor.

'What's up?' Cuttin' Edge demanded as they reached the flight cabin. The Doctor was all over the controls, leaping from one panel to the next, flicking switches and jabbing buttons with frenetic speed. 'Hey – what you doin', man?'

The Doctor was practically tearing his hair out. 'I'm trying to make contact with the refugees,' he gabbled. 'There must be a long-range transceiver system onboard a ship like this – but where? This thing's been repaired, replaced and reconditioned more times than my TARDIS!'

'Here,' said Scrum, sliding into one of the cockpit seats and activating a control unit. 'It's a hyperlink data-stream salvaged from an old Draconian battleship. It can tap into almost any major communications signal.'

'Brilliant!' The Doctor slipped on his glasses and studied the console over Scrum's shoulder. 'Send out a broad-contact beam. But scramble the signal. We don't want to be any more visible than we have to be, do we?'

'What's going on?' asked Bowman as he entered the flight deck. Koral was at his shoulder, a shadow among shadows.

'We've got to warn the people who left Auros,' said the Doctor without looking up. 'Tell them to turn around and head back home.'

'What?' Cuttin' Edge frowned. 'You gotta be kiddin', man...'

'Their home is burning,' Bowman said. 'They're running away, trying to put as much distance between themselves and the Daleks.'

'Are they?' The Doctor whipped off his glasses and looked straight at Bowman. 'This is the Daleks we're talking about, remember. They don't let people go. It's not in their nature.'

And in that instant Bowman understood. 'The Daleks will ambush the fleet. It's a trap.' He turned to Scrum and barked, 'For God's sake, man, get them on the hyperlink now.'

'I'm working on it,' Scrum assured him. His fingers flew over the communications controls, his tears forgotten as he concentrated on the task. 'Here we are. Looks like they left Auros in commercial passenger ships and cargo freighters, plus some private vessels. A convoy, packed with the entire population.'

'How could they have organised all that so quickly?' wondered Cuttin' Edge.

'There's probably not all that many of them in planetary terms,' said the Doctor. 'No more than a few thousand. They will all have been located near to the major spaceport, or owned spacecraft of their own. And fear is a great motivator. Once the countdown for the Osterhagen nukes started, I bet they all moved pretty fast.'

Bowman's face was a grim mask in the light of the control board. 'Too fast,' he growled.

'I still don't understand—' Cuttin' Edge began.

'Shh,' said Scrum. There was a rush of static from the panel. 'I've done it – I've hacked into the Auros convoy's communications network.'

The Doctor leant in and grabbed the microphone by its flexible neck. 'Auros convoy! Do you copy? This is the *Wayfarer* calling the Auros convoy – can you hear us?'

A burst of static, then: 'This is the Auros convoy.' The screen fizzled into life and the grainy image of a tired, anxious-looking woman came into view. 'I'm Vanessa Lakestaad—'

'Listen to me—' began the Doctor.

'Do you wish to join the fleet?'

'No, listen—'

'You can't miss us,' Vanessa Lakestaad said. 'There are nearly four hundred vessels in this convoy alone…'

'Stop!' yelled the Doctor. 'Turn back!'

'I'm sorry, you're breaking up,' said the woman, frowning. The image crackled. 'There's another signal interfering with yours. It's very powerful…'

The Doctor's grip tightened on the microphone and his knuckles turned white. 'Turn around!' he yelled. 'Tell the fleet to split up! Scatter! Run for your lives!'

'What? I can't hear you. Wait – here's that signal again. It's drowning you out.'

There was a loud crackle from the speakers and Scrum winced as the picture suddenly zigzagged and disappeared. 'We've lost contact…' He adjusted some controls. 'We can still hear them but they can't hear us. Someone's blocking our signal.'

The woman's voice came again, loud and clear, almost as if she was standing next to them on the flight deck of the *Wayfarer*. 'Unidentified vessel, this is Vanessa Lakestaad, Leader of the Auros refugee fleet. Our homeworld is destroyed. We are fleeing for our lives. Please identify yourself.'

There was a long pause. And then a harsh, grating voice filled the cabin: 'Survivors of Auros! Pay close attention!'

'Oh my God,' whispered Scrum.

The Doctor put his hand over his mouth in mute horror as the image on the screen slowly resolved into the familiar dome of a Dalek head. The eye glowed a bright blue, almost filling the screen.

'WE ARE THE DALEKS! YOUR EFFORTS TO ESCAPE ARE USELESS! PREPARE TO SURRENDER.'

'Please,' said Vanessa Lakestaad. Her voice now sounded small and frightened, suddenly almost childlike. 'You… you must let us pass. We are a refugee fleet, heading for the Inner Worlds. We can't—'

The metallic voice interrupted her. 'SILENCE! YOU WILL TRAVEL NO FURTHER. YOUR CONVOY IS SURROUNDED.'

'No, please, you can't mean that! You mustn't! We don't want to fight!' A sob broke through Lakestaad's words. 'We can't fight. We can't…! We're private vessels, merchant ships only. This is the entire population of Auros. We claim refugee status…'

'SILENCE! YOU HAVE DESTROYED YOUR OWN PLANET AND FLED INTO SPACE.' The Dalek voice rose in pitch as it grew more excited. 'YOU ARE NOW PRISONERS OF THE DALEKS!'

'I don't understand…' began Vanessa.

'YOUR SPACECRAFT WILL BE BOARDED AND YOUR PASSENGERS TAKEN AS PRISONERS. ANY ATTEMPT AT RESISTANCE WILL BE MET BY EXTERMINATION.'

'No! You can't!'

The Dalek's voice grated on: 'AS AN EXAMPLE TO THE REMAINDER OF THE REFUGEE FLEET, YOUR VESSEL WILL NOW BE DESTROYED.'

'Please, no…' whispered Vanessa.

Scrum turned in his seat and looked up at Bowman. 'We've got to do something!'

But Bowman stared impassively at the communications console, utterly powerless.

The Doctor closed his eyes.

'Please… Have mercy on us,' wept Vanessa. 'I beg you…'

'EXTERMINATE!' shrieked the Dalek.

There was a howl of feedback, echoing around the flight cabin like a blood-curdling scream. And then, abruptly, the signal died and the air was filled with white noise. The image of the Dalek faded slowly from the screen.

Scrum buried his head in his hands. Cuttin' Edge swore and looked down at his boots. Koral stepped closer to Bowman, who simply stood, rock-like, his eyes narrowed into grey slits as if his gaze could pierce the walls of the ship and see across space, to where the Auros fleet had once been.

There was complete silence on board the *Wayfarer* now. The Doctor gently switched off the radio.

'Gone…' Scrum was saying softly. 'That woman… All those people – just… gone. *Slaughtered.*'

Bowman turned his cold, steely eyes on the Doctor. 'You knew that was going to happen.'

'I guessed,' said the Doctor quietly. 'The Daleks knew the survivors would run for their lives. It was a simple matter to position the Dalek ships ready to intercept the convoy. A lot quicker and easier than attacking the planet itself. They kill the leaders and take the rest prisoner.'

'They never stood a chance.'

'No,' agreed the Doctor. 'They didn't.'

Bowman's lips compressed into a thin, bleak line and his face was white with anger. 'There's something going on here which I don't understand. First the Daleks turn up on Hurala, right out on the very edge of nowhere. And now this. Taking thousands of prisoners in one go. Why? What's going on?'

'I don't know.'

Bowman grabbed the Doctor by the lapels of his suit and slammed him up against the bulkhead wall. 'The hell you don't!' he roared. 'You never saw Auros before! Fields and oceans and blue skies! Men and women and kids! They had *everything*!'

'I'm sorry…'

'Sorry isn't enough!' Bowman swung the Doctor around, hurling him across the cabin. He crashed against the door and then slid to the ground in a crumpled heap. 'Sorry isn't *nearly* enough.'

The Doctor got to his knees slowly and painfully. He felt as if every bone in his body was still vibrating from the impact with the wall, and his mouth hurt. The front of his suit was creased where Bowman's giant fists had held him.

'Don't bother standing up,' Bowman growled menacingly, 'unless you want me to knock you down again.'

The Doctor touched a finger to his lip. There was blood where it had split.

'You know more than you're telling,' Bowman insisted. 'You know what all this is about. Don't you?'

Scrum and Cuttin' Edge were watching the altercation. Scrum looked nervous but Cuttin' Edge was sneering. 'You best tell us what you know, man. Otherwise we may have to make you.'

The Doctor stood up, slowly, to his full height. As tall as Bowman was, the Doctor could still look him in the eye. And he did this now, unflinchingly, his gaze cool and level. 'You can beat me up if you want to,' the Doctor told him. 'Here and now. Go on. Give it your best shot. If it helps, your two pals here can hold my arms. How about it, fellas? No?'

Scrum shook his head and even Cuttin' Edge looked away.

'Stop wasting my time,' Bowman said.

'I never waste time. So, come on. Here I am!' The Doctor held his arms out wide. 'Use your fists, do me some damage. Get rid of that anger and frustration. Don't hold back, Bowman, I'm not armed. I'm just a skinny guy in a suit. What's the problem? Here, I'll make it easier for you, shall I?' The Doctor put on his glasses. 'There! Now, come on, Bowman! Hit me hard! *Sort me out!*'

By now the Doctor was practically shouting in Bowman's face. The captain of the *Wayfarer* stared back, unmoving, but the muscles in his jaw and face were quivering with barely suppressed anger.

Then Koral stepped between them. 'That is enough. Everyone mourns for Auros. We should be fighting Daleks, not each other.'

There was a long, deadly pause.

Then the Doctor slowly folded his glasses and put them away. 'Thank you.'

Bowman was still seething, but, somehow, Koral had been able to prevent him losing his temper completely. He scowled at the Doctor. 'What were the Daleks doing on Hurala? What are they up to? We've stumbled across something big here, and I think you know what's going on.'

All eyes turned to look at the Doctor.

'I don't know,' he told them. 'Really, I don't. I shouldn't even be here. I'm in the wrong time and place altogether. In fact, I'm in the wrong time and place in more ways than you can imagine.'

'You always talk like that,' muttered Cuttin' Edge. 'Don't make no sense.'

'I just want to know what the Daleks were doing at the Lodestar station on Hurala,' repeated Bowman wearily.

'That's all.'

Scrum cleared his throat. 'Actually, captain, I think I may know a way we can find out.'

It was still cold in the cargo chamber, and the Dalek was still frozen.

But not as frozen as it was.

Now there was a steady trickle of water running down the segmented shoulders, dripping from the gun and sucker, pooling on the floor beneath the base. The head dome was almost completely clear of frost.

'What's happening?' asked Bowman.

'It's thawing out,' said the Doctor. His eyes were wide and anxious.

'Who asked you?' demanded Bowman. He turned to Scrum. 'I thought it was dead.'

'Perhaps it still is,' Scrum replied, circling the Dalek slowly, examining the casing. 'Perhaps this is some kind of automatic response by the armour.'

'But?'

'Yeah,' said Cuttin' Edge, 'I can sense a big "but" there, too.'

'But… I was thinking,' said Scrum, 'that the armour is actually a life-support system. Perhaps when the cryo-charge hit it didn't kill the creature inside but it froze it as well. Exactly what a cryo-charge is supposed to do, after all.'

'Wait,' said the Doctor. He stepped forward, right up to the Dalek. And then he hesitated, almost as if he was trying to convince himself of what he should do next. He took an old stethoscope out of his jacket pocket, clipped it into his ears, and placed the other end against the Dalek casing very, very softly.

Everyone was silent. All that could be heard was the steady background rumble of the ship's engines and the occasional drip of melting ice.

The Doctor had closed his eyes, concentrating. He moved the stethoscope to another area of the casing and listened again. Then, finally, he tried it against the black grille between the bronze neck rings.

Then the Doctor's eyes snapped open, the pupils dilating. He straightened up and backed away from the Dalek very quickly. 'It's alive,' he whispered. 'Inside. It's still alive.'

'I knew it,' breathed Scrum. A strange light came into his eyes as he watched the machine creature. More water trickled down through the frosted globes on its base unit. 'It's thawing itself out. The casing is doing it automatically.'

'This is bad news, man,' said Cuttin' Edge.

'The worst,' confirmed the Doctor. 'It's not strong enough to control the machinery yet, but it will be…'

Bowman said, 'Not really interested in your opinion, Doctor. All I know is we've caught ourselves a live Dalek here. I don't know anyone who's ever done that before.'

'It's better than that,' said Scrum excitedly. 'It's thawing out very slowly. We've got it totally under our control. If we disable the weaponry and self-destruct system we can render this thing completely harmless.'

The Doctor frowned at him. 'No Dalek is ever completely harmless.'

'So what are you suggesting, Scrum?' Bowman asked.

'I suggest we open this thing up,' Scrum replied. 'And ask it a few questions.'

Chapter
EIGHT

The *Wayfarer* suddenly became a hive of activity. Scrum and Cuttin' Edge set about securing the Dalek, wheeling in equipment and tools into the cargo hold with an air of professional urgency.

The Doctor caught up with Bowman in the corridor, heading for his cabin. 'You can't be serious about this.'

'I'm deadly serious,' replied Bowman over his shoulder. 'This is a golden opportunity to gain first-hand intelligence from an actual Dalek. No one's ever done that before.'

'Bowman, it's a golden opportunity to get us all *killed*,' the Doctor argued. 'Why don't you just take the thing back to Earth Command? Let them handle it.'

'No way. Earth Command is too far from here. We're in deep space, Doctor. Out here, no one can hear you whinge.'

'Bowman, I mean it—'

'Me too. We're on our own, Doctor. Just us and a Dalek. I've waited a long time for this.'

The Doctor let out an exasperated gasp. 'You're messing with things you just don't understand!'

Bowman rounded on him. 'No,' he growled. 'I understand the Daleks only too well, Doctor. I've fought them all my adult life. *Fought* them. I saw good soldiers and friends gunned down by those things, vaporised, like they never even existed. We *all* listened to the leaders of Auros being shot out of space in cold blood…'

'Believe me, no one knows the terrible things the Daleks can do better than me but—'

'Really?' Bowman paused in the doorway to his cabin. He looked doubtfully at the Doctor. 'That thing killed Stella. And you know how those Dalek guns work, don't you? On full power, they can blast a human being into atoms in a split second. But they never do that. Every Dalek dials down the power on its gun-stick to the specific level that will kill a human being. Then they lower the power setting just a tiny bit further, so that the beam burns away the central nervous system from the outside in, meaning that every human being dies in agony. So it takes a full two to three seconds for a Dalek to exterminate one of us – and that's *deliberate*.'

'I know,' said the Doctor. 'I know all that. But it still doesn't mean that what you're about to do is right. You can't just use it as an excuse to take your revenge for Stella's death.'

'But revenge is what I want,' said Bowman simply.

Cuttin' Edge had used the cargo loader to suspend the Dalek upside down from the ceiling. Its base unit was clamped into the lifter's giant metal slide grips. It hung in the middle of the chamber, its dome section level with Scrum's head.

'Perfect,' said Scrum, giving the thumbs up. 'See if you can secure the arm now.'

Cuttin' Edge was standing at the remote-control unit for the cargo loader. A few deft adjustments and a powerful metal clamp moved down from the lifting apparatus to grab hold of the Dalek's sucker arm. Cuttin' Edge increased the torque until the clamp began, very slowly, to dent the metallic tube which made up the arm. It was utterly immobilised.

The door to the cargo hold slid open and the Doctor moped in, hands in pockets. He looked up at the Dalek and tilted his head, frowning. 'Why upside down?'

'The loader's gravity field cancels out the Dalek's elevation units,' explained Scrum. He was moving around the Dalek, examining the neck and shoulder sections carefully. 'I've rigged a high-frequency radio-wave jamming field too, which should counteract the motive unit.'

The Doctor nodded, impressed. 'Yeah, that might work. I've done that a couple of times myself. It'll interfere with the guidance systems at least, and maybe the motive unit. But it won't last for ever. You'll get ten seconds, tops, before it finds a way to cancel the jamming field.'

'That's all we'll need.'

'You know this is wrong, don't you?' the Doctor asked. He picked up a couple of tools from a nearby table, checked them over, tossed them back down. 'Wrong, wrong, wrong. Wrong in so many ways.'

Cuttin' Edge looked scornful. 'We know what we're doin'.'

'And one of the many ways in which it is wrong,' continued the Doctor, 'is the way in which it is insanely, obviously and ludicrously *dangerous*.'

'Hey, we're Dalek hunters, dude. We do this for a livin'. Scrum's got everything covered.'

Scrum cleared his throat. 'Actually, I was rather hoping you would help, Doctor.'

'Not a chance.'

'You may not agree with what we're trying to do, but you must want to make sure the Dalek is truly defenceless.'

'No Dalek is ever truly defenceless.' The Doctor sighed. He pursed his lips thoughtfully. Sucked in his cheeks.

Blew out a long breath between his teeth and scratched the back of his neck. 'Oh, all right. But not because I approve of what you're doing. I just don't fancy my central nervous system being fried from the outside in – or watching yours being fried, for that matter.'

'We've immobilised the Dalek and secured the arm. It's effectively blind but—'

'Watch that sucker,' warned the Doctor, pulling Scrum away from the Dalek's reach. 'I've seen those things crush bricks like *that*.' He closed his fingers into a sudden fist.

'Uh, thanks. Well, as I said – the Dalek is effectively blind…'

'Vision impaired,' muttered the Doctor. 'That's how they like to put it. But don't forget it's got sensor systems all over its body.'

'It's the gun I'm worried about.'

'Yeah, you really want that out of action.' The Doctor slipped his glasses on and examined the weapon housing. 'Best thing is to remove it completely.'

'Is that possible?'

'While it's still thawing out we can try.'

The Doctor pulled a small set of steps over so that he could see the gun platform more easily. He took out his sonic screwdriver. 'There are four galvanised trintillium bolts securing the armour plate here around the ball-and-socket joint. See? We've got to get those out before we can see what's what.'

Scrum's eyes widened. 'Can you do that?'

'Let's give it a go,' answered the Doctor, clicking open the screwdriver.

Bowman kept an old bottle of Draconian branka in his cabin. He unscrewed the lid and sloshed some into a plastic cup. He stared at it for a second and then swallowed it down in one. The fire spread through his throat and stomach and he closed his eyes to appreciate the flavour. Then he grimaced.

'Yuck. Never did like that stuff.'

'Yet you still drink it?' Koral stepped into the pool of light that came from the captain's desk lamp.

'Sometimes.' Bowman placed the cup on the desk.

'Why?'

'It's tradition. Times like these, you need courage.'

'It gives you courage?'

'No. It just makes you think you have it. Drink enough and you think you've got all the courage in the world.'

'And what if you drink too much?'

'Then it doesn't really matter what you think.'

Koral sat on the edge of the desk. 'And what about the Doctor? What do you think of him?'

'Isn't it obvious? He's a jumped up little nerd who thinks he knows a bit about the Daleks.'

'Perhaps he does.'

Bowman regarded her carefully. 'You reckon?'

'He's not like you. But he does know a lot about the Daleks.'

'How can you tell?'

'Because of the fear in his eyes.'

'Huh.' Bowman reached for the plastic cup and the bottle again.

Koral put a hand on his arm, stopping him from pouring another drink. 'The more you know about the Daleks,' she said, 'the more you learn to fear them.'

Very carefully, the Doctor lifted the Dalek gun-stick out of its housing. The big black sphere at its base, which provided the weapon with an incredible field of fire, was attached to the interior of the rotating shoulder platform by a number of wires and flexible tubes.

'Hold that steady,' he told Scrum. Scrum took the gun-stick in his hands and watched the Doctor peer inside the open socket.

'You have to cut the right connections in the right order,' said the Doctor, aiming his sonic screwdriver inside and making a number of careful incisions. His voice was barely a whisper. 'It's a bit like defusing a bomb.'

'You've defused bombs before, then, have you?' asked Cuttin' Edge, looking over his shoulder.

'Yeah, loads.' The Doctor concentrated on the task at hand for a few more seconds and then said, 'Here we go! *Molto bene*! Out we come!'

He pulled the last wires out and the gun came free. Scrum carried it over to a workbench – it was heavier than it looked – and set it down carefully.

'You're right to be cautious,' the Doctor told him, wandering over. He was wiping his hands on a rag. 'There's a compressed power reservoir in the ball joint. There's still plenty of shooting to be done with that thing.' He pointed the sonic screwdriver at the base of the gun-stick and a shrill whine filled the air. Smoke started to drift out of the gun.

'There.' The Doctor flicked off the screwdriver. 'I've fused the control linkages. No more killing.'

'It was that easy?' queried Cuttin' Edge, looking from the gun-stick to the sonic screwdriver. 'An' that thing looks so *dinky*.'

'It's not dinky,' retorted the Doctor sharply. He held the screwdriver up, examining it. 'It's not at all dinky!'

'Whatever, it still made short work of that Dalek gun.'

The Doctor's face hardened and he took off his glasses. 'Only because it's disconnected from the Dalek itself. A sonic screwdriver wouldn't touch it otherwise.'

At that moment, Bowman strode in with Koral in tow. He took one look at the upside-down Dalek, and then glanced at the Doctor. 'What's he doing here?'

'He's been helping us,' said Scrum.

Bowman looked sceptical and the Doctor quickly shook his head. 'Oh no. No, not really. Not helping as such…'

'Yes, he has,' insisted Scrum, nodding at the gun-stick lying on the workbench. 'Couldn't have done that without him.'

'I'm not helping,' said the Doctor firmly. 'I just don't want any of you hurt.' He glanced at Bowman. 'Well, most of you.'

Bowman and Koral exchanged a look but said nothing. Eventually Bowman turned his back on the Doctor and addressed Scrum. 'Where are we up to?'

'We're ready. The casing is secured and disarmed. We can transmit a jamming field to interfere with any attempt by the creature inside to activate a self-destruct mechanism.'

'All we gotta do now is open the damn thing up,' said Cuttin' Edge.

Bowman walked slowly around the Dalek. It was completely inert. No movement from the single remaining appendage, no glimmer of light in the luminosity dischargers on its head. 'You're sure it's still alive in there?'

'Only one way to find out,' said Scrum.

'OK,' nodded Bowman. 'Let's get on with it. I've got a few questions I'd like answers to.'

'It won't work,' said the Doctor. He was leaning against the doorway, arms folded. 'Interrogating a Dalek is pointless. It won't give you any information. There's nothing you can do to it that will make it tell you anything.'

Bowman looked at him, raising an eyebrow. 'You ever tried?'

A pause. 'No.'

Bowman turned back to Scrum. 'Open it up.'

Cuttin' Edge powered up his laser and stepped forward.

'Wait!' cried the Doctor. 'Just one more thing. Don't forget that machine is also a life-support system. Open it up and you'll kill the creature inside.'

Bowman shrugged. 'Like I'm worried.'

'It's murder.'

All eyes turned on the Doctor, and he knew exactly what they were all thinking. Bowman said it out aloud: 'What about Stella? What do you call that?'

'You some kinda Dalek sympathiser now?' asked Cuttin' Edge bitterly.

'No. It's just…' The Doctor took a deep breath. 'It's just not right. I won't be a part of it.'

Bowman's lip curled as if his every worst opinion of the Doctor had been confirmed. He turned back to the others. 'Let's get on with it.'

Cuttin' Edge moved in with the laser, but Koral stepped forward and blocked his way. Puzzled, he switched off the laser, and the Doctor felt a surge of hope.

But Koral simply said, 'I wish to do this. For Stella.'

'It's OK,' said Bowman. 'Let her.'

Metallic claws sprang out of Koral's fingertips. They glinted, razor-sharp in the electric light. She stepped up to the Dalek and, turning her hand flat like the blade of a knife, pointed her fingertips at the centre of the shoulder section. It was here that the two halves of the weapons platform met, and, below this now that the Dalek was suspended upside down, the sections of the neck. There was an almost invisible join, less than a hair's breadth. Koral's red eyes narrowed as she concentrated and then, with explosive force, jabbed her fingers into the Dalek. The claws penetrated the metal with a flash of angry sparks.

There was no response. The Doctor was both appalled and fascinated. He realised that the claws must be diamond-hard and incredibly sharp, but even so – that kind of effort required immense mental focus and physical power.

Koral inserted her claws in the gap she had made and then suddenly, apparently with little effort, began to pull the two sections apart. At first the metal protested with a hideous grinding noise, but then, with a loud hiss of escaping gas, hydraulic motors opened the Dalek from within. Segments of armour split away, shifting on concealed hinges and slides.

Now the creature inside was visible. Something pale and wet moved like a slug among the exposed machinery, recoiling from the light.

'Get it out,' ordered Bowman.

Scrum and Cuttin' Edge picked up a pair of long metal staves, like boathooks, and approached the Dalek.

'Don't do this,' the Doctor urged them.

But they ignored him. Cuttin' Edge, grimacing in distaste, prodded the mutant creature a couple of times. The creature shrank back in its housing, but there was no escape. Scrum, his hands shaking, crouched low and inserted the end of his stave as well, trying to gain some kind of leverage.

And then, gradually, the creature began to emerge as they gouged it free, like an oyster from its shell. It was accompanied by a foul stench, a smell of pure *wrongness*, of something rotten sealed away for too long.

Instinctively, both Scrum and Cuttin' Edge backed away. Whether this was due to fear, or a strange kind of respect for their captive, it was impossible to tell. Cuttin' Edge dropped the stave and drew his blaster, a look of utter revulsion on his dark, sweating features.

Koral watched carefully, cautiously, ready to strike at a moment's notice. Bowman simply stood, arms folded, his face impassive.

The Dalek oozed slowly out of its cradle, leaving a thick film of mucus behind. There was a long, obscene sucking noise and then, all in a rush, the rest of the creature emerged. It plopped out in a tangle of slippery tentacles, some over a metre in length. It didn't fall onto the floor. Something caught inside the machine and the Dalek hung there, dripping slime, swaying from side to side. One of the tentacles reached down to the floor and rested there, unmoving.

'Is it dead?' Bowman asked.

'Damn waste of time,' muttered Cuttin' Edge, lowering his blaster.

'Wait,' breathed the Doctor quietly. 'Look…'

He was pointing at the centre of the beast. In among the dangling appendages and wires still connecting the flesh to the armoured machine, there was an eye.

And it was opening.

CHAPTER
NINE

The eye was yellow and bloodshot with a single black pupil.

No one said a word. The cargo chamber felt hot and claustrophobic now, more like a prison cell than a ship's hold. There was a genuine feeling that they were all witnessing something extraordinary.

The eye twitched, as if gaining some kind of focus, and began to move slightly in its socket.

'Dude,' said Cuttin' Edge, 'you are one *ugly* critter.'

'Be quiet,' said the Doctor sharply. 'I don't suppose you're the number one poster boy on Skaro yourself.'

'No, I guess that would be you,' said Cuttin' Edge.

'Only if they're "wanted" posters.'

'Shut up, the pair of you,' said Bowman. He stepped forward and looked down at the mutant. 'Can you hear me?'

There was a faint, gurgling reply. Bizarrely, the lights on the Dalek's dome flashed weakly.

'It's still connected,' Scrum realised, peering more closely at the nest of wires and tubes leading from the mutant's quivering flesh into the interior of the Dalek.

'Get back!' cried the Doctor, pulling Scrum to one side. As he moved, the black suction cup on the end of the Dalek's immobilised arm suddenly flexed as if trying to grab hold of Scrum's head.

'Whoa!' Cuttin' Edge cocked his blaster and aimed it at

the creature's blinking eye. 'Steady on there, boy.'

The sucker continued to grasp at thin air. The arm juddered in the vice-like grip of the cargo loader, and the Dalek let out a long, low groan of despair.

'You got it, dude,' said Cuttin' Edge. 'We got you by the—'

'That's enough,' growled Bowman. He turned back to the Dalek. 'You're on board the *Wayfarer*. I'm Captain Jon Bowman and this is my crew. You're our prisoner.'

'I think it's worked that part out,' said the Doctor.

'You stay out of this,' warned Bowman.

'I can't.'

'You can and you will. If you say another word, I'll have Cuttin' Edge throw you out. Got it?'

Cuttin' Edge gave the Doctor a stony look to reinforce the promise.

'You were one of a squad of Daleks on the planet Hurala,' Bowman continued, addressing the dangling mutant. 'What were you doing there?'

'It won't answer,' said the Doctor.

'Cuttin' Edge,' said Bowman.

The Doctor held his hands up as Cuttin' Edge started towards him. 'All right, all right! I won't say another word – and nor will the Dalek.'

Bowman smiled thinly. 'We'll see. Hey. Dalek. I know you can hear me. And I know you can understand me.' Bowman lowered himself to his haunches, so that he was eye-level with his prisoner. 'Now we're all humanoids here and we can be reasonable. It's your choice. Talk to us, tell us what we want to know, and things will be easier for you. If you don't cooperate – well, let's just say it won't be so easy. I don't want things getting ugly in here, but if they do... then so be it.'

The Dalek's single eye glared at Bowman with a fierce, palpable hatred. But it said nothing.

'That your final answer?'

The eye closed.

'Right,' said Bowman, standing up. 'You got that equipment I asked for, Scrum?'

Scrum wheeled a small instrument trolley forward. Laid across the tray were a number of tools.

'You can't be serious,' said the Doctor.

'You know I am,' said Bowman bleakly.

'I can't allow this.'

Bowman raised an eyebrow. 'You're not in charge around here, Doctor. I am. I want some answers from this ugly son of a bitch and I'm going to get them – by whatever means necessary.'

'You're better than this, Bowman!' the Doctor argued fiercely. 'You're a human being! Don't do this. Stand up for what you believe in.'

'I'm standing up for Stella. I'm standing up for the people of Auros. What are you standing up for, Doctor?'

'Something better than *that!*' The Doctor jabbed a finger at the mutant. 'Humanity!'

'Well, that's a very precious commodity,' Bowman sighed. 'But it isn't worth a damn to the Daleks. They don't even understand it. They just want to eradicate it. And they'll do anything and everything to achieve that aim. You know they will. They'll stop at nothing to destroy us, and so neither can I if I want to prevent them.'

'This is just one Dalek. It's as good as defenceless.'

'So I guess it's my lucky day.' Bowman picked up one of the tools from the tray and switched it on. A crackle of energy leapt from the business end. 'This one Dalek could tell me all I need to know. Now you can either stay in here and watch, or step outside if you've not got the stomach for it.'

'If you compromise your humanity now, Bowman, then the Dalek has won before you've even started.'

For a second, Bowman looked doubtful. He stared at the tip of the energy discharger, frowning. Eventually he said, 'I'm sorry, Doctor. I cannot afford the luxury of *humanity* right now.'

'I'll stop you!' growled the Doctor.

'No, you won't,' said Cuttin' Edge, levelling his gun at the Doctor's head. 'One more word an' you'll be able to sharpen pencils in your forehead.'

The Doctor glared icily at him. Then he turned to look at Scrum. 'What about you, Scrum? Are you a part of this, too?'

'You know I am,' replied Scrum quietly. He looked away. 'Just get out, Doctor, while you still can.'

The Doctor took a deep breath, realising that he was defeated. Koral watched him carefully from the other side of the cell, but her gaze was inscrutable.

Finally, the Doctor looked down at the Dalek creature. There was a slight gurgle, no more than a cough, and the dome lights sparked once. It could have been a nerve twitching, or an attempt at thanks, or even an insult. It could have been anything.

Tight-lipped, the Doctor stepped out of the room and the door hissed shut behind him.

He paced the corridor outside, seething. He had seldom felt so helpless. Of all the difficulties he had ever faced, all the strange and deadly encounters with creatures and aliens and monsters, it had to be a bunch of humans that finally stopped him in his tracks. Stupid, stubborn, infuriating *humans*.

Not for the first time, the Doctor felt incredibly alone. He longed for someone like Martha or Donna, someone who would understand, someone who could help. He thought of Stella, and a deep sense of grief suddenly washed over him. She would have understood. She would have helped.

With a heavy sigh, the Doctor leant against the wall opposite the cargo bay door. He could hear voices from inside the hold, but he couldn't tell what they were saying. He knew the Dalek wouldn't speak. He wasn't even sure if it *could* speak – there was no way of knowing how damaged it was after the cryo-charge had struck, or whether it had been harmed by the thawing process. Perhaps it was little more than a vegetable, incapable of thought or action.

He wished it was dead.

'*Think!*' he ordered himself, pressing the knuckles of his fists into his temples, running his hands backwards and forwards through his hair. He had to do something. *Anything.* There must be a way of stopping them.

Seized by a sudden need to take action, he turned towards the flight deck. Perhaps he could take control of the ship, force them to stop. Or divert all power from the cargo hold so that none of their instruments and tools would work.

The Doctor was already reaching into his pocket for the sonic screwdriver when the door hissed open. He looked up, surprised and hopeful.

It was Koral. The door hissed shut behind her and she stalked towards the Doctor. 'I've been sent out to stop you doing anything stupid.'

'I'm not the one who's doing anything stupid.'

'Put the sonic device away.'

The Doctor looked imploringly at her. 'Koral – you could put a stop to this madness. You know you could.'

'Perhaps. But I do not wish to.'

'But, Koral—'

'No buts.' She held up a hand and out jumped the steel talons. 'It would be much wiser to do as I ask.'

'Would it?' The Doctor's shoulders slumped and he put the screwdriver back in his pocket. 'All right. You've made your point.'

There was a hint of a smile as the claws were sheathed. 'Bowman guessed you would try to sabotage the ship or otherwise attempt to stop him.'

'He was right.'

'I will make sure that doesn't happen.'

The Doctor did not reply. He simply looked down as they both heard the sharp, galvanistic crackle of Bowman's energy discharger starting up, the noise slightly muffled by the cargo hold's heavy door.

The Doctor closed his eyes.

And then he heard an awful, shrill scream of pain as the discharger was used on the Dalek. It was followed by a long, involuntary gargle of relief as the agony ceased.

Koral stared straight ahead, utterly impassive.

The Doctor sank to the floor, his head in his hands.

CHAPTER
TEN

The screaming continued for another full minute before the Doctor cracked. He leapt to his feet and dived towards the cargo bay door. But Koral was there before him, steel claws at his throat. They felt cold and sharp on his skin.

'On my homeworld of Red Sky Lost, we hunted koogah beasts alone. Each koogah has a thick, armoured hide and poisoned tusks and we respected it as a formidable enemy. It is why we developed these claws.'

'Very useful, I'm sure.' The Doctor didn't move a muscle.

'With these, I could rip an adult koogah wide open with a single strike. I'm used to extreme violence and the spilling of blood. You mean less to me than a koogah beast, Doctor. I wouldn't hesitate to kill you if I had to.'

'Yes, I can see that.' Very carefully the Doctor backed away from the door, hands raised. 'But tell me, Koral – when you were hunting these koogah things... did you torture them as well?'

She made no reply. All they could hear was the crackle of the power discharger.

The Doctor leant back against the opposite wall. 'So, what are we going to do now? Stand out here and listen to that thing scream until it dies?'

'If necessary.'

'But that's just it.' The Doctor's teeth were grinding together as he bit off each individual word. 'It's *not* necessary.'

'Nor was the destruction of Red Sky Lost!' It was the first time the Doctor had seen Koral lose her cool, even slightly. 'The Daleks razed my planet to the ground. They slaughtered everyone. Everything. Genocide!'

'They are masters of it.'

'And you expect me to stand aside and allow them to go unpunished?' Koral glared hotly at him. 'I am the only survivor! The last of my people! After me, there is *nothing*.'

'Yes,' said the Doctor sadly. 'I know.'

She shook her head. 'You know nothing.'

He leant closer to her again, looking directly into her flaming eyes without flinching. 'Let me go back in there, Koral. Stop Bowman from tearing that creature apart and let *me* talk to it.'

'You?'

'Yes! *I* can make it talk!'

The corridor was filled with another round of screaming. Something thick and wet gurgled in the Dalek's vocal cords – or whatever it used to speak – and the noise suddenly choked off, replacing by a pathetic, ululating whimper.

'If it's not too late,' insisted the Doctor, 'I can make it speak. I know how to get information out of it.'

'You're bluffing.'

The Doctor didn't even blink. 'Trust me!'

The silence that followed was thick with possibilities. In the end it was broken by the sound of the cargo hold door opening.

The Doctor and Koral separated quickly, as if they were lovers caught by surprise, but no one was interested.

Bowman stood in the doorway. His big shoulders were slumped, and there was sweat on his face. A waft of hot air, carrying an indescribably fetid odour, seeped out of the hold.

'It's over,' he growled. 'It's dead.'

Scrum and Cuttin' Edge emerged behind him. Scrum looked white-faced and physically ill. Cuttin' Edge's face was etched with what could have been distaste or fear. He was still carrying the stave, and the end of it was covered in a sticky, green ichor.

Bowman stalked away, calling Scrum after him like an obedient dog. Cuttin' Edge paused, raising his head so he could look at the Doctor. 'If it's any consolation,' he said quietly, 'you were right. It never said a word.'

The Doctor just looked at him with contempt.

Cuttin' Edge turned to Koral. 'Skipper wants us all in the galley,' he told her. 'Team meeting.'

The door to the cargo bay remained open. Inside it was dark, except for a dull red glow from the emergency lights. The Doctor guessed that Bowman's power discharger had fused the illumination circuits at some point. Now the interior of the hold looked like a little pocket of Hell.

Ignoring the stench, the Doctor stepped inside.

The remains of the Dalek lay on the floor beneath the upended casing. It was quite small – the distended brain sac lying like a rotten melon in a pool of dark unguent. Some of its squid-like arms were coiled around the carcass, while others lay on the floor like dead worms, severed from the main body.

There were many more wires and cables dangling from the Dalek casing, evidence of how Scrum and Cuttin' Edge must have had to scrape the creature out of its shell. Strings of glistening slime hung down like the drool of some strange metal beast that had recently vomited the half-digested contents of its stomach onto the floor.

The Doctor knelt down carefully by the dead creature

and put his glasses on. It was difficult to see anything clearly in the red emergency lighting, but there was something that made him want to check. You could never trust a Dalek, even in death.

And, just fractionally, the single eye twitched.

'You're still alive,' breathed the Doctor. His voice was no more than an awed whisper.

The eye slowly closed.

'Oh, come on,' said the Doctor. 'You can't fool me.'

The eye opened again, swivelling jerkily in the broken socket until it was looking at the Doctor. There was no indication that it could actually see, let alone focus. Perhaps it was just registering the sound of his voice.

'It's me,' said the Doctor. 'The Oncoming Storm.'

The eye opened a little wider, and the red-black dot at its centre shrank. An inarticulate gurgle emerged faintly from the glistening remains.

'Or maybe you just know me as the Doctor.'

Another gurgle.

'That's the trouble with jumping the time lines,' said the Doctor, sitting down on the floor. 'It's difficult to work out where we're up to. Dalek history was confusing enough *before* the Time War.'

'DOC...TOR...'

The hairs on the back of his neck actually stood up. He swallowed, momentarily lost for words. Eventually he simply replied, 'Yes?'

'ONLY... AT... THE END... DO YOU COME...' The Dalek quivered with the effort of speaking, although it was hard to make out the actual words. 'TO GLOAT.'

'No,' the Doctor shook his head. 'No, I'm not gloating.'

'THEN... KILL... ME...'

'I can't.'

90

'COWARD.'

'There's no need to fight me,' said the Doctor.

'THEN... WHY HAVE YOU COME?'

'I'm not here for that. You're finished. Even you must admit that.'

'DALEKS... NEVER... CAPITULATE.'

'That's your problem. There's no reasoning with you. You've all got one-track minds. I bet if you could fire your gun now you'd exterminate me on the spot.'

'YES!'

'When any sane being would plead for their life. For mercy.'

'DALEKS DO NOT PLEAD.'

'I know. But you could have saved yourself a lot of bother if you'd spoken up sooner. Bowman only wanted to talk.'

'BOWMAN...?'

'The man who was… interrogating you.'

'HE FAILED.' There was a hint of triumph in the croaking voice. 'I SHOULD NOT... HAVE ALLOWED MYSELF... TO BE CAPTURED. BUT HIS FAILURE... WAS THE GREATER. NO MATTER WHAT HE DID TO ME... I WOULD NOT TALK.'

'Very impressive, I'm sure.'

'HUMANS DO NOT UNDERSTAND TORTURE.'

'Oh, I think they do. Unfortunately. It's not one of their more endearing traits, but they do know how to inflict pain and suffering, I'll give you that.'

'I EXPECTED NOTHING LESS.'

The Doctor stirred. 'No. That's wrong. Humans are capable of love and mercy as well. And generosity and charity too. There is no limit to the good they can do – or that they are capable of. Not like you. All you know is pain and suffering.'

'AND THAT IS WHY WE WILL SUCCEED.' said the Dalek. 'WE UNDERSTAND PAIN. HUMANS DO NOT.'

The Doctor wondered if the Dalek was speaking from experience. And when he considered the metal and plastic wires connecting the creature to its cramped life-support machine where, up until today, it had spent its entire waking life, he realised that it probably was.

The Dalek had not yet finished its rant. 'BUT THE HUMAN RACE WILL BE DEFEATED. ALL HUMANS WILL CEASE TO EXIST. THE DALEKS WILL ERADICATE THEM FROM THE UNIVERSE!'

'Never.'

'THE DALEKS WILL TRIUMPH! THERE IS NOTHING THAT CAN STOP US FROM CHANGING THE PATH OF HISTORY – NOT EVEN YOU. DOC-TOR!'

'You're delirious,' said the Doctor scornfully.

'THE DALEKS WILL CONQUER AND DESTROY,' grated the creature, seeming to regain some of its energy in its dying moments. 'WE WILL ELIMINATE ALL HUMAN LIFE FROM ITS VERY BEGINNINGS! WE WILL CONQUER TIME AND SPACE! THE FUTURE WILL BELONG TO THE DALEKS!'

The Doctor leant closer, suddenly angry. 'Oh yeah? Well, get this: I've seen the future. You lot are going to end up so hungry and mad for power that you bite off more than you can chew. And the whole conquest of time and space thing is going to blow up in your faces.' The Doctor moved even closer, until he could smell the toxic slime that covered the Dalek. 'You're all going to burn and no matter how much you try to come back, or which of you remain, I'm always gonna be there to stop you. So just remember: *there's a storm coming!*'

The Dalek shrank back a little. But there was still defiance, even in its last seconds of life. 'YOU THREATEN ME WHEN I CANNOT FIGHT BACK. YOU HAVE ONLY COME TO WATCH ME

DIE. BUT THE DALEKS WILL TRIUMPH! THE DALEKS WILL ALWAYS SURVIVE. WE WILL BE MASTERS OF THE UNIVERSE!'

The Dalek's final words died in a hysterical groan; the creature convulsed and then seemed to deflate as the eye closed for a final time. The Doctor was under no illusion that it was now truly dead. And for that he was profoundly grateful.

But then something seemed to click in his brain – a sudden connection, something the Dalek had said that flicked a switch of realisation in his head. He jumped up, wide-eyed and alert. His hair was practically standing up in spikes with agitation. 'Of course!' he exploded, smacking his forehead with the heel of one hand. 'That's what they were doing on Hurala!'

And then he turned and left the cargo hold at a run.

For a few seconds all was quiet in the room. And then a shadow detached itself from the corner of the hold and Koral followed the Doctor out.

There was silence in the galley. Bowman sat with his chin resting on one giant fist, locked in his own thoughts. Scrum sat at the mess table. Cuttin' Edge was sprawled on another seat, glumly nursing his assault rifle. None of them would look at the others.

'Total waste of time,' muttered Cuttin' Edge after a while. 'But I'm glad we did it.'

Scrum looked at him, hollow-eyed. 'Why?' he asked bitterly.

'Cos it felt good.'

'Did it?'

Cuttin' Edge looked away. 'OK, so maybe it *didn't* feel so good. It's like… it's like that thing was laughin' at us. Inside. Like it could just soak up anything we did to it. It was makin' monkeys outta all of us!'

'Don't be stupid.'

'It was never gonna tell us anything.'

'That wasn't the point,' said Bowman abruptly. He straightened up, looking at both crewmen. His grey eyes were tired and deep-set. 'We did it for Stella.'

'It didn't bring her back, though, did it?' said Scrum miserably.

'Wasn't meant to. But that Dalek had some pain coming to it.'

Scrum still looked unconvinced. 'I don't think Stella would have wanted that.'

'I don't think Stella wanted to be shot in the back by that scum either,' said Cuttin' Edge. 'Skip's right. Dalek had it comin'. End of.'

They lapsed into silence again, each man brooding on the argument.

And then the Doctor suddenly whirled into the room, fizzing with energy. 'What do you know about the Arkheon Threshold?' he demanded.

All three looked up at him. 'What?'

'I've just been having a little chat with your Dalek,' explained the Doctor. 'What was left of it, anyway.'

'You what?' growled Bowman.

'It's dead,' said Cuttin' Edge. 'We killed it.'

'Yes, it's dead *now*,' agreed the Doctor. 'And yes, you did kill it. But there was one last spark of life left in those old mutant genes and it suddenly felt quite chatty. Starting telling me all about the Daleks' big plan to wipe mankind from history.'

'You're lying,' Bowman stated, getting to his feet. He practically filled the small galley on his own.

'No,' said Koral, appearing in the doorway. 'He's not.'

The Doctor looked at her, puzzled.

'I was in the cargo hold with you,' she told him. 'I heard every word.'

'Really?' said the Doctor. He waited for her to say more, but she just returned his stare.

'Hang on,' interrupted Cuttin' Edge. 'How come it talked for *you*?'

'Dunno,' confessed the Doctor brightly. 'Maybe it was my winning personality. Maybe it was because I wasn't poking it with a sharp stick and discharging 50,000 volts through it at the time. Who knows?'

'Maybe it was a deathbed confession,' said Koral.

'Well, either way, we did exchange a few words in its final moments – although there was a lot of the usual kind of thing: Daleks are the supreme beings, Daleks will conquer and destroy, exterminate exterminate, et cetera. But it did let slip one tiny thing that could be important. Very, very important.'

Bowman folded his arms. 'Such as?'

'The Daleks must know about the Arkheon Threshold.'

The Doctor was met with four blank stares.

'The what?' said Bowman.

'*That's* what they were doing on Hurala,' the Doctor explained. 'They were sniffing around for information. The Lodestar station was a staging post for interstellar travel, remember – forgotten and dusty, but in its heyday quite an important little place. They used to call it "the gateway to the stars". Stella hit the nail on the head when she spotted the planet Arkheon in the station's list of nearby worlds. It didn't mean much to me at the time, but now I realise exactly why the Daleks were so interested in whoever turned up there! They want the Arkheon Threshold.'

'Which is…?'

'Don't tell me you've never heard of the Arkheon Threshold?'

Cautiously, Scrum raised a hand. 'Well, I have heard of the *planet* Arkheon…'

The Doctor spun around and pointed a finger straight at him. 'Give that man a star! The planet Arkheon – somewhere near the Crab Nebula, I seem to recall, just past the Pleiades and left at the Blue Star Worlds. You can't miss it.'

'Well you can now,' Scrum said. 'It was completely destroyed over forty years ago.'

The Doctor's face froze. 'What?'

'Arkheon was one of the planets that fell victim to the First Dalek Incursion,' Scrum explained. 'I think it was hit by one of those old planet-splitters. I was only a kid at the time.'

'Completely destroyed?'

'Yes.'

'What, *completely* completely?'

'Yes.'

'Doesn't matter!' The Doctor was instantly re-energised. 'Or rather, the actual planet itself doesn't matter. But the Threshold does.'

'The Arkheon Threshold,' Bowman repeatedly carefully.

'I think we ought to listen to the Doctor,' advised Koral. She was speaking directly to Bowman.

Bowman raised an eyebrow, considering. 'All right, Doctor. You'd better tell us what you know.'

CHAPTER
ELEVEN

'The planet Arkheon was famous for its ghosts,' began the Doctor, lowering his voice in a suitably sinister manner. He was sitting in the middle of the galley, with the crew of the *Wayfarer* arranged around him like children ready to hear a ghoulish campfire story. 'In fact, it was often called the Planet of Ghosts.'

A shiver seemed to pass through the little group.

'Well, I say ghosts,' the Doctor went on, 'but they were more like quasi-temporal personality echoes. But the Planet of Quasi-Temporal Personality Echoes just doesn't sound quite the same, does it? I won't bore you with the science – unless you really want me to – but the ghosts and spectral visions that haunted Arkheon were actually the usual sort of stuff you get with a planet that contains some sort of time rift.'

'Time rift?' echoed Scrum, frowning.

The Doctor pulled a face. 'Well, not actually a time rift. Not in your honest-to-goodness Cardiff kind of way...'

'Cardiff?'

'Never been to Cardiff? You haven't lived. Never mind. What I'm trying to say is that Arkheon was special. Located deep inside the planet was a small chronic schism – a little tear in time and space, if you like. It wasn't important. In fact it was largely ignored, except by the kind of scientists who liked to research that sort of thing. And the Arkheon Threshold – which is what the scientists called the temporal anomaly – was never actually found. After a while it was dismissed as nothing more than a theory.'

'What about the ghosts?' asked Scrum.

The Doctor grinned. 'Aw, what about 'em! Greatest ghost stories anywhere! Doesn't matter that they were nothing more than harmless echoes in time, they were still brilliant. I used to like the one about the sailor who had lost his head in a terrible battle. He could sometimes be seen just off the coast, rowing his way slowly around the bay in a small raft. They used to call him the Headless Oarsman.'

'Keep to the point,' said Bowman bluntly. He was sitting on the far side of the galley, massive arms folded across his chest and a sullen, distrustful look on his face. Koral sat nearby, cross-legged, her eyes half-closed like a dozing cat.

'OK,' said the Doctor with a sigh. 'Tough crowd. Never mind. The point is this – if Arkheon was destroyed by the Daleks like you say, then any little fracture in time and space at its centre will have remained. It wouldn't be a part of the actual rock and soil of the planet, you see, it'd be part of the fabric of time and space itself. You can't destroy a time fissure.'

'And this is really important because…?' prompted Cuttin' Edge.

'Because if the Daleks manage to locate the Arkheon Threshold then we're all in big trouble. I don't just mean the five of us in this ship. I'm thinking a little bigger than that – like the whole universe.'

'Why?' asked Bowman. 'How could the Daleks use this theoretical time thing – if it even exists?'

The Doctor looked grim. 'The Daleks are brilliant

scientists and engineers. Combine their indomitable hunger for power and conquest with the hitherto untapped potential of a time-space anomaly and… well, do I have to draw a diagram?'

'Yeah,' said Cuttin' Edge.

'He means they could use it to control time,' said Scrum.

The Doctor nodded gravely. 'Any foothold the Daleks can get in time they will exploit to the maximum. The Dalek you captured said that they intended to wipe mankind from history. It's easy to think that's just the usual Dalek rhetoric – but in this case it could be close to the truth.'

There was a short silence while the Doctor looked expectantly at them.

'So what are we supposed to do about it?' asked Bowman eventually.

'We have to stop them,' replied the Doctor simply. 'They must be looking for the Arkheon Threshold. We have to prevent them finding it. I suggest you contact Earth Command immediately and—'

'Hold it,' said Bowman, raising a hand. 'Forget that, Doctor. We can't contact Earth Command. For one thing, we don't have any official status with the authorities.'

'And no one on Earth will believe us anyway,' added Cuttin' Edge. 'We're bounty hunters, man. That's one step up from criminals as far as they're concerned. We tell them about this, they'll just laugh in our faces. We caught ourselves a live Dalek and interrogated it for the information? Yeah, right.'

Scrum nodded in agreement. 'You did say this time fissure was only a theory, Doctor. We haven't exactly got any hard evidence, have we? And we're light years from anywhere out here. By the time we reach Earth space and make contact, the Daleks will have found what they're looking for.'

The Doctor was looking worried. 'Even so—'

'We don't contact Earth Command,' said Bowman firmly. 'And that's final.'

He stared hard at the Doctor, absently rubbing the white scar on his forearm.

'All right.' The Doctor took a deep breath. 'So it's up to us to stop them.'

'Us?' Scrum looked around the galley, making a headcount. He didn't look very encouraged by the result.

'We've stumbled on something incredibly important here,' said the Doctor forcefully. 'We can't afford to ignore it.'

'It's only you who says it's important,' Bowman pointed out.

'You're the one who wanted to question the Dalek,' returned the Doctor acidly. 'Don't waste the answers.'

'It didn't give any answers – except a hint about some kind of legend. It's stupid.'

'For what it's worth,' said Koral, 'I think you should listen to what the Doctor says.'

Bowman frowned. 'I'm not promising anything. This whole thing sounds lame to me. Some old planet blown up way back when that can help the Daleks change history? It's a crazy idea, even for them.'

'But the Daleks *are* crazy,' said Scrum. 'They're arrogant and clever enough to take something like the Arkheon Threshold and use it against us. Against the whole human race. If there's even a chance of stopping them, then I think we should go for it. We owe Stella that much at least.'

After a short silence, Bowman said, 'OK. We'll check it out. For Stella.'

'There's one problem we're overlookin',' said Cuttin' Edge. 'If the Daleks don't even know where this Arkheon thing is, how can we hope to find it?'

'That's where you have an advantage,' smiled the Doctor. 'Me.'

The Doctor was soon sitting at the flight controls of the *Wayfarer* while Scrum showed him the navigation computer.

'It's programmed with all galactic coordinates for this sector of space,' Scrum explained, 'including star lanes and trade routes of every major solar system. It uses a hyperlink tachyon echo to the Earth satellite network.'

'Never did trust satnav,' sniffed the Doctor.

'You can't navigate your way through deep space without a proper guidance system.'

'I've got a proper guidance system,' the Doctor retorted. He tapped his forehead. 'Up here. Trust me, I never get lost. Well, hardly ever. Well, not often. All right, *sometimes*, perhaps... but more often than not I...' He started to tap his pockets. 'Where did I put my glasses? I've left them somewhere...'

'Well if you can't even find your glasses...!'

'No, here we are.' The Doctor found his glasses and slipped them on. He examined the navigation computer and then blew out a big raspberry. 'This is a bit primitive, isn't it?'

Scrum sounded hurt. 'This is state-of-the-art! It may not look like much but—'

'Yeah, yeah,' the Doctor waved him to silence. 'I don't mean to be rude, but... I was hoping for something a tiny bit more sophisticated. We need to get to the Arkheon system before the Daleks. We won't get there before Christmas using this stuff.' He rapped a knuckle on the navigation computer.

'The *Wayfarer*'s an old military vessel,' explained Scrum. 'She saw action in the First Dalek Incursion – there are still dents in her secondary hull where she was hit by a neutronic missile that failed to detonate.'

The Doctor whistled. 'She's a tough old bird, I'll give you that.'

'She was decommissioned and turned into a merchant ship,' Scrum continued as the Doctor began to work on the controls. 'Bowman had her reconditioned when he took her over. Her engines and flight controls have been completely replaced, much of it with stuff that isn't available on the commercial market. The *Wayfarer* may not be perfect, and she may be in need of repairs, but to us she's more than a ship, Doctor. She's home.'

'Reminds me of the TARDIS,' said the Doctor sadly.

'TARDIS?'

'My own ship. I left it on the planet Hurala.' The Doctor stared into space for a few seconds, lost in thought. Then he sniffed and gave Scrum a smile. 'Look, I couldn't help but notice that the *Wayfarer*'s engines were a bit rattly. It's probably just a loose regulator valve in the coolant pumps. I can fix it if you like.'

'Will you have time?'

'Course. It'll take a couple of hours for this old thing to get to Arkheon.'

'But what about the navigation? The coordinates?'

'All done.' The Doctor waved a hand at the flight controls. 'And I've set the autopilot. Straight past the Pleiades, left at the Blue Star Worlds. Like I said, can't miss it.'

'And the Daleks?'

'Oh, don't worry about them. They'll be using satnav. Probably going the wrong way round the Crab Nebula already.'

Scrum grinned. 'You remind me of Stella. No matter how bad things got, she was always able to cheer you up. She had a knack of saying just the right thing, you know?'

'I think I do.'

'And, for what it's worth...' Scrum added quietly, 'she would never have let Bowman do what he did to that Dalek. Stella was... better than that. She was someone you could rely on to do the right thing. And she could stand up for herself. I didn't like what was happening in that cargo hold, Doctor, but I was too weak to stop it. I was more scared of Bowman than the Dalek. But Stella would have stood up to him.'

'And Bowman would have listened to her?'

Scrum thought for a moment. 'Yes, I think he would.'

'I didn't know her for long, but she certainly seemed very special,' the Doctor agreed. 'You must really miss her.'

Scrum heaved a sigh. 'More than you can imagine.'

'Perhaps.'

In the cargo hold, Bowman and Cuttin' Edge were clearing out the remains of the Dalek. Bowman, wearing a pair of heavy, padded gauntlets from an old spacesuit, was scooping the remains of the Dalek mutant into a waste sack. His mouth was downturned, his nostrils pinched. The creature stank to high heaven.

Cuttin' Edge was detaching the empty casing and mechanisms from the cargo lifter, flinging bits of armour plate and lumps of wiring across the hold into a pile in the corner. Every so often he would throw a piece of the Dalek with more force than was necessary, accompanied by some very earthy language.

'Hey,' said Bowman. 'What's got into you?'

Cuttin' Edge paused, breathing hard. 'It was askin' for trouble,' he spat. 'Scum of the universe.'

Bowman straightened up. 'Say again?'

'We did the right thing,' Cuttin' Edge said. 'Didn't we?'

'Course,' said Bowman. 'It's warfare. You knew that; the Dalek knew it too.'

Cuttin' Edge wiped the sweat off his forehead with the back of his hand. 'I know that. But I only ever shot 'em up before. I never... did that. Not close up. It felt... it felt kinda wrong. An' the way the Doctor was goin' on... I just felt *confused*.'

Bowman sealed the bag and carried it across the hold. He dumped it on the floor alongside the jumble of machinery. 'Sometimes tough decisions have to be made. It's easy to take the moral high ground. The politicians and the civilians can do that. But we're the ones left to deal with the consequences.'

'Then why do I feel so bad?'

'No one said it was gonna be easy.'

Cuttin' Edge bristled. 'I know that. I ain't never had it easy. I had my Pa kickin' all kinds of zip outta me from day one on Gauda Prime. I had to drag myself out that hole an' into the army an' not even *they* wanted me. An' you know the fix I was in when you found me.'

Bowman looked at Cuttin' Edge for a long moment before replying. He suddenly felt very old, and Cuttin' Edge suddenly looked very young. 'Listen, son. You're one of the good guys. Don't let anyone tell you anything else. Not your folks, not the army, not even the Doctor.

You fight Daleks and that means you're on the right side when all is said and done, no matter what. And it takes courage to do what you did.'

'I didn't feel very brave when I was scrapin' that thing out of its barrel.'

'It's not how you feel that matters. It's what you do despite the way you feel. Look at Scrum. Damn near wetting himself the whole time but he still stuck it out. The only one not gettin' his hands dirty was the Doctor.'

Cuttin' Edge gave a shrug. 'Everyone has a point of view, I guess.'

'Yeah,' Bowman nodded. 'Only trouble is, his point of view is the wrong one. Now get that Dalek off my ship. Kick its tin backside out into space, along with the contents. I don't ever want another one of those things onboard.'

'You betcha.'

Bowman smirked. 'Whatever happened to "Yes, sir"?'

'You what?'

'Never mind, Cuttin' Edge. Never mind. Old days, long gone.' Bowman pulled off the gauntlets and threw them onto the rubbish heap. 'Best get rid of them too while you're at it. And then you can clear the rest of that slime off the floor. Smell's getting on my nerves.'

The Doctor and Scrum were discussing the technical specifications of the *Wayfarer*'s engines when Bowman strode onto the flight deck. He glared suspiciously at the Doctor and then spoke to Scrum. 'We've got rid of that thing, anyway. Dumped the casing and the mutant into deep space. Cuttin' Edge is cleaning out the cargo hold now.'

'The Doctor's plotted a course for Arkheon,' Scrum

informed him. 'Or at least, where it used to be. We should be there in a couple of hours.'

Bowman raised an eyebrow. 'That's quick, even for the *Wayfarer*.'

'Well, I know a few short cuts,' admitted the Doctor. 'And I picked up some clues on Hurala.'

'Maybe the Daleks did too.'

'True – which is why we need to push ahead at full speed.' The Doctor stood up and faced Bowman. 'With your permission, I'd like to tighten the regulator valves in the engine room. They're loose and costing us time.'

Bowman regarded him coolly. 'Just for the record, Doctor, I still don't like you. I've no idea what we're heading into, but I still say you know more than you're letting on. The only reason I haven't thrown you overboard with the remains of that Skaro slime is because of Koral. She's vouching for you and I'd trust *her* with my life. So if you betray that trust – if this is any kind of a trick or some sort of con – then I'll kill you myself, quickly and with pleasure. Got that?'

'Loud and clear.'

'And once we reach Arkheon, just remember one thing: I'm in charge. Not you.'

Chapter
Twelve

The Doctor was in his shirtsleeves, working on the *Wayfarer*'s engines, when Koral found him.

She stepped out of the shadows in a cloud of steam as the Doctor finished tightening the last of the regulator valves. He looked up when she arrived, the sonic screwdriver still clamped between his teeth.

'Gnnf gnn mmph gnn,' he said.

'Excuse me?'

The Doctor dropped the screwdriver into his hand. 'I said, you can't creep up on me like that any more.'

'I wasn't trying to.'

'Well, I've fixed these old engines so they're running like a sewing machine. Listen.' The Doctor cupped a hand to one ear and grinned. 'Not a rattle or a squeak. You could hear a pin drop anywhere onboard now.'

Koral frowned. The *Wayfarer*'s engines produced a constant, bass rumble. If you touched the bulkhead anywhere, you could feel the heavy vibration, and the deck plates trembled beneath your feet. This close, the engines sounded like more like the roar of a wild, mechanical animal.

The Doctor bounced to his feet and picked up his jacket from where he'd left it slung over a pipe. 'It's not often I get to fiddle with one of these old astronic propulsion systems. They're brilliant, in their own way. Rotten for the environment, of course, and prone to sudden

catastrophic ion implosion if they're not looked after –
but brilliant, even so.'

Koral gave him an odd look.

'It's a man thing,' he said.

'What did you mean, back in the cargo hold,' began
Koral, 'when you said that you'd seen the future?'

'Ah, sudden change of subject. Very good. Catch me off
guard. Won't work.'

'Don't avoid the question.'

The Doctor stopped and looked at her. 'I don't want to
talk about it. It's complicated.'

'When you first came onboard you said you were in the
wrong place and time.'

'It's just a saying. It means bad luck.'

'I think you meant it literally.'

The Doctor took a deep breath. 'Koral, let's say that I
have seen the future. Call it foresight or precognition or
just plain madness, I don't care. But when – if – the Daleks
manage to crack time wide open, it will lead to death and
destruction on a scale you simply can't comprehend.
The Daleks are more than capable of that. Worse, they're
willing to do it.'

Koral looked into his eyes and realised that, somewhere,
somehow, those eyes had witnessed that kind of death
and destruction. She shivered. 'You really intend to stop
them, don't you?'

'I can't.' He looked suddenly pained. 'I just… can't. But
maybe I can delay them, until the universe is ready. Or
as ready as it will ever be. I don't know. Like I said, it's
complicated. If you think about it too much your head
will hurt. Let's just say I'm in the wrong place and time,
but while I'm here I might as well try to help.'

'I think I understand,' Koral said eventually.

The Doctor nodded. 'And thanks for vouching for me, by the way. I think your pal Bowman is beginning to trust me.'

'Bowman does not trust anyone.'

'He trusts you. But he did say if I betray that trust he'll kill me.'

'Then he is mistaken,' Koral said. 'He will not kill you – I will.'

Thanks to the Doctor, the *Wayfarer* reached its destination in record time. The crew were met with something of a surprise when they reached the flight deck.

'I don't believe it,' said Scrum in an awed whisper. He was staring, open mouthed, at the forward viewscreen. The others crowded in behind him. 'What... the hell is it?'

'It's the remains of Arkheon,' said the Doctor. 'The Planet of Ghosts.'

It looked like the spectral remnant of a planet – a pale, wraithlike world shrouded in mists and shimmering ice. But there was something even more unnatural about it: a deformity, a terrible wrongness to its shape. This wasn't a complete globe – this was only one half of a planet, a giant hemisphere of frozen rock with the remains of its glowing, molten core exposed to space like a luminous scab.

As the *Wayfarer* descended into orbit, the pristine curvature of the horizon suddenly disappeared. The glittering white surface gave way to a dizzying chasm and a ragged, black interior. At its centre was a hard orange ball of superhot iron, crusted with burning rock.

'It's incredible,' breathed Koral. 'Impossible.'

'The Dalek planet-splitters do exactly what they say on the tin,' remarked the Doctor. 'That's all you're left with:

bits and pieces and a big, lifeless chunk of rock floating in space.' He glanced sourly at Bowman. 'Between them and your lot, it's a wonder there are any planets left in the galaxy.'

Bowman curled his lip but said nothing.

'It is both wonderful and terrible at the same time,' said Koral.

Scrum was checking the instruments. 'There's no sign of any other spaceships in the vicinity,' he reported. 'It's deserted. Looks like the Daleks are looking in the wrong place after all.'

'Couldn't be better,' said the Doctor, clapping Scrum on the shoulder. 'We've got the place to ourselves.'

'Do you think that Threshold thing is still down there?' wondered Cuttin' Edge.

'Let's find out,' said the Doctor. 'Take us in.'

Bowman gave a meaningful cough.

'Oh, sorry…'

The captain turned to Scrum.

'Take us in,' he ordered.

The *Wayfarer* swept through the tattered remains of Arkheon's atmosphere. Clouds parted like frightened wraiths as the ship thundered over mountain ranges and glaciers. There were deep, dry ravines where rivers and oceans once flowed, and towering crystals sculpted into strange shapes by harsh winds.

Finally, they flew over the ruins of a city. Crumbling spires stood among bridges and arched hallways, all covered in shrouds of snow that broke away in startled white flurries as the *Wayfarer* came in to land.

'It's fantastic,' said Scrum, his face reflecting the bright, wintery glare. 'Amazing.'

The Doctor peered out of the viewscreen, utterly captivated. 'The rulers of Arkheon built a city fit for a race of kings and queens,' he said appreciatively.

'Now all that's left is the wreckage,' growled Bowman, the blazing white light of the planet's surface bleaching the colour from his face.

'The atmosphere is borderline toxic,' reported Scrum. 'You can breathe it, but it won't be nice.'

'We won't be staying long,' said Bowman.

Scrum set the *Wayfarer* down on a rocky shelf overlooking the outskirts of the city. They assembled near the exit airlock and sorted out some cold-weather gear Bowman had stowed.

'You gotta be kiddin', man,' said Cuttin' Edge, pulling on a thick, padded jacket with a fur-trimmed hood. His bulky arms stretched the material taut across his shoulders. 'How am I expected to look cool in this stuff?'

'You're expected to look warm,' said Bowman. He pulled on his own parka and fastened the seal. 'These were Space Navy standard issue when the *Wayfarer* used to patrol the Iceworlds. They've got integral soft filament thermostats that will tune themselves in to your own natural body heat.'

He turned to look at the Doctor, who was struggling into one of the parkas. 'What exactly are we looking for, anyway? Ghosts?'

'No such thing,' replied the Doctor cheerfully. 'But keep an eye out for any quasi-temporal personality echoes, won't you?'

'Why? They dangerous?'

'No,' the Doctor sighed. 'I'd just like to see one, that's all.'

'So how do we find this Threshold?'

111

'Leave that to me.'

'Don't worry,' Bowman assured him. He rammed a charge pack into his blaster and holstered it. 'I'll be right behind you.'

The Doctor's plimsolls crunched into the snow. There was always something special about stepping onto a new planet and he tried to savour the moment.

'Move on out, dude,' said Cuttin' Edge behind him. 'There's a queue buildin' up here.'

The Doctor walked towards the remains of the city. Spires and towers and the jagged remains of rising walkways hung with long, glimmering icicles. Above him, thin strips of clouds glowed silver in the light of the stars. The planet – what was left of it – was on the edge of a vast, gaseous nebula which turned the night sky into a field of verdant, glittering green lights.

'Well?' Bowman asked, trudging through the snow.

'Fine, thanks,' nodded the Doctor. 'You?'

'Don't get funny, I'm not in the mood.'

'Where's Koral?' asked the Doctor.

'Why? Worried she isn't around to protect you?'

'No, I just thought she would enjoy a bit of shore leave. We could all do with stretching our legs.'

Bowman turned away, scanning the horizon. 'She's around. Koral likes to keep a low profile.'

'Even here?'

The Doctor was impressed. There didn't appear to be anywhere in this white wilderness that even Koral could hide.

'You'd be surprised.'

Scrum crunched his way through the snow to join them. 'Ship's secure. Any luck with the Threshold?'

'Haven't started looking yet,' said the Doctor. 'We're just admiring the view.'

'*He's* admiring the view,' grunted Bowman. 'I'm not.'

Cuttin' Edge had climbed up onto a high wall. 'Hey, guys. Check this out.'

They clambered up to join him, using a succession of broken rocks and icy ledges to reach the top. On the other side, a long, shallow ravine stretched away from them, littered with boulders and lumps of what looked like rusted machinery.

'What the hell?' growled Bowman.

'It's a road,' Scrum realised. 'Look – leading out of the city. Sweeping off in that direction. You can see where the ice has formed.'

Cuttin' Edge pointed at the machinery. 'What are they? Cars?'

'Some sort of transport, yes,' said the Doctor. 'All heading out of the city. Probably running for their lives when the planet-splitter missiles were detected heading straight for them. They never stood a chance. Clogged up with all these vehicles, the road would have become a death trap. When the missile struck, the seismic shock would have been enough to shift continental plates. Tidal waves, volcanoes, earthquakes, fire, poisonous fumes – all at once. There probably wasn't even time for all those cataclysms to have an effect. The entire planet would have broken apart, right down to the centre, like an apple hit by an axe. The atmosphere would have been torn to shreds. These people would have perished in an instant, turned to jelly by the initial shockwave.'

They stood and stared at the fossilised cars for several minutes, each trying to take in the size of the catastrophe in their own way. It was barely possible.

'Hold it,' said Cuttin' Edge, raising his assault rifle. 'Thought I saw somethin'.'

'What?' asked Scrum.

'I dunno. Somethin' movin'. In the distance.'

'Impossible,' said Bowman.

Cuttin' Edge was scanning the road through the gunsight on his rifle. After a minute he lowered the weapon. 'Gone now. If there was anythin' at all.'

'Maybe it was just some snow falling,' suggested Scrum. 'Or an icicle breaking.'

'Yeah.' Cuttin' Edge didn't sound convinced.

Bowman whistled – a short, sharp note that was carried eerily away on the cold breeze. A moment later, a dark figure scampered up onto the wall alongside him. It was Koral; she wasn't wearing a parka but appeared completely at ease in the biting cold.

'Cuttin' Edge thinks he saw some movement down there,' Bowman told her. 'Check it out.'

Without a word, Koral turned and darted away, jumping lithely down the rubble where the wall had collapsed. She ran onto the road and quickly disappeared among the dead cars. Soon, the sound of her feet in the snow was covered by the thick blanket of silence.

'Koral can scout ahead,' Bowman said to the others. 'Let's get on with it, Doctor.'

The Doctor took out his sonic screwdriver and clicked it on. Holding the device out in front of him at arm's length, he appeared to take a number of readings from all points of the compass. 'This way,' he said at last, following Koral down towards the ancient highway.

'OK,' nodded Bowman. 'Let's move out.'

CHAPTER
THIRTEEN

'I can't see Koral anywhere,' said Scrum nervously. He was standing on the remains of a collapsed footbridge. All he could see were the ruins, stretching away into the distance, cut through by wide boulevards full of debris.

'Her tracking skills are second to none,' said Bowman. There was a hint of pride in his voice. 'And if she doesn't want to be seen, she won't be. First her prey knew about her on Red Sky Lost was when their throats got ripped out.'

'They must have loved that,' said the Doctor drily. He was walking slightly ahead of the *Wayfarer's* captain, moving the sonic screwdriver slowly from side to side. The tip pulsed blue and a low, wavering hum could just be heard.

'This place is spooky,' said Cuttin' Edge. He was walking a little to the left, his assault rifle held ready across his chest as his eyes roved from side to side, scanning in his own way.

'Well, it is the Planet of Ghosts,' Scrum called over.

'Ha ha.'

Occasionally, Cuttin' Edge would raise his rifle and peer through the scope, roving the electronic crosshairs around the terrain, clicking through a variety of image enhancers: thermal, infrared, macroscopic. Nothing showed up, but they could all feel a definite tension in the crisp polar air. Scrum said it was almost as if they were being watched.

The road had collapsed in on itself, and their progress slowed as they tried to negotiate a series of rocks, boulders and crushed, rusting cars.

'Whoa,' said Cuttin' Edge, approaching an overturned vehicle. Sprawling out of the driver's seat was a thin, snow-crusted jumble of bones. The skull lay at an angle, neck broken but still attached to the body by scraps of leathery skin and dried tendon. One skeletal hand kept a fingertip grip on the steering column. Jewellery glittered on the blackened wrist and arm.

'People died here,' Scrum said, climbing up to look. 'Real people, living real lives. Families, friends, lovers. Men and women and children – laughing, playing, working. Doing all the things people do. I wonder where this poor soul was going when the planet-splitter hit?'

'Nowhere,' answered Bowman. His tone was blunt. 'Let's keep going.'

They marched on, the Doctor leading them further down the crumbling roadway, and Koral suddenly appeared, bounding up the slope.

'There you are,' said the Doctor, still concentrating on the screwdriver. 'Wondered where you'd got to.'

Koral reported only to Bowman. 'I've scouted ahead but I can't find anything. The ground gives way further on – sheer drops, then some sort of escarpment. I can't see much beyond that.'

'We're probably right on the edge of a massive area of subsidence,' noted the Doctor. 'It must've been seismic chaos here.'

'Anything else? Any movement, sign of life?' Bowman asked Koral.

'Any sign of ghosts?' Cuttin' Edge added.

'No. But there is a… smell.'

Cuttin' Edge snorted. 'Babe, this whole planet stinks.'

'It's the atmosphere,' said Scrum. 'All sorts of pollutant gases and reactions were thrown up when the planet was split.'

Koral shook her head. 'I do not mean that kind of smell. I mean something else. Something I can't define. Something not right.'

'OK,' Cuttin' Edge cocked his rifle loudly. 'Now you're makin' me nervous.'

Bowman turned to the Doctor. 'What have you got? Anything? If this is some sort of wild goose chase, Doctor…'

'Shh.' The Doctor now had the sonic screwdriver against his ear, listening intently for some faint signal or another. He made a couple of tiny adjustments and listened again, screwing up his face in concentration. 'We're definitely getting warmer,' he said. 'I'm picking up all sorts of stray chronon activity. It's hard to be sure. There's a lot of background radiation, muons, huons, tachyonic decay… and… and…' He shook the screwdriver and listened again, closing his eyes and holding up a hand for silence.

'And what?' asked Bowman regardless.

The Doctor frowned and shook the sonic again. 'And sand, I think. Dropped it on Scarborough beach last month. Took me ages to find it.'

Bowman sighed. 'This is getting us nowhere.'

'No! Wait!' the Doctor suddenly yelled, his voice echoing around the rocks.

Cuttin' Edge and Bowman instantly dropped into defensive crouches, weapons brought to bear. When nothing happened, they straightened slowly and glared at him.

'I've got it again,' declared the Doctor. 'This way!'

He sprang forward, hopping down the rocks as if the land had become a series of enormous steps. On either side, Cuttin' Edge and Bowman dropped from ledge to ledge, their guns and equipment rattling.

'You think there is something down here, don't you?' asked Scrum, hurrying to keep up.

'What makes you say that?' the Doctor asked.

'I saw the way you listened to Koral. You took her seriously.'

'Sometimes you have to trust your instincts, Scrum. Or someone else's. Koral's hackles were raised – the hair on the back of her neck. Stood up like a brush. A primal reaction as old as time. She sensed something all right, she just doesn't know what.'

'Something dangerous?'

The Doctor shrugged casually. 'It usually is.'

'Ghosts?'

A smile. 'Unlikely – although the sonic screwdriver is registering some kind of time drift. Oh! I've just had a thought.' The Doctor stopped in his tracks. 'Time drift. I wonder…'

'Wonder what?'

'Well, nothing really. It's just a bit of a coincidence, when you think about it. Coming here, looking for some sort of temporal disturbance – and when I've already jumped a time track to a period in history when…'

'When what?'

The Doctor ran a hand roughly back and forth over his spiky hair, as if trying to dislodge an unwelcome train of thought. 'Nothing important. Just thinking aloud. Take no notice. Wibbly wobbly timey wimey. You really don't want to know.' Then the sonic screwdriver buzzed and the blue light winked faster. The Doctor was instantly galvanised into action. 'Aha! Oh, yes! We're really getting warm now!'

The Doctor scampered away, screwdriver aloft.

They moved on, heading down all the time. Further on, they couldn't see anything any more – as if they were approaching the edge of a cliff. Beyond that was a distant mist.

Looking back up the slope, Scrum was surprised to see how far they had descended. He could just make out the broken spires of the old Arkheon city, and beyond that a dark green sky full of stars.

'Movement!'

The word was barked out by Cuttin' Edge. He was already down on one knee, bringing the rifle sight up to his eyes. Bowman had swung around to cover him. Scrum stood, wide-eyed, peering at a patch of broken ground way to their left, his heart racing.

Everyone stood still. There was complete silence.

'I thought I saw it too,' said Scrum after a minute. He spoke very, very quietly. 'Out of the corner of my eye.'

'Yeah,' said Cuttin' Edge. 'That's what I saw. Definitely somethin' movin' past those rocks. We're bein' followed.'

The Doctor put a finger to his lips. There was a tangle of metal half-hidden in the soil, the remains of another rusting hulk. Flakes of snow drifted off the sharp edges, carried up and away into the night sky by the faintest breath of wind.

The Doctor crept slowly towards it. Behind him, Bowman and Cuttin' Edge aimed their weapons.

When the thing launched its attack, flying over the wreckage with a shocking, awful wail, everyone froze. Like a spectral demon from the planet's darkest shadows, the creature dragged the Doctor to the ground.

CHAPTER
FOURTEEN

Two guns roared. Bowman and Cuttin' Edge had the thing in their sights before it had even reached the Doctor. The two rounds struck simultaneously, throwing the creature backwards like a discarded rag against the rocks. It slid to the ground in a heap of tattered grey material.

The Doctor was already on his feet, racing to its side.

Bowman and Cuttin' Edge closed in, their weapons trained on the inert figure.

'Don't get too close,' ordered Bowman.

The Doctor ignored him, kneeling down. It was roughly humanoid – but strangely distorted and wrapped in a rough grey shroud. There were two large smouldering holes in the material, and a pale light shone out from inside.

'Is it dead?' asked Scrum, approaching warily.

'Course it's dead,' snapped Cuttin' Edge. 'High-impact rounds, hollow tipped. We ain't messin', dude.'

The creature gave a last, nervous twitch and slumped sideways. The cowl that hid its head slipped and revealed the face beneath.

'Holy cow,' muttered Cuttin' Edge. 'It's a freakin' ghost.'

The face was pale and glowing. The skin was actually luminous, shining like the moon, with two eyes set so deep and so immersed in wrinkles that they looked like those of a newborn rat. A gaping mouth revealed yellow teeth and dark, withered gums. The pallid flesh was covered in iridescent spots and pustules.

'We just shot ourselves a *ghost*,' Cuttin' Edge repeated. He sounded fearful and thrilled, all at once.

'Be quiet,' ordered Bowman. He bent down to examine the features more closely. 'What is it?'

The Doctor shook his head. 'I don't know. The devolved remains of the native Arkheonites, perhaps. Irradiated, desperate, scavenging among the ruins. More wild animal than anything.'

'It's disgustin',' said Cuttin' Edge.

The Doctor stood up. 'It's dead,' he said solemnly.

The creature's glowing face had begun to darken. As they watched, a black stain seemed to spread across its skin, which sagged and crumpled like ancient paper in a fire. Soon the creature was little more than a blackened husk.

'Whatever it is,' growled Bowman, 'it won't be alone. Look sharp and stay focused.'

No sooner had he spoken than there was a noise behind them. They turned to see two more of the mutant figures scrambling towards them. They moved with an awkward, urgent gait across the uneven terrain.

Bowman's gun cracked twice and the figures reeled back. The foremost staggered a few more steps, his tattered hood thrown back to reveal the bright, snarling face and gaping black mouth. Then it collapsed and lay still, face down in the snow.

'More of them!' shouted Scrum, pointing further back. Half a dozen of the grey, shambling creatures surged into view.

'Incomin',' muttered Cuttin' Edge, squaring his boots and pulling up his rifle to aim. He and Bowman dropped the first three between them with quick, precise shots.

The fourth loped across the intervening scrub with a surprising turn of speed, closing in on Koral. She bared her fangs and claws, preparing for battle, but the Doctor stepped nimbly forward, pulling her to one side as he flicked a lump of snow up with the toe of his trainer, straight into the mutant's face. 'Don't touch them! The blood will be contaminated – poisonous! You start digging your claws into this lot and it could be the last thing you ever do.'

'I will die fighting!'

'Very likely – but not just yet.'

The Doctor ducked, pulling her down with him despite her protests, as a volley of fire from Cuttin' Edge's rifle tore through the cold air.

'They're all over the place!' cried Scrum, helping the Doctor and Koral away.

'We've stirred up a nest or somethin',' said Cuttin' Edge. He was picking off more of them as he spoke, the heavy boom of the rifle echoing around the wreckage. The mutants were crawling from holes in the ground, their black teeth bared in the middle of glowing, growling faces. 'There's too many of 'em. We need to move out.'

'This way,' Bowman called. He shot another mutant through the head and climbed swiftly up the slope behind them. 'Get to the high ground.'

They scrambled up the rocks after him, Cuttin' Edge bringing up the rear. Every couple of paces he would turn and shoot. The creatures were starting to recognise the danger and moved quickly from rock to rock, car to car, staying low.

'We can't get back to the ship,' Scrum panted. 'They've cut off our retreat.' He had drawn his own blaster and was looking around uncertainly for a target.

'Cuttin' Edge!' barked Bowman. 'Left flank! Clear a path!'

'Yo.' Cuttin' Edge dropped to one knee, turning to the left, and switched his rifle to automatic fire. The barrage ripped through the air and tore into a group of mutants climbing up the slope towards them. Their strange, whimpering cries merged into a funereal wail.

Bowman led the way down, jumping from rock to rock. The Doctor, Koral and Scrum followed.

'This way!' yelled the Doctor, pointing to a gap in the horde.

Bowman's blaster roared repeatedly, mercilessly clearing mutants from his path. He strode through the carnage, wreathed in the smoke from his weapon. His boots crunched over the corpses as he led his party onward. Behind them, more mutants were filling the night with hungry snarls.

'We're being herded,' realised the Doctor, skidding to a halt.

'What?'

There was a wind blowing now, cold and harsh, and it took the Doctor's words straight from his lips. He cupped a hand over his mouth and yelled, 'We're being herded! They're forcing us to go this way.'

Craggy rocks reared ahead of them. They couldn't see what lay beyond, but thin, ragged flurries of snow kept drifting past them, blown down from the summit. They hesitated, uncertain now. Bowman looked back with dark, angry eyes. 'We can't afford to stop,' he growled.

'They're closing in!' said Scrum, looking back at the approaching mutants.

Bowman turned and began to climb steadily up the rocks, setting the example. The Doctor, Scrum and Koral hurried after him. Cuttin' Edge gritted his teeth, squeezing off half a dozen more shots, and then turned to follow. Behind him, the pale, glowing creatures were converging on the slope.

Near the summit, Koral was helping Scrum. 'Th-thanks,' he stammered, breathing heavily. 'I don't think I can go... much further.'

'Just a little more,' Koral urged.

'Keep moving!' thundered Bowman.

Koral hooked an arm around Scrum and supported him as they struggled up the last few metres.

'What's over the ridge?' asked Cuttin' Edge.

'No idea,' Bowman said. 'But we're gonna found out.'

With a final series of lung-bursting steps, they made it to the top. As each of them crested the rise, they halted in their tracks and gaped. A strange, massive silence weighed down on them, crushing them.

'My God,' breathed Bowman, awestruck.

'It's... it's impossible,' said Cuttin' Edge.

Scrum started hyperventilating as a panic attack rushed through him. Koral simply stared, open mouthed.

They had reached the very edge of the world. Literally – because the ground simply fell away at their feet in a gigantic, immeasurable cliff stretching from side to side, horizon to horizon. The sheer face sank down and down, into a dark, mist-shrouded distance. And below them – far, far below – was the curved edge of a glowing ball of molten rock.

'Cor!' exclaimed the Doctor. His face was a picture of boyish excitement. His eyes were wide, his hair standing on end, as he practically danced along the cliff edge. 'I mean – *core!*'

'It's… it's…' Cuttin' Edge was, finally, lost for words.

'It's the edge of the world!' cried the Doctor. He was jumping up and down, barely able to contain his excitement. 'Look at it! The very edge! It's a sheer drop, right down to the core! Amazing! Fantastic! Brilliant! Have you *ever* seen anything like that in your life before? You haven't, have you? You haven't!' He bounced around among them, whooping and laughing. 'I haven't either! Never, ever before! Not like this! It's a new sight! *A new sight!*'

Somehow, heat radiated from the distant knot of burning iron, rising up to carry flakes of snow from the edge of the cliff into the air. The snow danced faintly in the air, rising like pale, spectral flames.

'I feel sick,' Scrum said.

'It's just vertigo,' said the Doctor happily. 'Perfectly natural. It's quite a view, isn't it? Brilliant! *Molto bene!*' He roared the last two words into the night sky, feet planted wide, arms thrown up into the air.

'Before you get too carried away,' warned Bowman, 'you might like to think about our position in purely strategic terms.'

'He means this ain't no sightseein' trip,' said Cuttin' Edge, pointing behind them. A crowd of glowing mutants were dragging themselves up the rise, murmuring and growling.

'Oh, *them*,' nodded the Doctor. 'No, I hadn't forgotten. I'm just multitasking.' He whipped out his sonic screwdriver, held it out over the cliff edge and clicked it on. The sonic bleeped faintly, slowly at first but then with sudden, thrilling urgency. 'Aha!' The Doctor's face broke into another huge grin. 'There it is! We've found it – the Arkheon Threshold. Remember that? The little tear in space-time – it's right near the heart of this planet… right in the dying core!'

'Doctor,' Cuttin' Edge said. 'They're gettin' closer.'

'Working on it, working on it…'

Bowman turned to Cuttin' Edge with a frown. 'Since when did *he* become leader?'

'Oh no.'

The Doctor's voice cut through the air like a knife. He was staring over the cliff edge again, but with none of the giddy delight he had previously shown. He looked suddenly stiff and uncertain.

'What is it?' asked Scrum. 'What's the matter?'

'A thought has just occurred to me,' the Doctor said. His tone was bleak, almost angry. 'Why didn't I think of it before?'

'What?'

The Doctor pointed downwards, towards the exposed centre of the shattered world. 'The planetary core!' He suddenly snapped his hand upwards, smacking himself on the forehead. 'D'oh!'

Koral frowned. 'I don't understand…'

'I think things are about to get a lot worse,' the Doctor sighed.

'Worse?' repeated Cuttin' Edge scornfully. 'We're trapped on the edge of the biggest cliff in the universe, facin' an army of zombie ghosts from hell. What could be *worse*?'

The Doctor looked at him sadly, at all of them, and his expression was as cold and terrible as the planet they stood on. 'I'm sorry,' he said, his eyes full of anguish. 'I'm so sorry…'

And then, behind him, rising up beyond the cliff edge, seemingly borne aloft on the flickering curtain of snow, they came: metallic bronze shapes, bristling with arms and weaponry which wavered and twitched like insect antennae.

Eyestalks swivelled, fixing on the Doctor and his little party as they cowered on the edge of the cliff. Implacable, glowing blue eyes stared down at them.

'HALT!' screeched the nearest Dalek, its dome lights flickering in triumph. 'DO NOT MOVE – OR YOU WILL BE EXTERMINATED!'

There was nowhere to go, nowhere to run. They just stood and stared helplessly as the Daleks floated towards them.

'YOU ARE NOW PRISONERS OF THE DALEKS!'

Chapter
Fifteen

The Daleks slowly descended until they were skimming the surface of the escarpment.

The native mutants of Arkheon immediately scattered, turning and running for cover or slipping down boltholes, their thin rags snaking after them as they disappeared from sight. Within moments, there was no sign that they had ever existed – ghosts in every sense.

'RESIST AND YOU WILL BE EXTERMINATED,' grated the first Dalek. It glided over to where the *Wayfarer* crew stood huddled together. The eyestalk roved up and down, examining them contemptuously.

'YOU ARE OUR PRISONERS,' the Dalek repeated loudly. 'YOU WILL OBEY THE DALEKS!'

Bowman was gripping his blaster so hard his knuckles were bone-white. He was a fraction of a second from opening fire when the Doctor said, 'Leave it. Try anything stupid and you'll be exterminated on the spot.'

'Then what do we do?' hissed Cuttin' Edge, his voice cracking with anger and fear. He, too, was a single jittery moment away from bringing his rifle to bear.

The Doctor simply raised his hands. 'Surrender.'

There was a tense moment, but neither Bowman nor Cuttin' Edge moved.

The Dalek swivelled to address the Doctor. 'ARE YOU THE LEADER OF THIS GROUP?'

'No, he isn't,' said Bowman. 'I am.'

The Dalek's dome turned, the eye focusing on Bowman. His face reflected the blue glow like stone. 'DISCARD YOUR WEAPONS,' it ordered.

Nobody moved.

'IMMEDIATELY!' screeched the Dalek. 'OBEY!'

'Do it,' said Bowman, after a pause.

He let go of his blaster and it dropped to the ground at his feet. Cuttin' Edge threw down his rifle. Scrum dropped his handgun.

'I'm not carrying any weapons,' said the Doctor. 'And neither is this person.' He indicated Koral with a nod of his head.

A Dalek moved forward, extending its sucker arm. It scanned the Doctor and Koral briefly. 'NO ENERGY OR PROJECTILE WEAPONS DETECTED.'

'Told you,' said the Doctor quietly.

'SILENCE!' barked the Dalek. It turned its head towards another pair of Daleks. 'DESTROY THE WEAPONS.'

The Daleks glided forward, their gun-sticks swivelling to point at the blasters lying in the dirt. There was a bright flare and the discarded weaponry was melted into slag.

Koral was trembling violently. The Doctor could sense that she was about to run or attack. And knowing Koral, he guessed it would probably be the latter. Either action would result in death.

Bowman had sensed it too. He reached out a hand and rested it on her shoulder. 'Easy.'

Koral turned to look at him, her eyes blazing. Bowman simply nodded. He understood. 'You're the last of the Red Sky Lost,' he said gently. His voice sounded like the purr of a tiger. 'You've got to stay alive.'

Scrum, also, was visibly shaking. But this was due to simple terror. He had one hand clamped over his mouth, as if trying to stop himself from being sick. Cuttin' Edge nudged him with his elbow. 'Dude. Chill out.'

Scrum nodded but kept his hand on his mouth. His eyes were so wide they were almost circles.

'WALK THIS WAY,' grated the lead Dalek, turning towards the cliff edge.

'I couldn't walk that way if I tried,' muttered the Doctor under his breath. 'At least, not without castors…'

The Dalek's dome swivelled right round, the eyestalk glaring at him.

'Nothing,' the Doctor said, innocently.

'WALK IN FRONT OF ME,' the Dalek said, gliding round to position itself behind the group. 'MOVE! DISOBEDIENCE WILL RESULT IN INSTANT EXTERMINATION.'

'Come on,' said the Doctor, adopting as jaunty a tone as he could manage. He stuck his hands in his trouser pockets and sauntered towards the cliff edge, whispering into Scrum's ear as he passed. 'Stick with me. I'll handle this.'

Scrum looked uncertainly at him. 'Really?'

The Doctor raised his eyebrows and pulled an *of course!* face. 'I've done this loads of times,' he said.

So Scrum stuck with him, walking stiffly towards the cliff edge, the direction in which the Daleks were herding them. When they reached the precipice, they stopped. Bowman, Koral and Cuttin' Edge joined them. No one wanted to go too near to the abyss.

'What they gonna do?' asked Cuttin' Edge. 'Throw us off?'

But a heavy whine of machinery was already filling the air as a large, flat metal surface suddenly rose up adjacent to the cliff top. There were two Daleks on the platform, one of them positioned next to a small control podium. It made an adjustment with its sucker and the platform moved closer to the edge, hovering on antigravity thrusters.

'A lift!' exclaimed the Doctor. 'That's handy. Come on, everybody, hop on.'

He led the way, springing lightly onto the metal platform. It bobbed fractionally under his weight, like a raft floating on a pond. There was room for a dozen or so, but the other Daleks simply floated off the cliff top alongside the platform.

'Looks like we were expected,' Bowman remarked.

'Yeah,' nodded the Doctor. He took a deep breath. 'Gravity, atmosphere, the lot. They're giving us the VIP treatment.' He looked carefully at Bowman. 'Why d'you think that is?'

Bowman shrugged but did not reply.

The platform started to descend. Eventually they couldn't even see the top of the cliff, it just rose up like a vast, dark wall, blotting out half of space. The Doctor wandered over to the edge of the platform and peeked over. Below, the exposed centre of Arkheon broiled and spat like a cauldron of fire. 'Y'know,' he said conversationally to the Dalek at the controls, 'that really is an incredible view. Absolutely *amazing*. Pity you lot had to come and spoil it.'

The Dalek said nothing. The platform continued to descend.

'So, what's it all for, then?' the Doctor asked. 'Let me guess. You're gonna replace the molten core with a drive system, start flying the planet around the galaxy? See the sights?'

'SILENCE!' grated the Dalek.

'I'm only trying to make conversation,' the Doctor retorted, sounding hurt. He waited for a response but there was nothing.

132

The platform cleared the upper edge of an enormous cavern. The solid wall of the planetary magma had suddenly given way to a vast hollow in the rock. Whether it was a natural chasm or deliberately excavated it was impossible to tell, but there was enough room for several spacecraft hangars. The platform veered into the cavern, moving slowly inside the planet itself. Below them was an immense, metallic web of criss-crossing walkways and landing areas. There were Daleks gliding along the walkways, across platforms, through corridors. On one level there were serried ranks of Daleks, all moving in unison, disappearing into a deeper, darker cavern.

'Hell and damnation,' breathed Cuttin' Edge. He had never in his life seen so many Daleks in one place. 'Now we're really in the—'

'Should have seen this coming,' interrupted the Doctor. There was no attempt at a casual demeanour now. 'I really should.'

'What do you mean?' asked Scrum.

'They've been here all the time,' the Doctor said. The expression on his face was dark, rueful. 'Look at this place! It must have taken years to build and develop a base like this. We thought the Daleks were searching for Arkheon. Turns out they found it ages ago and moved in.'

'I think it's worse than that,' said Bowman.

Cuttin' Edge let out a hiss of frustration. 'Will you guys stop sayin' that? "It's worse than that" and "It's worse than I thought"! Hell! How much *worse* is this gonna get?'

'A lot,' said Bowman. 'I think I know what this place is. I heard rumours. The Daleks had a top-secret base where they took all their high-level prisoners for interrogation and experimentation.'

'No *way*,' Cuttin' Edge spat out in disbelief.

'Interrogation? *Experimentation*? Are you serious?'

'Daleks love prisoners,' the Doctor said. 'Gives them such a sense of power. They love nothing more than lording it over the inferior species. Humiliation, torment, slavery. That's their thing.'

Cuttin' Edge shook his head. 'You ain't makin' it sound any better, dude.'

The Doctor turned to Bowman. 'This top-secret interrogation base. Is there anything else you can remember about it?'

'Why?' Bowman's tone was bleak. His face was retreating into its stone-like appearance as he prepared himself for what lay ahead.

'Anything could be useful.'

'Don't count on it. They used to call it "the Black Hole" – as in nothing ever came out again. No one – and I mean *no one* – ever escaped from this place. It's a one-way ticket.'

'CEASE TALKING!' One of the Daleks moved towards them, gun and arm twitching eagerly. 'PRISONERS WILL BE SILENT.'

No one spoke again as the platform continued its descent into the Dalek prison. Whenever they passed more Daleks, eyestalks would slowly turn, domes swivelling, observing. It was as if every Dalek that saw them was minutely examining them, glaring at them with a mixture of hatred and resentment and, perhaps, just a hint of curiosity. The prisoners huddled together, Koral moving closer to Bowman so that he could put a hand on her shoulder.

Presently the platform lowered itself into a wide reception area. Daleks glided to and fro, watching them carefully. Two Daleks came forward to meet the platform.

'STEP OFF THE LANDING PLATFORM,' grated the first.

Slowly the prisoners filed onto the metal floor. The Dalek on the platform prodded Cuttin' Edge in the back with its sucker arm, pushing him forward so that he stumbled. 'MOVE! FASTER! OBEY THE DALEKS!'

Cuttin' Edge glared back. 'Don't push me, you metal creep.'

The Dalek floated forward, the bulbous blue eye fixed on the human. 'BE SILENT!'

Cuttin' Edge stared back, his face reflecting the light. 'Don't wave that eyestalk in my face, creep. I can get good money for that back home.'

'BE SILENT OR YOU WILL BE EXTERMINATED!'

'All right, cool it,' said Bowman. 'That's enough, Cuttin' Edge. Let's not rile them. It's too easy.'

With a snort, Cuttin' Edge turned away. 'Whatever you say, skip.'

The Dalek circled slowly around Cuttin' Edge, examining him from every angle. 'YOU WILL OBEY THE DALEKS. FROM NOW ON YOU WILL TAKE ORDERS ONLY FROM DALEKS. THIS HUMAN IS NO LONGER YOUR COMMANDING OFFICER.'

'He never was my commanding officer,' shrugged Cuttin' Edge. 'He's just a guy I kinda like.'

The Doctor, keeping very much to the background, watched the exchange carefully. He didn't know whether to wince or cheer out loud. But Cuttin' Edge was playing a dangerous game; the line between defiance and suicide was a very thin one when baiting Daleks.

This particular Dalek had already reached screeching level. 'OBEY THE DALEKS! YOU WILL OBEY!'

'Just remember,' Cuttin' Edge said coolly, 'that eyestalk's *mine*.'

'BE SILENT!' The Dalek's sucker arm suddenly extended and grasped Cuttin' Edge's chest. The black cup gripped and squeezed and Cuttin' Edge howled. Then the Dalek released him and he fell to the floor, gasping for breath and rubbing his chest.

Scrum helped him to his feet. 'You're going to get yourself killed!'

'THE NEXT PERSON TO SPEAK WITHOUT PERMISSION WILL BE EXTERMINATED,' grated one of the other Daleks. 'NOW REMOVE YOUR OUTER GARMENTS.'

Slowly the prisoners unfastened their heavy winter jackets and dropped them on the floor. Cuttin' Edge's bravado may have been inspirational, but he had very nearly paid for it with his life. The Doctor was trying to keep a low profile and merge in with the group, keeping his head down. But Koral had already seen enough. She was looking at him curiously, but the Doctor pretended not to notice and stared down at his canvas trainers.

Two Daleks approached the group, sucker arms extended. 'PRISONERS WILL BE SCANNED AND CATEGORISED,' said one. 'STAND APART! MOVE!'

The little group shuffled around until they were all separate and in a line. First to be scanned was Scrum. The suckers roved all over him, emitting strange electronic warbling noises. 'SPECIES – HUMAN.' The Dalek spoke the word as if it tasted foul. 'MALE. PHYSICAL CAPACITY – LEVEL FIVE POINT NINE. MARGINAL USE.'

'Marginal?' echoed Scrum, affronted.

The Daleks scanned Cuttin' Edge. 'SPECIES – HUMAN. MALE. PHYSICAL CAPACITY – LEVEL SEVEN POINT FIVE. SUITABLE. YOU WILL BE TAKEN TO THE MINE TO WORK FOR THE DALEKS.'

The Daleks then moved on to Koral, who was standing next to Bowman.

'SPECIES – UNKNOWN,' announced one of the Daleks. 'FEMALE. PHYSICAL CAPACITY – LEVEL NINE POINT FOUR.

SUITABLE. YOU WILL BE TAKEN TO THE MINE TO WORK FOR THE DALEKS.'

Koral looked fearfully at Bowman. He reached out and squeezed her hand gently; and it was easy for Koral to see the relief in his eyes – relief that she hadn't been declared too dangerous and killed on the spot.

The Daleks moved on, scanning Bowman next. He stood straight, shoulders back, chin up, almost as if he was back on the parade ground.

'SPECIES – HUMAN. MALE. PHYSICAL CAPACITY – LEVEL SEVEN POINT SIX. WAIT!' Something had attracted the Dalek's attention. 'EXTEND YOUR ARM.'

After a brief pause, Bowman thrust out his left arm.

The Dalek's eye focused on the small white scar running down his forearm. 'EVIDENCE OF SUBCUTANEOUS TRANSMITTER REMOVAL!'

Another Dalek moved forward, its blue eye zeroing in on the scar. 'X-RAY CONFIRMS TRANSMITTER HAS BEEN REMOVED.'

'Transmitter?' Scrum whispered. 'What transmitter?'

'Hell, I dunno, pal,' Cuttin' Edge whispered back. 'But Bowman don't look happy.'

Bowman glared stonily at the Dalek and lowered his arm. 'Guess it's your lucky day,' he growled.

'What's going on?' Scrum wanted to know. Like the others, he could sense something was up, and his curiosity – kindled by panic – was enough to make him forget the orders not to speak.

But the Daleks were too preoccupied with Bowman to notice. 'STEP FORWARD! KNEEL!'

'I'm not kneeling for you,' Bowman replied simply.

The Dalek behind Bowman simply thrust out its sucker arm, aiming for the back of Bowman's left knee. His leg folded and Bowman hit the metal floor with a grunt.

Koral started forward, clearly alarmed. But the Doctor reached out and took her arm, shaking his head fractionally. She looked at him in despair.

'INITIATE BRAIN SCAN!' Two Daleks extended their suckers, closing them around Bowman's head. There was a shrill, piercing whine and Bowman gasped loudly, flecks of saliva jumping from his lips.

'Leave him alone!' yelled Scrum, moving forward, but Cuttin' Edge grabbed him and pulled him back.

The Doctor, too, had to grab hold of Koral again to prevent her from physically attacking the Daleks. 'Don't be stupid!' he hissed.

The suction cups retracted and Bowman fell forward, onto his hands and knees. He was trembling violently, his head hanging low between his arms, fighting the urge to vomit. There were angry red weals on his face where the suckers had gripped him.

The Daleks were screeching at each other with excitement. 'ALERT! INFORM COMMAND! PRISONER IDENTIFIED AS SPACE MAJOR JON BOWMAN!'

'WE OBEY!' shrieked a pair of Daleks.

'Space Major?' echoed Cuttin' Edge. He sounded shocked. '*Space Major?*'

'Since when?' Scrum asked.

'Since the very beginning,' said the Doctor. 'Remember when Auros was destroyed? Bowman knew about the Osterhagen Principle. Only senior members of the Earth military would have access to that kind of information. No wonder the Daleks are so excited... it can't be often they catch someone as important as this.'

'Important?' Cuttin' Edge frowned. 'He ain't important. Well, not that kinda important.'

'The Daleks would appear to disagree.'

At this point a new Dalek arrived – it had a similar bronze shell to all the others but they obviously deferred to it as chief, backing away slightly to allow it access to the prisoners. The Doctor surmised that this would be the Dalek designated as overall commander of the prison.

'STAND!' ordered the Command Dalek, looming over Bowman. 'STAND IMMEDIATELY!'

Koral helped Bowman to his feet. He was unsteady, uncharacteristically pale and listless. His eyes were cloudy and he looked confused. Koral turned and spat at the Command Dalek. 'Leave him alone! Do not touch him or I will rip out your guts!'

'RELEASE THE PRISONER!' Already, the spittle was evaporating from the Dalek's head dome in a tiny, pathetic puff of steam. 'HE IS TO BE TAKEN FOR FULL BRAIN EXCORIATION.'

'You will have to kill me first!' Koral roared. She lunged at the nearest Dalek, flicking out her claws and gouging bright sparks from its armour plate.

But two Daleks fitted with claw manipulators had already moved in and seized her. They gripped her arms and practically lifted her off her feet, kicking and struggling.

'YOU WILL OBEY THE DALEKS,' said the Command Dalek.

'Why don't you just exterminate me!' Koral yelled.

'IT IS NOT NECESSARY,' intoned the Dalek. 'YOU ARE REQUIRED FOR WORK IN THE MINES. BUT YOU HAVE DISOBEYED THE DALEKS. ONE OF YOUR PARTY WILL BE PUNISHED.'

Bowman looked up groggily. 'No…' he croaked.

The Dalek glided forward. 'THE WEAKEST MEMBER WILL DIE,' it said.

Cuttin' Edge choked. 'No!' he bellowed, knowing exactly what this would mean.

'DISABLE THIS HUMAN,' ordered the Command Dalek. One of the others lowered its gun-stick, aiming for Cuttin' Edge's legs, and fired. A bright blue flash lit the area and Cuttin' Edge collapsed to the floor. He then lay there, hands scrabbling at the metal, unable to get a grip. His legs were completely immobile.

'I can't feel my legs!' he cried.

'YOU HAVE SUFFERED TEMPORARY NEUROLOGICAL DAMAGE,' one of the Daleks informed him. 'MOBILITY WILL RETURN IN DUE COURSE.'

Cuttin' Edge swore at the Dalek, completely unable to stand. Tears of pain and frustration ran hotly down his cheeks.

Scrum was watching all this, his face white with fear. He could hardly breathe. He knew exactly what was coming next, but his brain, normally so quick, had simply stopped thinking. He was completely unable to speak. His mouth dropped open wordlessly as two Daleks slowly turned to face him.

'EXTERMINATE THIS HUMAN,' ordered the Command Dalek.

The twin beams caught Scrum full in the chest, illuminating him with a deadly, coruscating charge. He screamed and flung his arms out wide, the bones darkly visible through the irradiated flesh. And then he fell to the floor, sprawled across the metal next to Cuttin' Edge.

'No…' said Cuttin' Edge, almost silently. '*Please, no…*'

Then Scrum's face tipped slowly over, and Cuttin' Edge saw that his eyes were still open, but they were charred black and utterly dead.

CHAPTER
SIXTEEN

Scrum's smoking corpse lay between the prisoners and the Daleks.

All that could be heard in the minutes that followed was the dull, persistent throb of the Dalek machinery.

'There was no need for that,' said the Doctor quietly. He didn't look up. He was staring down at the body, his fists clenched hard. 'He wouldn't have harmed anyone.'

'HE WAS OF NO USE TO US,' replied the Command Dalek.

Its voice grated on the Doctor's nerves, and he closed his eyes to shut out the sight.

'You'll pay for this,' said Cuttin' Edge. He tried to sit up on the floor, teeth gritted as his legs filled with agonising pain. 'I'll make you pay.'

One of the Daleks circled around Cuttin' Edge, eyestalk fixed on him. 'SILENCE. YOU WILL BE TAKEN TO THE MINES AND MADE TO SERVE THE DALEKS.'

'No! Never! Kill me now, you metal b—'

'Cuttin' Edge!' barked Bowman. 'Leave it. Just… stay alive as long as you can.'

Cuttin' Edge looked up at him, his eyes wet with tears. There was a world of despair in those eyes, and they had turned to the only person who had ever believed in him, looking for hope, for reason, for anything. 'How?' he asked, eventually.

'Kid,' said Bowman, 'Just do your best.'

The Command Dalek approached Bowman. 'YOU

141

WILL BE TAKEN FOR DEEP-LEVEL INTERROGATION. THE PROCESS INVOLVES BRAIN EXCORIATION AND SURGERY. YOU WILL NOT SURVIVE THIS PROCESS.'

Bowman did not reply. He merely looked the Dalek straight in the eye, his face as impassive as rock.

The Dalek moved a little closer, and then rasped, almost gloatingly, 'THE INFORMATION YOU POSSESS WILL SERVE THE DALEKS. IT WILL BE USED TO AID US IN OUR VICTORY AND HELP IN THE DESTRUCTION OF THE HUMAN RACE.'

'Yeah, right,' Bowman grunted. 'Tell me something I don't know.'

'YOU WILL OBEY THE DALEKS!'

Bowman raised an eyebrow. 'That a fact? What if I choose not to? What if I say you can take your gun-stick and—'

'SILENCE!'

'Why? What are you going to do to me, Dalek? I'm too valuable for you to exterminate. You need me alive for interrogation, remember? To help you wipe out mankind or something.'

The Dalek quivered, its arm and gun twitching with annoyance. The lights on its head flashed manically as it replied: 'YOU WILL BE MADE TO COOPERATE. IF NECESSARY YOU WILL BE PERMANENTLY DISABLED AND TAKEN TO THE INTERROGATION CHAMBER BY FORCE.'

Bowman straightened up, squaring his shoulders. 'Forget it. I'll walk. Which way is this interrogation chamber, anyway?'

Once again, the Doctor felt like he wanted to punch the air. There was Scrum, murdered in cold blood, and Cuttin' Edge with his legs paralysed, about to be dragged off with Koral to who knew what. But Bowman, the great, bloody-minded, thick-skinned and irresistible human being that he was, had still found a way to maintain his dignity.

Koral had other ideas. She tried to free herself from the grip of her guards, but it was useless. Not even her alien sinews could break the grip of the Dalek claws. She pulled towards Bowman, her spine bent like a bow and her fangs bared, but it was no good.

Bowman saw her and just shook his head. 'I'll be OK,' he lied.

'No,' Koral said. Her voice came out as a pathetic croak. She turned to the Doctor. 'Please… You can't let them take him away.'

The Doctor swallowed. 'I can't stop them, Koral.'

'You can! You *know* you can!'

He shook his head. 'I can't.'

'What's she talkin' about, man?' asked Cuttin' Edge. 'What's she sayin'?'

The Doctor looked away. 'Nothing. She doesn't know what she's talking about.'

'I do!' Koral's eyes flamed. She looked across at Bowman, who stood watching with a slightly puzzled frown on his old, craggy face. Then she turned back to the Doctor. 'You know the future. You've *seen* it. You know what happens. You know *more* than him.'

'Koral, stop it,' ordered the Doctor. 'You don't understand!'

'I understand that they are going to take him and cut out his brain!' Koral yelled. 'And you're just standing there, letting them do it! And he doesn't know *anything*. Not compared with you!'

The Doctor took a step towards her. Around them, all the Daleks had also turned to watch the altercation. 'It doesn't work like that. I can't let that happen.'

This time Koral did not reply. She simply stared at the Doctor, a look of utter desperation on her face.

The Doctor looked away.

Bowman caught his eye and shook his head slowly. His meaning was clear: *don't do it.*

'TAKE JON BOWMAN TO THE INTERROGATION LEVEL,' ordered the Command Dalek.

Two Daleks began to herd Bowman towards a ramp leading further down into the Dalek base. He walked ahead of them, head high and shoulders squared. He didn't look back.

'Wait,' said the Doctor.

The Command Dalek swung round to face him.

The Doctor cleared his throat. 'Can I have a private word?'

'SPEAK,' ordered the Dalek.

'Well, this is probably going to be a bit embarrassing…'

'EXPLAIN!'

'Look, I really hate it when people say this sort of thing, but… *Do you know who I am?*'

The Dalek said nothing. It simply stared.

The Doctor stepped towards it, lowering his head slightly so that his mouth was level with the Dalek's neck grille. Ignoring the oily, noxious vapour that came from within, he leant a little closer.

And whispered something.

The effect on the Dalek was literally electric. Its head lamps flashed involuntarily and it suddenly jerked away, arm, gun and eye quivering like the antennae of an alarmed cockroach.

'ALERT!' it cried, head spinning from side to side. 'ALERT! SCAN THIS PRISONER!'

Two Daleks glided forward, suckers extended.

The Doctor stood, hands held wide. 'Come on,' he said with a smile and a wink. 'You know you want to.'

The sucker arms scanned his body up and down and then both Daleks became agitated. Ever so slightly, they seemed to move back, giving the prisoner a little more space. 'EMERGENCY!' one of them shrieked. 'EMERGENCY! IT IS THE DOC-TOR!'

'It's the twin hearts, isn't it?' asked the Doctor. 'They're such a giveaway.'

Several Daleks took up the chant, a note of hysteria entering their voices: 'IT IS THE DOC-TOR! IT IS THE DOC-TOR!'

'Please,' smiled the Doctor modestly. 'No autographs.'

The Command Dalek aimed its blaster at the Doctor. 'DO NOT MOVE! DO NOT MOVE! YOU ARE THE DOC-TOR! YOU ARE AN ENEMY OF THE DALEKS. YOU WILL BE EXTERMINATED!'

'Oh, come off it. Not before you've had a chance to interrogate me, surely?' The Doctor looked around the assembled Daleks. 'At least a quick question-and-answer session. No?'

Throughout the vast, metallic cavern, a ripple of agitation spread through the Dalek ranks, with the Doctor at its very centre.

Despite himself, Cuttin' Edge was impressed. 'Dude, you got some *serious* presence. What the hell did you say to them?'

'Just enough to make Space Major Bowman look like third prize in the Christmas raffle. Sorry about that.' The Doctor turned to Bowman with an apologetic shrug. 'I'm afraid they're not going to be all that interested in you now. Try not to feel too downhearted.'

'I always knew there was something you weren't telling us,' replied Bowman. 'Turns out you're Dalek Enemy Number One. Congratulations.'

The Doctor nodded sadly. 'I know. Funny how things turn out, isn't it?'

'Silence!' shouted the Command Dalek. 'Do not speak! You are a prisoner of the Daleks! You will be taken for interrogation! And then you will be exterminated! Exterminated!'

'You always make me feel so welcome.'

This was now altogether too much for the Dalek. Its sucker arm thudded into the Doctor's stomach and he folded, the wind whooshing out of him. As he lay on the floor, gasping for air, the Command Dalek turned back to Bowman. 'You will be taken to await your interrogation. The other members of your crew will be taken to work in the core mines.'

Two Daleks lifted Cuttin' Edge and, dangling him like a puppet, took him away with Koral, heading for a doorway that led deeper into the prison.

Koral looked back at Bowman, shouting, 'I will come back for you!'

And then the door closed and Bowman knew that would be the last he ever saw of her.

CHAPTER
SEVENTEEN

The Doctor was marched into a security room to be scanned again. Though he was naturally optimistic, even he had to admit that things weren't looking too good right now. He was uncomfortably reminded of an electric chair as he was forced to sit down in the machine.

The equipment hummed and circular screens around the scanning area filled with information as the Doctor was examined on a molecular level. Daleks roved around the room, checking instruments and displays. The atmosphere was electric, in more ways than one: the Doctor could tell that his arrival had really set the cat among the pigeons.

The Command Dalek glided forward. 'YOU WILL BE TAKEN TO A MAXIMUM-SECURITY HOLDING CHAMBER TO AWAIT FULL INTERROGATION.'

'Really, I don't want to put you to any trouble…' said the Doctor.

'NOTIFICATION OF YOUR CAPTURE HAS REACHED SKARO.'

'Ah. Well, they say bad news travels fast.'

'THE SUPREME DALEK HAS AUTHORISED THE PRIMARY INTELLIGENCE UNIT TO EXTRACT ALL NECESSARY INTELLIGENCE VIA MIND PROBE EXTRACTION. THE PROCEDURE WILL ULTIMATELY PROVE FATAL. THE INTERROGATION WILL BE LED BY THE DALEK INQUISITOR GENERAL.'

The Doctor raised his eyebrows in surprise. 'You mean the Supreme Dalek has *sent* someone to question me?

That's an insult. It's outrageous. The least he could do was come himself. Better fish to fry, has he?'

The Command Dalek's eye loomed large as it drew closer, the lights on its head flashing with calculated menace. 'THE SUPREME DALEK IS FULLY ENGAGED DIRECTING THE WAR AGAINST EARTH! BUT BY THE TIME THE INQUISITOR GENERAL HAS COMPLETED YOUR INTERROGATION, YOU WILL WISH THE SUPREME DALEK HAD COME HERE!'

Koral tried to blank Bowman from her mind. She had been consumed by rage and fear in the reception area, and it could have cost her everything. She had to stay alive and get back to him, somehow. The Doctor had diverted the Daleks' attention, but Koral knew it was only a temporary reprieve.

The base crackled with static electricity and the metallic air smelled of machine oil and hate. Cuttin' Edge could barely walk and he was forced to lean on Koral for support. They staggered slightly as the lift that carried them down into the prison vaults slowed to a stop and the doors slid open. The Daleks pushed them out onto a narrow walkway overlooking a vast cavern. Its rough-hewn walls rose up to a jagged, cathedral arch of stalactites.

It was incredibly hot. Emerging from the lift had been like stepping into an oven. As they moved down the ramp, descending through a layer of thick, searing mist, the ground suddenly came into view: irregular blocks of black granite separated by streams of bubbling, red-hot lava and volcanic slag.

And all around, everywhere, there were people: human beings manacled together and set to work with pickaxes and shovels, breaking rocks and carrying them to heavy, primitive barrows.

Floating through the clouds of steam and hovering over the glowing lava were Dalek guards, their bronze armour plate pockmarked and stained, their domes constantly revolving, looking for signs of trouble or weakness from the slaves. The blue eyes shone out of the burning haze with deadly, implacable purpose.

'WORK UNIT DELTA,' grated one of the Daleks. 'YOUR PRODUCTION RATE HAS DROPPED BELOW MINIMUM TOLERANCE. YOUR OUTPUT IS UNSATISFACTORY!'

Four men looked up fearfully as the Dalek approached. They were thin, emaciated, clearly exhausted – and all chained together. One of the men, a few wisps of grey hair left on his skull, simply sat down heavily on a nearby rock and put his face in his hands. 'I can't go on...'

'It's not our fault!' cried one of the other men. He was younger, healthier. He pointed at the weakened old man on the rock, his chains rattling as he moved. 'He's holding us all back. He can't work any longer. He's sick!'

'INEFFICIENT WORK UNITS WILL BE REPLACED,' said the Dalek remorselessly.

Two more Daleks descended slowly to join the first. 'EXTERMINATE!'

They opened fire without another word, shooting all four members of the slave group. The men screamed and twisted in the blaze of energy and then sank into the lava. Within minutes, they had disappeared, leaving nothing but a layer of bubbling slime on the surface of the molten rock and the stench of roasting meat in the air.

'STEP FORWARD,' ordered the Dalek who had brought Koral and Cuttin' Edge to the mine.

They shuffled forward, Koral trying to keep Cuttin' Edge on his feet. His legs were shaking as he tried to walk.

The mine Dalek swung around, glaring at them both for a long moment before saying, 'YOU WILL NOW BE WORK UNIT DELTA.'

'This man is injured,' Koral pointed out. 'His legs have been damaged. He cannot work.'

'THEN HE WILL BE EXTERMINATED!'

'No, wait!' cried Cuttin' Edge, raising a hand. 'Wait. I'll be OK. I can work.'

'CAN YOU STAND UNAIDED?' grated the Dalek.

'Yeah.'

Cuttin' Edge let go of Koral's arm. His teeth were bared – he was clearly in great pain – but he managed to stand on his own two feet. Koral could see that Cuttin' Edge simply wasn't going to give the Daleks the satisfaction of killing of him.

'SATISFACTORY,' droned the Dalek.

Cuttin' Edge smiled through the pain.

'Damn right.'

Bowman paced back and forth like a wild animal in a cage. The cell was no more than a few metres square, solid walls and floor. No windows. A harsh white light beat down on his head.

Two narrow benches ran along opposite walls. Bowman tried sitting down but he couldn't keep skill. The anger inside him raged like a beast. He wanted to punch the walls, kick the door, tear apart the first thing that came through it with his bare hands.

The cell door hummed open and the Doctor was thrown inside. He hit the floor heavily and groaned. The door closed behind him with a solid clang.

Bowman stalked backwards and forwards but made no attempt to help him up.

The Doctor crawled up onto a bench and stared at Bowman for a full minute before saying, 'All that pacing up and down is going to wear you out. It's making me tired just watching you.'

'Shut up.'

'Sorry. What are you doing, thinking up a way to escape?'

'You don't escape from a place like this,' Bowman snarled back. 'You just wait until they come and kill you.'

The Doctor blew out his cheeks in a long sigh. 'You're a big comfort, aren't you? Some cellmate.'

'I'm just telling it like it is.'

'Sounds more like you're giving in.'

'Don't you see?' Bowman suddenly roared. 'Don't you care? They're gonna rip our brains out! It's the end of the line!'

'Well, technically, they're going to take my brain apart neuron by neuron. But yes, they'll probably just rip yours out.' Under his breath, the Doctor added, 'If they can find it…'

'You think this is all one big joke, don't you?'

The Doctor stretched out his legs and folded his arms. 'No. I think it's a disaster. And, worst of all, I should have seen it coming.'

'What?'

'We've been set up. This was a trap all along. A great big gold-plated trap. With the words "this is a trap" written on it in mile-high luminous letters. And we just walked right into it.'

Bowman frowned dangerously. 'What the hell do you mean?'

'The Dalek on the *Wayfarer*,' explained the Doctor. 'It tricked us. When it finally talked, it left us just enough clues to lead us here, to Arkheon.'

'You mean it tricked *you*,' Bowman said. '*You* brought us here, remember.'

'Yeah, well, if you want to point the finger, then maybe – *maybe* – I should have seen it coming. I did exactly what I told you not to – which is underestimate the Daleks. They're always thinking, always conniving, always planning. You can't trust them an inch. Even in its last, dying moments that Dalek – having been torn out of its life-support machine and tortured – managed to trick us. Sold us half a line about the Arkheon Threshold and left my imagination to do the rest. It knew who I was, it knew who you were. And it tricked us into taking ourselves straight to the biggest Dalek prison this side of Skaro.' The Doctor's eyes narrowed as he stared into space. 'Clever, that. Really, really clever.'

Bowman leant down so that he was right in the Doctor's face. 'For your information, I don't admire the Daleks. Never have done. I respect them, but I don't admire them.'

The Doctor smiled. 'Nah. It's not respect, Bowman. It's fear.'

'What did you say?'

'I said it's fear. That's what you're feeling now.'

'No chance.'

'It's fear of what the Daleks can do to you, of what they can do to your friends and family and loved ones. What they can do to all of us – everyone and everything that isn't a Dalek. Cos you know they won't stop until they're the only creatures left in the universe.'

'The supreme beings?' Bowman sneered. 'In their dreams.'

'That's more like it,' grinned the Doctor. 'There's life in the old dog yet.'

*

In the caverns, two more prisoners – a woman and a girl – were marched over to where Cuttin' Edge and Koral stood. Manacles and chains were quickly fixed to their wrists and ankles so that all four were bound together. The woman and the girl clung to each other, not even looking up.

'YOUR TASK IS TO REMOVE ROCK DEBRIS FROM THE DRILL AREA,' a Dalek informed them. 'IF YOU DO NOT WORK HARD ENOUGH YOU WILL BE EXTERMINATED!'

Cuttin' Edge looked at the woman and the girl. They were probably mother and daughter, the girl perhaps only eleven or twelve years old. Both kept their heads down. Cuttin' Edge felt his stomach churn with anger.

'You gotta be kiddin',' he told the Dalek. 'They can't work. She's only a kid.'

The Dalek glided forward, gun-stick revolving in its socket. 'THE DALEKS DO NOT MAKE EXCEPTIONS. YOU ARE TO WORK AS A UNIT. IF YOU FAIL YOU WILL BE EXTERMINATED.'

'I'm tellin' you, she can't work—'

'DO NOT ARGUE WITH THE DALEKS! YOU WILL OBEY!'

Cuttin' Edge felt a cool hand on his arm. It was the woman – looking up at him through a thin curtain of dirty hair with imploring eyes. She didn't say anything. She didn't have to. The meaning was clear. *Be quiet, please. Don't argue. Don't provoke them.*

The woman had kept one arm tight around the girl's shoulders, holding her close. She was doing her best to protect her daughter. The anger in Cuttin' Edge's guts turned into a sense of helplessness. He looked back at the Dalek, but its single blue eye only blazed, challenging him, daring him to argue. *Wanting* him to argue.

'OK,' he muttered. 'OK. You win. For now. We'll move rocks.'

'SPEAK LOUDER,' grated the Dalek.

'I said OK! We'll work!'

Cuttin' Edge turned to Koral. She was staring listlessly at the rocky ground, the chains hanging heavily on her wrists. She looked utterly defeated.

'Hey, don't let your head go down, babe,' he said quietly. 'Come on. Let's go.'

Cuttin' Edge had been leaning on Koral for support, but his legs were now full of an agonising pins and needles sensation, which he presumed was a good sign. It meant that the feeling was finally coming back. He could walk a little, although it was still painful.

'I can manage,' he told Koral quietly. 'Don't help me any more. If they think I can't walk on my own they'll shoot, remember.'

Koral nodded and let him stand unaided. Cuttin' Edge took a deep breath. The nerves in his legs felt like they were burning up. But he was determined to walk alone. That's what Jon Bowman would have done.

The four of them trooped slowly, awkwardly, across the cavern, winding their way through the other slaves and clouds of steam. They were taken to an area littered with rocks and rubble, where several work units – groups of four humans chained together – were picking up rocks and passing them along the line to a large metal skip.

'They don't need us to do this,' said Cuttin' Edge in disgust. 'They could do this faster an' better with machines. Why use us?'

'Because they can,' said Koral. 'Because they like to. Subjugation of the lower races. It's Dalek policy.'

A Dalek rolled by, watching them, and Cuttin' Edge picked up a rock. 'Best get started,' he said. 'Pass it along.'

Koral passed the rock to the woman, who let her daughter take it to the skip and throw it in. The girl moved quickly back to stand close to her mother, waiting for the next rock. The chains that bound them all together rattled with every movement.

Again, Cuttin' Edge felt the fury building inside him. But they were surrounded by Daleks – all of them looking for an excuse to exterminate. There was nothing he could do.

Except, he realised numbly, whatever the Daleks wanted.

'All the detention cells they must have in this place, and I get to share one with you.'

The Doctor sat up on the bench. 'It could be worse. You could have been having your brain scooped out of your skull and dissected by now.'

'Tough choice.' Bowman sat back on a narrow metal bench and folded his arms.

'At least this way we've got a bit more time. You've been put on the back burner while they think what to do with me.'

'Whatever.'

'And they've put us together deliberately,' said the Doctor, looking upwards. The cell was metal and otherwise featureless – apart from a protected light fitting in the ceiling and a camera mounted high up on one wall which resembled a Dalek eyestalk. 'They'll be watching everything we do. They want to hear what we've got to say to each other.'

'Which is nothing.'

'Oh come on. Talking is good! I like talking.'

Bowman closed his eyes. 'Yeah, I'd noticed.'

They sat in silence for a minute before the Doctor said, 'So. *Space Major* Bowman. You're a bit of a dark horse, aren't you?'

Bowman looked balefully at the Doctor. 'Don't you ever give up?'

'Never. So come on. How come *you're* so important to the Daleks?'

'I thought you said they'd be listening to us,' Bowman growled, jerking a thumb at the eyestalk on the wall.

'Yeah, but they'll know all this stuff already. They'll probably just turn over and watch whatever's on the other side.' The Doctor sat forward and pointed at the white scar on Bowman's forearm. 'That's what gave you away, isn't it? Where you took the old Earth Command transmitter out of your arm. Everyone over the rank of captain has one surgically implanted when they're commissioned. It's a little microchip that transmits your location and health status – basically whether you're alive or dead – back to base. Helps Earth Command keep track of all its important military assets right across the galaxy. But you took yours out, which is strictly against orders. Are you a *deserter*, Space Major Bowman?'

Bowman's eyes narrowed. The Doctor was staring at him, eyes huge, mouth hanging open in a half grin. Bowman felt like punching his lights out.

'It's a bit more complicated than that,' he said eventually.

The Doctor sat back, put his hands behind his head and stretched his long legs out on the bench. 'Go on, I'm listening.'

'Well,' Bowman rumbled, 'maybe it just *seemed* complicated at the time. Thing is, I was once a good soldier with a bright future. Did some good stuff in the

First Dalek Incursion. Got promoted. Somehow ended up a Space Major and before I knew it I was helping to design the defence system for Earth Central. I'd gone from being a fighting soldier on the front line to a security consultant sitting behind a desk. Didn't like it one bit – but I did a good job.'

A bitter look flashed across his face at the memory. 'When I finished, Earth Command decided that I was now a security risk because I knew so much and the safest thing to do was wipe my memory.'

The Doctor winced sympathetically. 'No wonder you didn't want to involve Earth Command in this business.'

'Yeah, well, I didn't fancy a future as a brainless old trooper in some spacers' home. So I got out.'

'You deserted.'

'I cut the chip out of my arm and buried it in the desert on the planet Mykron. And then I went on the run.'

'But carried on doing the only thing you knew – killing Daleks.'

'The only thing I *wanted* to do. Worked around the fringes of the Earth worlds for a while, on the *Wayfarer*. But eventually, when Earth was getting desperate, they started recruiting bounty hunters to harass the Dalek forces on the frontier planets. I jumped at the chance to kill some Daleks, and it paid good money.'

'Bit of a comedown, though, for a high-ranking officer in the Space Service.'

'Better than winding up a brainless old trooper.' Bowman considered where he was and then added, 'Looks like that's gonna happen now anyhow. The defence system for Earth Central is still wet-wired into my brain. The Daleks know that – I've been on their most wanted list for years. Now I'm here and I can't help thinking I should have taken the brain-wipe when it was first offered.'

'Rubbish. While you're still alive and you've still got all your marbles, there's always hope. Always.'

Bowman raised an eyebrow. 'You're pretty optimistic for a man who's sitting in a cell at the very centre of the Daleks' biggest prison and interrogation centre.'

The Doctor was suddenly struck by a thought. 'Have you ever heard of something called the Dalek Inquisitor General?'

Bowman's eyes opened fractionally. 'Where did you hear that name?'

'The Command Dalek said I was going to be interrogated by the Dalek Inquisitor General. Mean anything to you?'

Bowman sat upright. His whole demeanour had subtly changed: he was alert, tense, and his eyes were uncharacteristically wide. 'You've got to be kidding. You've never heard of *Dalek X*?'

'Should I have?'

Bowman drew a deep breath.

'The Dalek Inquisitor General is one of Earth Command's priority targets. His Space Service security designation is X. Hence the nickname – Dalek X. If they've called *him* in then you're in more trouble than I thought. In fact, you must have put every damned Dalek from here to Skaro on red alert.' He leant forward, staring intently at his cellmate as if examining him properly for the very first time. 'Just who the hell are you? Really?'

'Never mind about me. Tell me what you know about this Dalek X.'

'Well, he's a whole deal of trouble. It's not very often a particular Dalek gets a reputation – but he's one of the Supreme Dalek's top commanders and a helluva tough customer. They say he's put the order in to exterminate more humans than anyone else in history. I've heard him described as the Devil in Dalek form.'

The Doctor sagged. 'Suddenly I'm not feeling quite so optimistic.'

Chapter
Eighteen

Cuttin' Edge was still hurting. He was starting to shake, almost as if he had a fever. Spasms of burning pain ran through his legs every few seconds. Occasionally he would stumble, or fall painfully on one knee, and Koral would have to pull him quickly to his feet before the Daleks noticed. His heart hammered in his chest every time a Dalek came near.

The Daleks glided among the workers, some armed with a kind of electric tine in place of the usual sucker. Any slave thought to be slacking was prodded. There would be a loud crackle and the slave would instantly move faster, blinking away hot tears of pain.

'I can't stand much more of this,' muttered Cuttin' Edge.

Koral looked at him. 'Don't stop now. You are stronger than almost anyone else here.'

'I don't mean that. I can keep on shiftin' rocks from now until doomsday, if my legs hold out. I'm talkin' about watching those scumbuckets torturin' innocent people.'

'Just keep working,' said a voice from the back of the line. It was the woman. Her voice wavered as she spoke, but her green eyes were steady and determined. 'If you do anything stupid, the Daleks will kill all of us. Me and my daughter included.'

Cuttin' Edge lowered his gaze.

'I'm Jenifa,' said the woman. There was the ghost of a

smile on her lips. 'This is Kuli.'

'Hi,' said Kuli in a small voice.

Cuttin' Edge found himself waving back at the little girl. She was just like her mother – long, straight hair, determined eyes. 'How long you been here?' he asked.

'Long enough to know that you're badly injured,' Jenifa replied.

'I'm OK.'

'You can barely stand. You're shaking.'

Koral said, 'He was shot in the legs by a Dalek. Some kind of stun blast.'

'It's neurological shock,' Jenifa explained. 'I was a nurse on the planet Auros. When the Daleks intercepted the refugee fleet, we were all brought here to work. But I've helped treat injuries like yours before.'

'Is he going to die, Mummy?' asked Kuli. She stared at Cuttin' Edge in wonder, as if expecting him to keel over any minute.

'Hey,' said Cuttin' Edge. 'I ain't goin' anywhere yet, babe.'

'Does it matter?' asked Jenifa. 'Looks to me like we're already in Hell as it is.'

A Dalek descended through the mist. 'DO NOT SPEAK. YOU ARE HERE TO WORK. TALKING IS FORBIDDEN. OBEY THE DALEKS.'

'Yeah, yeah,' grumbled Cuttin' Edge. 'Same old same old.'

The Dalek's electric prod extended and a spark leapt into Cuttin' Edge's chest. He cried out and sat down heavily, chains rattling. Koral grabbed him and tried to pull him upright. It was difficult. Cuttin' Edge felt as if his legs were on fire, and they were as weak as a newborn lamb's. He held on to her for support, teeth gritted.

'YOU CANNOT STAND,' observed the Dalek. 'IF YOU CANNOT STAND YOU CANNOT WORK.'

'We've been through this already,' snarled Cuttin' Edge. 'An' I've told you: I'm still standin'. And I'll still be standin' when you're a pile of rust on the floor. Got that?'

The Dalek eyed him implacably. 'IF YOU DO NOT WORK YOU WILL BE EXTERMINATED.'

'Yeah,' nodded Cuttin' Edge, bending down and picking up a rock. 'So you said.' For a moment he contemplated ramming the rock into the Dalek's eye. Wouldn't do it a whole lot of harm, but it might make him feel a bit better. Just for a second. But then he thought of Koral and Jenifa and Kuli. And he turned and passed the rock on. It was transferred down the line and dropped into the skip with a loud clang.

Satisfied, the Dalek moved on.

And, teeth grinding as he fought back the overwhelming pain, Cuttin' Edge bent down and picked up another rock. His legs trembled and his heart pounded. But he continued working.

In the main control room, the Command Dalek swung around to face a subordinate. 'REPORT!'

'EXCAVATION WORK ON THE PLANETARY CORE IS BEHIND SCHEDULE,' said the Dalek. 'SLAVE OUTPUT IS FALLING. RESOURCES HAVE BEEN DIVERTED TO ENSURE MAXIMUM SECURITY ON LEVEL NINE ZERO ONE.'

Level nine zero one was Arkheon's most secure area. That was where the Doctor was being held.

'UNDERSTOOD,' replied the Command Dalek. 'REPORT ON THE SCIENTIFIC RESEARCH TEAM.'

'PROGRESS CONTINUES. THE RESEARCH TEAM ESTIMATES THRESHOLD BREAKTHROUGH IN THREE SOLAR DAYS.'

'THAT IS UNSATISFACTORY! THE ARKHEON THRESHOLD MUST BE BROKEN AS SOON AS POSSIBLE. DIVERT ALL AVAILABLE RESOURCES. PRIORITY ONE!' The Command Dalek glided over to one of the main control panels, where several circular screens showed views of the surrounding cosmos. 'THE DALEK INQUISITOR GENERAL IS DUE TO ARRIVE IN FOUR HUNDRED RELS! THE FLEET HAS BEEN PLACED ON FULL ALERT ON THE EDGE OF THE ARKHEON SYSTEM. WE MUST BE READY!'

There was no mistaking the rising pitch of the Command Dalek's voice. The subordinate's lights flashed urgently. 'I OBEY!' it shrieked, and turned to leave the room quickly.

The Command Dalek watched the screens. One showed a fleet of Dalek saucers flying in formation towards Arkheon space. A tiny thrill of anticipation passed through the shrunken creature inside the bronze casing. Anticipation and fear. It could sense, like every other Dalek in the room, that history was about to be made. Or, if not actually made, then torn apart.

Dalek X was coming.

The Inquisitor General had adopted the security designation given to him by Earth Command. He understood that it inspired fear in humans – fear of the unknown, fear of his ruthlessness, fear of his complete devotion to the Supreme Dalek.

Dalek X had just one purpose, one goal: the total and utter destruction of the human race. Mastery over every other life form. Domination of the universe at any cost. These were the central beliefs of every Dalek in existence, but Dalek X was driven by something else: the certain knowledge that the only way the Dalek race would ever achieve its ultimate aim was by conquering both space *and* time. He reported only to the Supreme Dalek on Skaro. He was feared by everyone and everything in the galaxy.

And he was coming for the Doctor.

'We've got to get out of here,' said the Doctor. He was moving around the cell, checking the walls and floor.

'Don't be stupid,' growled Bowman.

'You can either sit there and criticise, or you can help.'

Bowman snorted. 'What are you looking for? A trap door?'

'Anything. Anything at all.' The Doctor dropped to his hands and knees, pressing his ear to the metal floor. 'I can't hear a thing. I think we're on the lowest level.'

'Figures.'

The Doctor jumped to his feet. 'Well, it means one good thing: the only way is up!'

'Feeling optimistic again?'

'Oh yes!'

'You're insane.'

'I'm in here. And I want to be out there.' The Doctor pointed at the door. 'Is that so crazy?'

'Save your breath, Doctor. You'll need it for screaming when Dalek X gets hold of you.'

'By the time Dalek X gets here, I intend to be long gone. But if you see him, pass on my regards.'

'You're never gonna give up, are you?'

'Are *you*?'

'Have you ever escaped from a Dalek prison cell before, Doctor?'

'Loads of times. Been there, done that, got the T-shirt. "I visited Skaro and all I got was this lousy T-shirt." Believe me, it can be done.'

'All right.' Bowman got slowly to his feet. He was as tall as the Doctor but he was a lot broader. He seemed to fill the little cell. 'What do we do?'

'Bang on the door. Yell for the guards. You say I'm sick – I'm having a fit or something. Or I'm dead! Yes, tell 'em I'm dead. I've just collapsed on the floor – double heart attack. That'll bring them running.' The Doctor quickly lay on the floor, spread-eagled with his eyes shut. 'Go on!'

Bowman thumped on the door. 'Hey, Dalek!' he called. 'I know you're out there. You better come in and check this out. The Doctor's collapsed. I think he's dead.'

Silence.

The Doctor opened one eye. 'Any sign?'

'Yeah, I think they've sent for an ambulance.'

'This is no time to develop a sense of humour, Bowman.' The Doctor got back up on his feet. 'I thought I could rely on you to be dour and pessimistic.'

'Hey, I'm just killing time until they come to rip my brains out. Meanwhile, I'm wondering exactly what they must be thinking, watching you do all this.' He pointed up at the camera eye on the wall. 'Or had you forgotten they're watching our every move and listening to our every word?'

The Doctor looked up at the eyestalk, almost comically surprised. Then he turned to face Bowman, and, together, they burst out laughing.

'Well,' gasped the Doctor after a few moments, wiping his eyes, 'it was worth a try!'

Bowman shook his head in wonderment. The two men stared at each other, a unique moment of comradeship passing between them. Locked together in the deepest dungeon of a Dalek prison, they both knew the end was in sight.

In the distance, echoing through the steel walls of their cell, a klaxon sounded. A warning alarm. It was the kind of noise that made the guts turn over.

Bowman swallowed. 'Dalek X is here,' he said.

CHAPTER
NINETEEN

On the edge of the Arkheon solar system, a squadron of Dalek saucers emerged from hyperspace and swept towards the broken planet that glittered like a tiny diamond in the glare of its distant sun.

Six outrider saucers zoomed ahead of the giant *Exterminator*-class flagship belonging to the Supreme Dalek's Inquisitor General.

It was the first of its kind; the ultimate expression of Dalek power. Ten immense antigravity impeller engines thrust the ship onwards, so powerful that they left a trail of time distortion in its wake. The neutronic reactor at the ship's centre supplied gigantic power to the vast array of particle-beam weapons, missiles and energy-shield repulsors. The saucer carried a standard crew complement of five hundred Daleks plus ten ranking commanders and, at the very top, secure in his Dalekenium plate-armoured control dome, Dalek X.

This squadron of ships had broken away from the command battle fleet, redirected from Skaro, for one purpose only: to bring the Primary Intelligence Unit, led by the Inquisitor General, to Arkheon. Its mission: to interrogate and destroy the definitive enemy of the Daleks – the renegade Time Lord known only as the Doctor.

The ships swooped into orbit around the shattered remains of the prison planet, scything through what was left of the upper atmosphere and cracking the deserted ruins of its once-beautiful cities with a succession of giant sonic booms.

The *Exterminator* settled into a geostationary orbit level with the huge cavern that housed the landing port and upper tiers of the Dalek prison facility. The saucer was far too big to land in the cavern or even dry dock. It simply hovered, its engines throbbing with enough suppressed power to shake loose stones from the edges of the cave.

Hatches slid open around the saucer's edge, and a phalanx of Daleks poured out in strict formation, heading for the landing platforms.

There were many more Daleks assembled in ranks on the various levels of the Arkheon base. At the very front was the gleaming bronze shape of the Command Dalek.

The *Exterminator* Daleks hovered as a small unit broke away and floated down towards the reception area. There were two elite guard Daleks, their black domes continually sweeping from side to side, double gun-sticks raised, and they came in to land first. Behind them were four assault Daleks, fitted with laser-cutting claws rather than suckers.

And then there was Dalek X.

The armour casing was gunmetal black where the other Daleks were bronze. But the globes which studded the base unit and the thick armour slats on the weapons platform were all gold. He glided imperiously onto the landing level and swept straight past the Command Dalek without even acknowledging it.

The Command Dalek slid hurriedly in behind the Inquisitor General.

'REPORT!' barked Dalek X.

The Command Dalek edged closer as they moved towards the prison interior, flanked by the assault and elite guards. 'CORE SEPARATION IS PROCEEDING AS ORDERED – BUT THE SCHEDULE HAS BEEN DELAYED BY THE ARRIVAL AND APPREHENSION OF THE DOCTOR!'

'HOW LONG UNTIL THE ARKHEON THRESHOLD IS BREACHED?'

'RESEARCH TEAM ESTIMATES TWO SOLAR DAYS UNTIL THE THRESHOLD IS EXPOSED. PARTICLE ACCELERATION BOMBARDMENT WILL FOLLOW IMMEDIATELY!'

They had reached the interior hallway. Dalek X swept around and allowed his cold blue gaze to fall on the Command Dalek for the first time. 'THE DELAY IS UNACCEPTABLE,' he grated. 'SUMMON THE DALEKS RESPONSIBLE FOR MAGNETIC CORE SEPARATION.'

'I OBEY!'

Led by Dalek X, the group moved into the prison control centre. The guard Daleks took up positions behind and either side of their master. Very soon, three Dalek mine overseers arrived. Their normal bronze casings were covered in grime and dust and lava splashes from the cave systems that surrounded the planet's molten core.

Dalek X's dome lights flashed menacingly. 'EXPLAIN THE DELAY IN MAGNETIC CORE SEPARATION!'

One of the Daleks moved forwards, twitching nervously. 'DISRUPTION DUE TO THE ARRIVAL OF THE DOCTOR HAS DIVERTED RESOURCES FROM THE MINE WORKINGS. THE HUMAN SLAVES ARE NOT STRONG ENOUGH TO ABSORB THE INCREASED WORKLOAD.'

'THIS DELAY IS UNACCEPTABLE,' repeated Dalek X implacably. 'YOU HAVE FAILED THE DALEKS! FAILURE CANNOT BE TOLERATED! EXTERMINATE!'

The two elite guard Daleks on either side of him instantly opened fire, unleashing twin bursts of neutronic energy at the mine Dalek. The creature inside was fried alive, its harsh, dying shriek nearly drowned by the piercing screech of the beams. A moment later, all that was left of the Dalek was a blackened shell, the oily smoke belching from the neck grille accompanied by a quiet sizzling noise.

'Recycle the casing,' ordered Dalek X, addressing the remaining mine Daleks. 'Continue with the separation schedule. Force the humans to work harder and faster. Select the weakest human every hour and exterminate it in front of the other slaves. They will redouble their efforts. Continue!'

'We obey!' shouted the Daleks. They turned and hurried away.

The Doctor was listening at the door of the cell with his stethoscope. He moved the diaphragm carefully around the metal frame and then raised his eyebrows.

'Lots of activity outside,' he murmured. 'Something's really stirred them up.'

'I told you,' said Bowman. 'It's Dalek X.'

The Doctor straightened up and folded away the stethoscope. 'We've got to get out of here.'

'Why didn't I think of that?' wondered Bowman drily. He was sitting along one of the benches watching the Doctor run his hands through his hair in agitation.

'We can't all be geniuses,' replied the Doctor, but he wasn't smiling. He started to go through his pockets.

'This is the top Dalek detention and interrogation facility. No one gets out of here alive.'

'You're being negative again.'

'I tell you it's impossible,' growled Bowman, losing patience.

'I *like* impossible!'

*

Cuttin' Edge stumbled again, crashing to his knees and almost pulling Koral over with him.

She staggered, grabbed him quickly by the arm and hauled him to his feet.

'Another slip like that will cost us all our lives!' she hissed in his ear.

He shook her hand away. 'You think I don't know that?' He looked down at his legs, where the tough material of his fatigues was stained with blood. He couldn't feel the pain, not properly. His legs were still riddled with nerves and it took all his concentration not to let them shake. Bending down and picking up rocks was becoming more and more problematic.

'Please, don't argue,' said Jenifa. She looked past Koral at Cuttin' Edge. 'It just attracts attention.'

'Not pickin' up rocks is gonna attract attention,' said Cuttin' Edge bitterly.

'Let's change places, then,' Jenifa suggested. She pulled a strand of sweat-soaked hair back behind her ear; her fingers were sore and bleeding from the work but she never complained. Behind her, Kuli watched silently, eyes wide and fearful.

Cuttin' Edge felt ashamed.

'I'll go to the head of the line,' explained Jenifa quickly. 'You stand at the back. Then you won't have to bend down so much.'

'I ain't no invalid,' said Cuttin' Edge.

'The Daleks might not agree,' Koral said.

'Look out,' Jenifa whispered suddenly. 'They're back.'

Two overseer Daleks had swept back into the cavern. They floated over the bubbling streams of lava, eyestalks roving over the human slaves.

'ATTENTION! THE WORK RATE IS UNACCEPTABLE! YOU WILL

173

INCREASE YOUR EFFORTS IMMEDIATELY! IMMEDIATELY!'

'We can't work any harder,' argued one old woman bravely. She stood up straight, right in front of one of the Daleks. Her grey hair stood out on her scalp like wires, but there was a burning defiance in her eyes. 'You're just being ridiculous.'

'DO NOT ARGUE WITH THE DALEKS!' screamed the overseer. Its sucker arm extended and grabbed her by the face.

Unable to breathe, she was forced quickly to her knees. The suction cup released its grip and the old woman sagged to the ground, heaving. Those in her work unit gathered around, helping her back up as quickly as they could. Everyone knew that any untoward sign of weakness could result in death for them all.

'FROM THIS POINT ON WE WILL IDENTIFY THE WEAKEST WORK UNIT EVERY HOUR,' the Dalek continued, addressing the entire cavern. Its harsh, metallic voice echoed around the stalagmites. 'THAT WORK UNIT WILL BE EXTERMINATED.'

'NO FURTHER WARNING WILL BE GIVEN!' the second Dalek added.

There was a murmur of fear throughout the crowd – but no one wanted to argue too loudly.

'They're in one bad mood,' observed Cuttin' Edge quietly. 'I mean, worse than usual. Wonder what got into them?'

'Fear,' said Koral.

The Daleks swept through the lines of slaves, domes rotating. 'THE FIRST WORK UNIT TO BE EXTERMINATED WILL BE CHOSEN NOW.'

The slaves milled around in a quiet panic, all trying to look stronger, taller, fitter than their neighbours. Cuttin' Edge gritted his teeth as his legs started to shake. The sweat was pouring down his face and chest, his shirt stuck to his skin, and he knew he must look awful. Everyone else around him seemed to be healthier and more upright. Even the old woman who'd been suckered looked livelier than him.

The Daleks cornered a work unit on the edge of the cavern. From where they stood, Cuttin' Edge and Koral could not see the prisoners. Were they old? Weak? Injured? It was impossible to tell. All they heard was the savage metallic cry, 'EXTERMINATE!' and then a brilliant blue flash as the neutronic beams struck home.

Then silence.

'CONTINUE WORKING!' ordered the Daleks.

The remaining slaves set to their tasks with desperate energy, each work unit competing with the next as if it was some macabre contest.

Cuttin' Edge picked up rocks and passed them quickly down the chain. Kuli tossed them into the skip, giving a tiny little grunt of exertion every time. The whole process was repeated, again, again, faster, faster. Cuttin' Edge was shaking now, his legs on fire. Tears burned his eyes. Whoever they were – the ones that the Daleks had murdered – they couldn't have been any weaker than him. He felt ill with fear and guilt. How long would it be before they came for him?

In the prison control centre, the Command Dalek was studying a bank of monitors. Circular screens projected images of the mines, the core, the research laboratories, and the prison levels. One large monitor was showing the interior of the Doctor's cell on level nine zero one. The Doctor and Bowman were sitting opposite each other, talking.

Dalek X glided over and stared intently at the image.

'WHICH ONE IS THE DOC-TOR?'

The Command Dalek indicated. The thin figure on the screen made the creature that lurked inside the bronze casing squirm. But Dalek X seemed completely unfazed. He studied the Time Lord with fierce intent, the blue light in his eye growing stronger by the second. And then, bizarrely, the Doctor looked up, straight at the camera lens. His wide, alien eyes stared out of the screen at the observers.

'HE KNOWS THAT WE ARE OBSERVING HIM!' said the Command Dalek.

'IT IS UNIMPORTANT. THE DOC-TOR HAS A HIGHER THAN AVERAGE INTELLIGENCE RATING FOR A HUMANOID. CERTAIN REACTIONS ARE EXPECTED.'

The Command Dalek touched a control and a succession of images flicked rapidly across the screen – different men: old, young, tall, short. The faces flicked past at bewildering speed. 'THIS PERSON DOES NOT MATCH ANY PREVIOUS IDENTIFIABLE VERSIONS OF THE DOC-TOR IN OUR DATABANKS.'

'HE CONTINUALLY CHANGES HIS PHYSICAL APPEARANCE IN A FUTILE EFFORT TO AVOID DETECTION,' explained Dalek X. His eyestalk never left the Doctor on the screen. 'HE HAS INTERFERED WITH DALEK PLANS ON MANY OCCASIONS. BUT HE WILL INTERFERE NO LONGER.'

'HE IS RESOURCEFUL AND CUNNING,' warned the Command Dalek.

'HE RELIES ON FORTUITY. HIS ARROGANCE WILL PROVE TO BE HIS DOWNFALL.' Dalek X turned away. 'BRING HIM TO THE INTERROGATION CHAMBER!'

The Doctor and Bowman had emptied their pockets to see what they could muster between them. It was the

Doctor's idea; Bowman complied simply because he was too tired to argue.

On the floor in the centre of the cell was a little pile of junk: the Doctor's sonic screwdriver, his psychic paper, glasses, the TARDIS key, a pencil, a handful of strange coins, some string and a couple of rubber bands. He studied the assorted odds and ends as he chewed the earpiece on his stethoscope.

'No blaster,' observed Bowman.

'Guns are not the only weapons,' replied the Doctor tartly. 'It's all a matter of resources – and using our brains. Or rather my brain.'

'You going to take out the guard with a pencil?'

The Doctor picked through the junk. The sonic screwdriver was useless; all Dalek doors were deadlock sealed. The screwdriver wouldn't even scratch them. He picked up the TARDIS key and looked at it sadly. Then he closed his fist tightly around it. 'Come on, Doctor, *think!*'

Bowman sat back with a sigh.

'There must be more,' insisted the Doctor. 'Come on, anything. Are you sure you've checked all your pockets? No one travels that light.'

'I do.'

'You're just not trying. You've given up!'

Bowman raised an eyebrow. 'I think I gave up a long, long time ago.'

Something in his voice made the Doctor stop. He watched Bowman carefully for a second or two before saying, 'You mean when you first went on the run? I don't think Cuttin' Edge would believe that. He thinks the world of you.'

'Cuttin' Edge is just a kid.' Bowman rubbed a big hand across his eyes. 'No, I gave up long before all that.'

He reached into a side pocket and withdrew a small card. He threw it down in front of the Doctor. It was an old photograph, slightly creased and dog-eared – and the same picture that the Doctor had already seen as a hologram in Bowman's cabin aboard the *Wayfarer*. A very young, smooth-faced Jon Bowman with his proud parents.

'There,' growled Bowman. 'That's everything I have. There's nothing else.'

The Doctor picked up the photo and studied it. Bowman was smiling out from the past, caught in an unguarded moment when he knew nothing of the future. The Doctor wondered if that smile would have been so bright if he could have seen what lay ahead: older, tougher, disowned and disheartened, sitting on the floor of a Dalek prison cell.

'Ever since we came here,' said Bowman thickly, 'ever since I met *you*… I've had a feeling that this was it. The end of the line. I looked at Stella when she was lying in the sickbay and I knew – I just knew – what was coming.' He took the photo back and stared at the picture. 'The end of the line.'

'Not yet,' the Doctor said. 'You mustn't ever give up. There's always a chance.'

He grunted, unconvinced.

'Are your parents still alive?'

Bowman shrugged, 'Maybe. I haven't seen them in a long, long time. I doubt they even think of me any more. Why would they? I'm just a bad memory. When I went on the run, the army would have called on them, told them.' Bowman's words faded as his lips grew tight. He stared at the image in the photo, at the smiling eyes of his parents. He knew they weren't smiling at him.

'It's not too late...' began the Doctor.

The door to the cell suddenly whirred open, revealing two Daleks.

'End of the line. Doctor.' said Bowman.

CHAPTER
TWENTY

They were taken out of the cell and marched down a series of featureless metal corridors. The Doctor could see that Bowman was getting very anxious now. His skin was a horrible grey colour, his lips compressed into a thin white line. His eyes were sunk deep into his head, full of visions of what lay ahead.

The Doctor's own hearts were hammering in his chest, the blood pounding away in his head. He was trying to think, trying to come up with a last-minute escape plan or brilliant idea, but his mind felt paralysed.

They passed a number of doorways and laboratories, with wide windows allowing views of Daleks at work: the Doctor saw one room with a native Arkheon mutant strapped to the wall, its skin glowing brightly under the harsh electric light. A Dalek opened fire at the mutant, which blackened and died like an autumn leaf. Another Dalek was calculating exactly what firepower was required to exterminate the creature.

Sickened, the Doctor looked away.

They arrived at a junction. Bowman was led to one door, while the Doctor was pushed towards another.

'Looks like this is it,' said Bowman. 'Time to give them a piece of my mind.'

The Doctor gamely tried to smile at Bowman's joke, but all he felt was a profound, helpless sadness. He swallowed with difficulty and then looked at Bowman.

'I'm sorry,' he said.

Bowman touched his forehead with a finger in ironic salute as the door began to close. 'Good luck.'

'Never give up!' the Doctor shouted after him. 'Never!' Then the door slammed shut.

'MOVE!' ordered the Dalek next to him.

The Doctor drew a breath, and followed the Dalek into a darkened room. He was marched over to a metal wall and forced to stand upright against it. It felt uncomfortably like being made ready for the firing squad. His ankles and wrists were secured with tight steel bands so that he was utterly immobilised. The Daleks then withdrew and the door clanged shut behind them. The Doctor was left in complete darkness.

It was cold. He had no idea how big the room was or what else was in there with him. He couldn't see a thing. All he could hear was the heavy, metallic throb of Dalek machinery and behind that some kind of hard, electric vibration. The air tasted of static.

Something cold and metal embraced his head. The Doctor gasped as his skull was clamped into position and a hundred fine needles pricked his scalp. *This is it,* he thought, his hearts racing. *The beginning of the end.*

Eventually, a light appeared in the darkness – a blue disc. The eye of a Dalek. He sensed rather than saw the familiar shape as it circled, its single blue eye always on him.

Eventually a harsh, grating voice said, 'DOC-TOR...'

The lights on the Dalek's head flashed slowly, in time with each syllable. The Doctor swallowed. This Dalek was in no hurry. He licked his lips and, as brightly as he could manage, replied, 'That's me.' His voice sounded more brittle than he would have liked.

'I AM DALEK X.'

'Can't say I'm pleased to meet you, sorry.'

'YOU ARE ATTACHED TO A DALEK MIND-PROBE MACHINE. IT HAS BEEN CALIBRATED TO YOUR SPECIFIC BRAINWAVE FREQUENCY.'

'You won't get anything out of me,' the Doctor blurted.

'THAT IS NOT THE INTENTION,' replied Dalek X. 'YET.'

The Doctor couldn't turn his head because of the mind probe. It felt like a vice clamped around his skull. A couple of extra turns on the screw would crack the bone. 'So…' he said at last, 'what do you want? If it's my secret recipe for bread and butter pudding you can forget it. I'm taking that little beauty to my grave.'

'I INTEND TO MEASURE YOUR CAPACITY FOR PHYSICAL PAIN,' said Dalek X.

'Oh. Why?'

'BECAUSE I WISH TO.'

The Dalek's sucker touched a control on the mind-probe machine and turned it minutely. There was a fierce, galvanistic crackle of power, and the Doctor's body arched like a bow, straining against its bonds. A howl of anguish echoed through the darkness, torn from his lips with sudden, shocking ease.

How long it was before the control was released the Doctor could not tell. Time passed in an abstract sense amid a kaleidoscope of pain. It could have been seconds, minutes or even hours. It left him drained, limp, his hair stuck to his head with perspiration and his throat raw from screaming.

'EXPECT NO MERCY,' Dalek X informed him.

'I'm not stupid,' the Doctor croaked, feeling very stupid indeed. Partly because his head felt so foggy with pain but also because he couldn't for the life of him work

183

out how it had all come to this: helpless, friendless and homeless, chained to a wall and tortured by the Devil in Dalek form. That's how Bowman had described him, and it was difficult to argue.

'DALEKS DO NOT SHOW MERCY,' said Dalek X.

'Yes,' the Doctor replied. 'I know.'

'MERCY IS WEAKNESS.'

'Really? Why don't you just give it a try? Go on, I won't tell anyone.' The Doctor tensed, ready for the next onslaught. Out of the corner of his eye he could see the Dalek's suction arm hovering over the probe control. Any second now and he would be plunged back into the abyss of pain. 'On second thoughts, maybe I'm wasting my breath. And I've reconsidered the bread and butter pudding thing. You can have it if you want.'

'YOU DO NOT BEG FOR MERCY LIKE THE OTHERS.'

'What others?'

'THE FUGITIVES OF AUROS.'

A chill ran through the Doctor. 'Was that you?'

'I GAVE THE ORDER FOR THE REFUGEES TO BE EXTERMINATED,' Dalek X confirmed. 'THE PEOPLE OF AUROS HAD FLED AND LEFT THEIR PLANET IN RUINS. THEY COULD HAVE BEEN SLAVES. INSTEAD THEY CHOSE DEATH.'

'No they didn't. They had no choice at all. You murdered them all in cold blood. An entire colony.'

'DALEKS SHOW NO MERCY.'

'Or common sense, for that matter. Don't you realise that when news of that attack gets back to Earth they will launch a counter-offensive?' The Doctor suddenly stopped speaking and marshalled his thoughts. 'Ah. Now I see. That was the whole point, wasn't it?'

'EARTH COMMAND WILL RESPOND AS YOU HAVE PREDICTED. THE DALEKS WILL BE PREPARED. THE HUMANS WILL BE CRUSHED.'

'It's a bit desperate, though. Or is that the real reason? Are you losing the war with Earth? Is this one last shake of the dice?'

The response was unequivocal: a savage twist of the probe control and a series of wracking, nerve-shredding waves of pain. His brain felt like it was about to burst, but when the torment ended the Doctor was laughing.

'That's it, isn't it?' he panted, his breath ragged and thin. 'You're losing! This whole plan – the slaughter of the Auros fugitives, the attempt to break through the Arkheon Threshold… it's a last-ditch attempt to worm your way out of defeat. *Well it won't work!*'

He lifted his head and yelled the last four words.

'YOU UNDERESTIMATE OUR POWER,' grated Dalek X. 'YOU DO NOT REALISE WHAT THE ARKHEON THRESHOLD MEANS TO US – AND TO THE REST OF THE UNIVERSE.'

'Well I'm a bit of an expert on time travel and that sort of thing, and I can tell you it won't work. I was there, on Skaro, right at the very beginning when you lot were first slugging it out with the Thals and losing. And I'll be there right at the end, too – and guess what? You lose. Again.'

'IN THIS UNIVERSE,' conceded the Dalek. 'BUT NOT IN THE NEXT.'

Another chill of fear passed through the Doctor. His mind was racing. 'If you think you can use the Arkheon Threshold to change the entire universe, you're mistaken.'

'WE WILL CHANGE HISTORY.'

'But you'd need a massive power source to break down the Threshold. It's a minor fissure in space-time. A dead end. Blink and you'd miss it. What makes *you* think you've got what it takes?'

Dalek X approached the wall, his eyestalk boring into the Doctor. 'I WILL SHOW YOU.'

The Doctor was released from the mind probe. He sagged for a second as the bonds slid away, but then stood up stiffly, rubbing his wrists. He felt unsteady on his feet but tried not to show it, ruffling his hair back into its usual spiky fringe and clearing his throat. 'Find anything?' he asked, giving the probe a tap with his knuckle.

'THE MIND PROBE CONFIRMS THAT YOU ARE THE TIME LORD KNOWN AS THE DOC-TOR. BUT YOU DO NOT MATCH ANY OF THE PHYSICAL DESCRIPTIONS WE CURRENTLY HOLD IN OUR DATABASE.'

'Oh, shame. Maybe your records aren't as up to date as you think.'

Dalek X swivelled round to glare at him. 'THE MOST LIKELY CONCLUSION IS THAT YOU ARE FROM THE FUTURE.'

'What?' The Doctor looked horrified. 'Don't be ridiculous! As if!'

'IT HAS HAPPENED BEFORE.'

The Doctor pursed his lips. 'Ah, well, yes, now you mention it… but never mind. I hate all that continuity stuff. Tell me all about your plans for the Arkheon Threshold instead. That's much more interesting.'

Dalek X led the Doctor out of the mind-probe chamber into a long, low room with a wide viewing window stretched across the far wall. The room was in darkness, but there was a flickering orange glow coming through the window, as if it overlooked a furnace. The Doctor strolled across to the window and found himself looking out across a vast, subterranean vault. Dark crags were separated by winding, straggling rivers of molten rock. Daleks hovered amid clouds of sulphurous smoke, overlooking a hundred or more human slaves as they toiled in the searing conditions.

'Your own private view of Hades?' asked the Doctor as Dalek X joined him.

'WE ARE CLOSE TO THE MAGNETIC CORE OF ARKHEON,' Dalek X replied. Lit from below by the bubbling red light, his black and gold casing appeared to run with blood.

'Getting humans to do your dirty work again, eh? It's always the same with you lot. Of course, I blame the suckers.'

'EXPLAIN.'

'I mean,' the Doctor said, 'does stealing planetary cores really compensate for having no hands?'

'IF THE DALEKS ARE TO ACHIEVE TOTAL UNIVERSAL DOMINATION AND TAKE OUR RIGHTFUL PLACE AS THE SUPREME BEINGS THEN WE MUST MASTER TIME TRAVEL,' said Dalek X. 'THAT THE TIME LORDS HAVE FAILED TO ACHIEVE THE SAME GOAL IS A SIGN OF THEIR WEAKNESS AND INFERIORITY.'

'Or perhaps a sign that they don't want to rule the universe.'

'THEN THEY WILL CAPITULATE TO THE POWER OF THE DALEKS.'

'Forget it. If future Daleks gained mastery of time travel then you'd already know about it. They'd be here right this minute. In fact we'd *all* be trundling around in the old Mark Three Travel Machine chanting "exterminate" by now.'

'INCORRECT. DALEK TIME-TRAVEL THEORY STATES THIS IS AN ERRONEOUS VIEWPOINT. MASTERY OF TIME WILL BEGIN WITH THE DESTRUCTION OF THE TIME LORDS AND CONTROL OF THE TIME VORTEX. AND IT WILL END IN THE COMPLETE SUBJUGATION OF THE HUMAN RACE!' For the first time, Dalek X's voice increased in pitch as he grew more excited. 'WITH THE ARKHEON THRESHOLD WE WILL FIND A WAY INTO THE VORTEX!'

Bowman was pushed into a brightly lit laboratory bustling with Daleks. He turned angrily on the Dalek behind him. 'Keep your filthy sucker off me!'

The Dalek threw Bowman backwards. He landed on his back, winded.

'OBEY THE DALEKS!' shouted the metallic shape as it loomed over him.

'Never.'

'STAND!'

'Or what?' asked Bowman from his position on the floor. 'You ain't gonna exterminate me, remember. Not until you've picked *this* to bits.' He tapped his head.

The Dalek regarded him sourly for a moment but said nothing.

With a humourless smile, Bowman got slowly to his feet. 'I'll stand, but not because you tell me to. I'll stand because this way I'm *taller*.' He squared his shoulders and stared down the Dalek's eyestalk. 'Just remember that. Cos every human being you ever meet will look *down* at you.'

The Dalek glided forward. 'PAY ATTENTION TO THIS SCANNER SCREEN.'

Bowman looked at the bank of instruments to which it pointed. There was a circular monitor showing what looked like the surface of Arkheon – frozen, elegant ruins. The image zoomed in to one particular spot: a heavy, rough-looking spaceship that Bowman recognised only too easily.

'The *Wayfarer*,' he said aloud, momentarily stunned. It made his heart heave when he saw the old ship, left exactly where it had touched down only hours before. Almost as if it was waiting for him. Silent and patient.

'WE HAVE LOCATED YOUR SPACECRAFT,' the Dalek stated.

Bowman blinked. Was the Dalek expecting him to say *thanks*?

And then a shadow passed over the *Wayfarer*, and a Dalek saucer came into view on the screen, hovering above the old ship. Bowman automatically identified the saucer: an assault craft, *Aggressor*-class, small, highly manoeuvrable and heavily armed. As he watched, missiles streaked from the underside of the saucer and struck the *Wayfarer* amidships. It exploded into a giant, silent fireball and the debris scarred the snow around it for hundreds of metres.

'TARGET DESTROYED,' stated the Dalek.

It felt like a punch to the solar plexus. Bowman had to fight the urge to physically wilt. He took a deep, shuddering breath and stood up straighter, stronger. He looked at the Dalek.

'Think I've never seen a ship blown up before?' he snarled. 'I'm Space Major Jon Bowman. I've been blowing up spaceships and Daleks all my life. When are you going to get it? *I'm not scared of you.*'

'MOVE!' ordered the Dalek. It was joined by two others, and together they herded Bowman across the laboratory.

There were several benches arranged with clinical precision around the room. They were metal and looked like mortuary slabs. On each of them was a human being, lying face up, head shaved and exposed to the Daleks surrounding them. Some of the Daleks had surgical implements attached to their arms rather than suction cups or claws. Bowman felt physically sick.

'LIE DOWN.'

'This where you cut my head open?'

'LIE DOWN! OBEY!' The Dalek used its sucker arm to force Bowman back against the mortuary slab, so that he was bent awkwardly over it. Suddenly he twisted, lashing out with his foot, but the Dalek barely moved. Two more Daleks joined the first and together they manipulated him, kicking and fighting, onto the bench. Metal straps secured his wrists, ankles and throat.

He struggled, but uselessly. A sudden, wild fear swept through him, the kind of panic he had never experienced in his life before. His chest heaved and sweat broke from every pore. The bench felt hard and unyielding beneath him.

'NOW YOU FEAR THE DALEKS!' observed one of his captors triumphantly.

'PREPARE FOR FULL BRAIN EXCORIATION,' said another.

A surgical Dalek glided over, a small metal saw whirring into life on the end of its arm.

'Go on, then!' roared Bowman. 'Do it! You might as well get your kicks, cos I did the same thing to one of you not so long ago.'

The Daleks ignored him, going about their business with meticulous care.

'I had to scrape him out of his shell like a snail!' Bowman screamed. 'And you know what? He didn't make a damn sound. *And neither will I!*'

Cuttin' Edge winced, straightened up, took a deep breath. He caught Koral's eyes, and she nodded at the woman and the girl. They were clearly exhausted, perhaps only minutes from collapse.

'Don't give in now,' Koral whispered.

Jenifa looked up wearily through bloodshot eyes. 'There's nothing more we can do,' she croaked.

Kuli wept. 'I don't want to die, Mummy! I don't want to die.'

'Hush,' said Koral. 'You will attract attention.'

Jenifa scowled. 'We can't go on much longer. None of us can. They're going to kill us sooner or later and that will be it.' She put her arm around her daughter. 'I'm sorry, Kuli. I love you. I will always love you.'

190

Kuli squeezed her mother tight, and Jenifa looked back at Cuttin' Edge and Koral with a sad smile. 'Thank you for helping us,' she said.

Cuttin' Edge gritted his teeth. 'No, you helped *me*. I could hardly stand and you kept me goin'. All of you.'

'It's not over yet,' Koral said.

'It is now,' said Cuttin' Edge. He was looking past them, to where a cloud of sulphur had dispersed to reveal two Daleks.

'WORK UNIT DELTA!' grated the first. The hard, metallic words were full of cold menace. 'STEP FORWARD!'

Chapter
Twenty-One

'So this is the guided tour, is it?' asked the Doctor airily. Dalek X had taken him down into the granite bowels of Arkheon. Two of the Inquisitor General's black-domed guard Daleks had joined them. They hung back slightly, gun-sticks trained on the Doctor at all times.

Dalek X glided along a metal walkway installed the length of the cavern. Clouds of evil-smelling steam drifted by. The Doctor strolled along, hands in pockets, gazing all around him like a tourist on a holiday excursion. 'It's a bit stuffy down here,' he said. 'You need to get the heating fixed.'

Despite his casual demeanour, the Doctor was very worried. For a Dalek, the Inquisitor General was one cool customer. He was impossible to taunt. And he seemed to be two steps ahead all the time, out-guessing the Doctor at every turn. The Doctor was waiting for the chance to somehow turn the tables, but it was never coming – or showing any sign of coming.

'I suppose we're pretty close to the core here,' said the Doctor chattily. He tried a few light bounces, his trainers squeaking loudly on the metal walkway. 'I can feel the fluctuations in the magnetic field. Must be playing hell with you.'

'I AM IMMUNE TO THE EFFECTS,' Dalek X replied.

'Well,' said the Doctor. 'Good for you.'

They came to another part of the cavern and turned a

corner. The Doctor stopped in his tracks. After a moment he let out a low, appreciative whistle. In front of them was an enormous machine, five storeys high and just as wide, filling the length of a massive tunnel. It curved away into the distance on either side.

'It's a particle accelerator,' said the Doctor, gazing at the towering apparatus. Dalek scientists hovered around the machinery, adjusting and monitoring the complex systems. 'A very big one.'

'THIS IS THE LARGE CHRONON COLLIDER,' explained Dalek X. 'WE WILL BOMBARD DISCRETE PARTICLES OF TIME AGAINST EACH OTHER AT SUPRALIGHT SPEEDS. THE RESULTING HUON SHOWER WILL BE USED TO TRACE THE TEMPORAL PROFILE OF THE ARKHEON THRESHOLD. WE WILL THEN BE ABLE TO ACHIEVE MAGNETIC SEPARATION AND BREAK THROUGH TO THE TIME VORTEX.'

'Oh, that was good,' nodded the Doctor. 'You've been taking gobbledegook lessons. I like it.'

'IT WILL WORK.'

'Ah, well, yes – it might.' The Doctor craned his neck, looking up at the highest parts with a critical eye. 'It's *possible*, I'll give you that. But it is also insanely dangerous.'

'NOTHING IMPORTANT CAN BE ACHIEVED WITHOUT RISK.'

The Doctor frowned.

'Was that a bit of Dalek philosophy I just heard? You're going soft.'

'YOU CONCEDE THAT OUR PLAN IS VIABLE.'

The Doctor couldn't tell if this was a statement or a query. But it was true, nonetheless. He nodded thoughtfully, suddenly serious. 'Yes. It will work. But – and it's a big but – you'll need some sort of control element to stabilise it. Then it will work *properly*.'

'A CONTROL ELEMENT?'

'Yeah.' The Doctor sniffed, scratched his ear, looked away.

'SUCH AS A TARDIS.'

There it was again. Statement or question? The Doctor wasn't sure. He pulled a face, weighed up the factors involved, shrugged. 'Well, yeah. That'd do it. I suppose.'

'SUCH AS YOUR TARDIS?'

A grim look stole across the Doctor's face and his eyes became deep, dark pools. 'No,' he said bluntly. 'Absolutely no.'

'YOU ARE NOT IN A POSITION TO REFUSE THE DALEKS.'

That was definitely a statement. And it was also a fact. But the Doctor shook his head nevertheless. 'No. Sorry. No. N-O spells no. It's not even negotiable.'

'YOU WILL PROVIDE YOUR TARDIS, DOC-TOR!'

'Never.'

'THE DALEKS WILL USE ITS CONTROL SYSTEMS TO ACCESS THE TIME VORTEX!'

'I said never.'

Dalek X moved closer. His voice continued to grate out calm, unhurried statements as if they were facts. 'YOU REQUIRE PERSUASION.'

'I do not.'

'COERCION.'

'Not possible.'

'LET US INVESTIGATE.' Dalek X turned to one of the other Daleks as it glided by. The Dalek almost seem to cringe as the black and gold machine addressed it peremptorily: 'ALERT THE COMMAND DALEK!'

The Doctor was taken back to the detention levels and then into the high-speed lift to the prison control room. He walked out into the busy chamber with Dalek X in tow, as if they were old buddies. The feeling made the Doctor's skin crawl.

The Command Dalek swivelled hurriedly to face the Inquisitor General. 'YOUR ORDERS HAVE BEEN CARRIED OUT!'

The Doctor had an uneasy feeling. Dalek X glided silently forward and then turned. 'SUMMON THE PRISONERS.'

A door opened and four people shuffled into the control room.

'Koral! Cuttin' Edge!' the Doctor exclaimed in delight. His face fell. They looked awful. 'Are you all right?'

Cuttin' Edge was limping badly, and he seemed smaller than before, his shoulders hunched and his face haggard. Koral also seemed bowed, and her red eyes looked cloudy. Behind them, in chains, were a woman and a girl the Doctor had never seen before. They looked equally weak, and the girl was crying.

'Hi there,' said Cuttin' Edge. His smile looked fake, although the Doctor sensed he was genuinely pleased to see him. At least at first. When he looked around the brightly lit control room, saw the Doctor standing with the Daleks, his expression turned sour. 'What's goin' on? You colludin' with this scum now?'

'No,' said the Doctor. Then he cleared his throat and said, more firmly, 'No, I'm not.'

'THE DOC-TOR IS REFUSING TO COOPERATE WITH THE DALEKS,' stated Dalek X. 'THAT POSITION IS ABOUT TO BE REVERSED.'

'No,' said the Doctor again. 'You can't do this...'

'INCORRECT!'

The Command Dalek said, 'BRING FORWARD THE PRISONERS WHO CAME TO ARKHEON WITH THE DOC-TOR.'

Two guards unfastened the chains that connected Cuttin' Edge and Koral to Jenifa and Kuli. They were marched forward into the centre of the room. Koral looked uncertainly at the Doctor, as if wondering whether to attack him or the Daleks.

Dalek X moved forward, fixing the Doctor with his steady glare. 'IF YOU DO NOT COMPLY WITH DALEK INSTRUCTIONS THEN INNOCENT LIVES WILL BE LOST. IT IS YOUR DECISION.'

'I won't be bullied into helping you,' replied the Doctor. His voice was steely. 'There's too much at stake!'

Dalek X looked at Cuttin' Edge and Koral for a long moment and then said, 'THESE TWO PRISONERS ARE COMBATANTS. THEY EXPECT TO DIE IN THE LINE OF DUTY. THEREFORE THERE IS NO VALUE IN THEIR EXTERMINATION.'

'What's that supposed to mean?' Cuttin' Edge demanded.

Dalek X turned away, addressing the Doctor only. 'THESE PRISONERS WILL NOT BE KILLED.' There was a longer, colder pause. 'BRING FORWARD THE HUMAN MOTHER AND HER OFFSPRING.'

'No!' said the Doctor.

'No!' Cuttin' Edge shouted. 'Kill us instead!'

Jenifa and Kuli were herded forward, looking panicky and frightened. Jenifa had her arms around her daughter, her fingers were rigid and white on her shoulders.

'FORMATION THREE!' ordered the Command Dalek.

A trio of Dalek guards lined up in front of the woman and her daughter. There was no doubt that it was an execution squad. They turned their faces away from the Daleks, hugging each other tightly. No one drew so much as a breath and the only sound that could be heard was Kuli's muffled sobs.

'EX—' began the Command Dalek.

'*All right!*' yelled the Doctor. His voice echoed around the control room. 'All right! All right. Stop! I'll do it.'

Dalek X's eye swivelled slowly to face him.

'I'll give you the TARDIS,' said the Doctor quietly.

The eye glowed, full of greed. It bathed the Doctor's face in its cold blue light.

'But there are conditions,' the Doctor added.

'NOT VALID.'

'Wait. It's important.'

The Doctor took a deep breath, his face solemn.

'I'm giving you everything here. All of history opened up like a book for you to rip the pages out and start again!' His voice was shaking with fury. 'The very least you can do is hear me out!'

'CONTINUE.'

'My TARDIS requires a crew of six to function properly. Together with myself, I need Koral, Cuttin' Edge and Space Major Bowman.'

'THAT IS ONLY FOUR,' said Dalek X.

The Doctor indicated Jenifa and Kuli. They were looking up at him with haunted, disbelieving eyes. He hardly dared give them hope but he had to try. 'These two make six.'

'THESE HUMANS ARE NOT CREW MEMBERS.'

'I know. But they can be trained. They can help. I can show them what to do—'

'NEGATIVE.' The three syllables were ground out like pieces of broken rock. There would be no negotiation on this. 'YOU WILL HAVE FOUR CREW MEMBERS ONLY.'

'It can't be done!' the Doctor argued.

'IT WILL BE DONE! THESE HUMANS ARE NOT MEMBERS OF YOUR CREW. THEY ARE NOT NECESSARY. THEREFORE THEY WILL BE EXTERMINATED!'

The Doctor leapt forward. 'No! No, wait. They must be allowed to live. Even if they can't come, they must be allowed to live.'

The execution squad was already moving back towards the Jenifa and Kuli, taking up extermination positions again. The Doctor ran over and placed himself between the Daleks and the women. 'If you really want to kill them then you'll have to go through me first.'

'YOU CAN BE DISABLED,' warned Dalek X.

'Try it.'

The Dalek guns twitched impatiently in their sockets. All eyes were on the Doctor, but he met the pitiless blue stares unflinchingly.

'Harm them in any way and I will not cooperate. You can disable me and torture me and kill me but you will *never* get the TARDIS.'

Dalek X seemed to consider. Then: 'AGREED. BUT THAT IS THE LAST OF YOUR CONDITIONS. THERE WILL BE NO FURTHER COMPROMISE.'

'All right. You win.' The Doctor's shoulders were slumped in miserable defeat. 'But I do need Space Major Bowman.'

Dalek X turned to the Command Dalek. 'RELEASE THE HUMAN PRISONER AND HAVE HIM BROUGHT HERE.'

'I OBEY!'

Dalek X swivelled back to face the Doctor, his gun, arm and eye quivering hungrily. 'TELL ME THE LOCATION OF YOUR TARDIS.'

Through gritted teeth the Doctor said, 'Hurala.'

The Command Dalek twitched excitedly as it processed the information. 'PLANETOID KX-NINE IN THE LASRON SOLAR REGION!'

'Of course you'd know it,' muttered the Doctor resignedly. 'That's where all this started, after all.'

'WE WILL PROCEED IMMEDIATELY,' said Dalek X. 'PREPARE THE EXTERMINATOR FOR DEPARTURE.'

'There is just one another thing...' ventured the Doctor.

'NO MORE CONDITIONS!'

'This isn't a condition. It's just a word of advice.' The Doctor sounded apologetic. 'The TARDIS is actually grounded at the moment.'

'EXPLAIN!'

'Its spatial motivator is all to cock,' the Doctor said matter-of-factly. 'Why else d'you think I left it on Hurala? It'll be fine for what you want, but you'll need to remove the time rotor.'

'SUMMON THE TEMPORAL RESEARCH TEAM,' ordered Dalek X. 'IT CAN MAKE THE NECESSARY TECHNICAL ARRANGEMENTS ON HURALA.'

The Doctor joined Cuttin' Edge and Koral. 'Crew members?' Koral frowned.

'Don't mention it.' The Doctor murmured, and then he turned to the mother and daughter. 'I'm sorry,' he said. 'I did my best...'

'I know,' said Jenifa. She smiled weakly. 'Thank you.'

The Doctor nodded.

A door opened and Bowman walked through, covered with ugly bruises and cuts but still standing tall. Two Daleks glided in behind him. 'MOVE! WAIT IN THE CENTRE OF THE ROOM!'

Bowman sneered at them and then crossed over to Koral. She suddenly seemed to be filled with renewed hope, her eyes glowing strongly.

'Bowman!'

'Didn't think you'd get rid of me that easy, did you?' he asked.

'Are you OK?' asked the Doctor.

'Yeah. They pushed me around a bit but they never got

as far as the knives.' Bowman gave the Doctor a wry look. 'I take it you're to blame?'

'He's cut a deal with the Daleks,' said Cuttin' Edge. 'Like some sorta collaborator.'

'Easy, kid.' Bowman placed a hand on Cuttin' Edge's shoulder. 'You're still breathing, aren't you?'

'Yeah, but for how much longer?'

'PROCEED TO LANDING PORT!' Dalek X interrupted them loudly.

The Command Dalek and its guards started to herd the Doctor and his friends towards the exit. 'MOVE!'

The Doctor, Bowman, Koral and Cuttin' Edge marched out in sombre formation. Dalek X watched them go. Then he turned to follow, his head swivelling to address the elite Daleks that were still guarding the other prisoners.

'RETURN THEM TO THE CORE MINES,' he said.

'WE OBEY!' screeched the Daleks. Instantly, they turned back to face Jenifa and Kuli.

And the dark shape of Dalek X glided smoothly through the door as Jenifa broke down and wept.

CHAPTER
TWENTY-TWO

The interior of the Dalek cruiser was typical in its design: dark and functional, studded with control pillars and instrument banks, and teeming with Daleks. It was difficult not to see it as a kind of giant nest, with the Daleks crawling and hovering busily around the vaguely honeycombed interior.

The Doctor, Bowman, Cuttin' Edge and Koral were transported from Arkheon to the *Exterminator* via antigravity discs – large circular platforms fitted with handrails suitable for the transportation of individual prisoners, equipment or even Daleks that were damaged beyond their ability to fly.

Then they were led from the vast docking slot on the edge of the huge saucer through several levels until they reached the central command dome at its very heart.

'It stinks in here,' growled Bowman.

Koral, who had not left his side since they had been reunited, agreed. 'The stench of metal and hate.'

The Doctor was rather more impressed. 'Look at it this way,' he said. 'Very few human beings have ever been aboard a Dalek saucer, let alone one as big as this.'

'And we're bein' taken right to the top spot,' noted Cuttin' Edge ruefully. 'Guess they must really like us.'

Two guard Daleks herded them into a small area to one side of the circular flight deck. Then the ever-present assault Daleks, outriders for Dalek X, took up positions on either side of the raised podium. A section of the deck plate in the centre of the dais ground open like a steel iris and the now-familiar black-and-gold shape of the Dalek Inquisitor General rose slowly up through the aperture.

'SET COURSE FOR THE PLANET HURALA!' Dalek X ordered. 'MAXIMUM SPEED!'

'WE OBEY,' chorused the bridge crew, turning to face their individual flight stations. From his raised position at the centre, Dalek X could easily watch all of the instruments by simply swivelling his head.

Bowman watched the Daleks at the control panels carefully, but the Doctor shook his head. 'Don't bother trying to memorise what they do,' he warned quietly. 'The controls can only be activated by Daleks – they each have a code signal aligned to the ship's computer systems to allow them access.'

Bowman raised an eyebrow. 'Is there *anything* you don't know about the Daleks?'

'Yes,' the Doctor admitted. He kept his voice low. 'I don't know how we're going to stop them.'

'I don't think we can.'

'You didn't think there was any way to get out of Arkheon,' the Doctor reminded him. 'And yet here we are.'

'On a Dalek battle cruiser. Not exactly *free*.'

'Well it's a start.'

The *Exterminator*'s huge engines fired up and a heavy rumble passed through the ship. The deep, persistent background throb of the control room rose in pitch as, on the main viewscreen, the broken orb of Arkheon began to move slowly away.

Then the saucer powered up, suddenly leaving the planet behind until it was little more than a shimmering white dot.

'That's some acceleration,' marvelled Cuttin' Edge.

'Yeah, hardly felt a thing,' Bowman agreed. Even he was struggling to keep a note of admiration out of his voice.

'Superb inertia-dampening fields,' explained the Doctor. 'Whatever you think of the Daleks, they are brilliant scientists and engineers.'

'This must be the pride of the fleet.'

'Yes,' the Doctor said thoughtfully, looking up at Dalek X. 'It must be.'

The *Exterminator* paid scant attention to the laws of physics that governed normal space flight. The immense ion thrusters warped the space around the saucer to a point where time could, temporarily, be condensed. It wasn't time travel per se, the Doctor told the others, but it did mean the ship was incredibly fast. It made the *Wayfarer* on its best days look like a complete sluggard.

The journey took no more than an hour. The cruiser slammed out of maximum speed on the edge of the Hurala solar system, and again no one inside the craft could discern any real change. Space simply warped back into its normal shape around the vessel. Even decelerating, the ship took only another twenty minutes to complete the trip.

Hurala quickly filled the viewscreen, swelling up like a ball of dried mud. The *Exterminator* and its outrider saucers burst through the thin atmosphere and swept across the deserted terrain until they reached the old Lodestar depot.

The battle cruiser was too big to land, so it remained hovering over the rusting hulks and abandoned refinery buildings like a giant metal hand poised to crush a spider. Squadrons of Daleks flooded out of the saucer towards the desolate settlement, flying in strict formation. The Doctor and his friends were transported on antigrav discs once again, to be joined on the surface by the Command Dalek. Dalek X and his elite guards arrived moments later.

'WHERE IS YOUR TARDIS?' demanded Dalek X.

'I'm not sure,' replied the Doctor, turning slowly on his heel and scanning the surrounding buildings. 'All these alleyways look the same to me.'

Dalek X turned to one of his subordinates. 'INSTRUCT THE COMMAND SHIP TO SCAN THE AREA.'

The Doctor laughed softly. 'It won't be that easy to find the TARDIS,' he said. 'It's designed to blend in with its surroundings, to come and go like a whisper in the night.'

'TARDIS LOCATED,' grated the Command Dalek as it received the response signal from the *Exterminator*. 'GRID COORDINATES TWELVE-ZERO-NINE-GAMMA.'

'Ouch,' said the Doctor.

'MOVE!'

The Daleks glided effortlessly over the scrubby earth, leaving little trails of dust floating behind them in the wake of their gravity repulsors, as they marched their prisoners into the town.

'Never did like this dump,' muttered Cuttin' Edge, kicking at the dust. 'Back end of nowhere and smells like it too.'

'Stella said it reeked of death,' noted Bowman. 'I think I see what she meant now.'

'We're not dead yet,' the Doctor reminded them.

'CEASE TALKING!' ordered a nearby Dalek.

'I trust you have a plan,' whispered Bowman after a few minutes.

'Who, me?' The Doctor shook his head. 'Nah. Have you?'

'Not a clue.'

'At least we're thinking along the same lines, then.'

They arrived at the TARDIS soon enough. The old police box was waiting for them at the end of the little alley where it had originally materialised several days earlier.

'Is that it?' asked Cuttin' Edge, disappointed. 'The Daleks have come all the way here for *that*?'

'It may not look like much, but... oh, forget it.' The Doctor brushed some dust off the doors and regarded his ship sadly. 'What do they know?'

Dalek X glided forward. 'THIS TARDIS WILL PROVIDE THE CONTROL SYSTEM FOR THE ARKHEON THRESHOLD! SUMMON THE TEMPORAL RESEARCH TEAM!'

Moments later a number of Dalek scientists descended and approached the police box. Their eyes glowed hungrily. 'OPEN IT!' demanded the leader.

'Say please,' the Doctor said. 'Oh, sorry, I forgot. That word isn't in the Dalek vocabulary, is it? Along with "thank you", "joke" and "blancmange". You lot must be *so* miserable.'

'STOP WASTING TIME,' said Dalek X menacingly. 'OPEN THE TARDIS.'

'All right, all right.' The Doctor fished in his pocket for the key. Then he tried another pocket. Hurriedly he went through all his pockets, looking more and more worried. 'I can't find it!' he said. 'The TARDIS key – it's gone...'

'BLAST OPEN THE DOORS,' ordered the Command Dalek.

'NEGATIVE!' Dalek X countermanded. 'THE TARDIS IS PROTECTED BY A TEMPORAL FORCE FIELD. DALEK WEAPONRY WILL NOT PENETRATE THE SHIELDING. IT MUST BE OPENED WITH THE CORRECT KEY!'

The Doctor was still checking and double-checking his

pockets, handing various bits and pieces to Bowman and Cuttin' Edge in an effort to minimise the clutter. 'I don't understand it…' he complained. 'How could I lose the TARDIS key? I've *never* lost it!'

'Hurry!' ordered Dalek X. 'The TARDIS must be opened!'

'It's not that simple,' the Doctor insisted. 'It's a triple-curtain trimonic lock. It's got twenty-seven different tumblers in four separate dimensions. If I don't find the key, *I'm* absolutely stuck, never mind you.'

There was a ridiculous few seconds while Bowman, Cuttin' Edge, Koral and all the assembled and various Daleks watched the Doctor going through his pockets one last time.

'It's no good,' he said eventually, slumping in defeat.

Dalek X was starting to twitch. 'Where did you last have it?'

'I don't know.' The Doctor suddenly leapt up straight with a sharp cry. 'Wait! I know! It was *here* – on Hurala. I was trapped in one of the cellars down below. I must have dropped it there!'

'You are lying,' stated Dalek X.

'No, honestly!' The Doctor looked at Bowman and Cuttin' Edge. 'Don't you remember? You had to open the door to the cellar. I'd been locked in by an automated trap.'

'He's right,' said Cuttin' Edge.

The Doctor looked earnestly from one Dalek to another. 'We were all chased off the planet by a Dalek scout team,' he explained.

'It's true,' said Koral. 'We had to run for our lives.'

The Command Dalek turned to Dalek X. 'There is a report from a Dalek scout unit that several humanoids were recently discovered here and pursued. They match the description of these humanoids.'

'That's it,' nodded the Doctor. 'It was a close thing, too. I didn't exactly have time to check my pockets properly before I left.'

'One of our crew was killed by a Dalek,' added Bowman darkly. 'We were rather preoccupied with her at the time.'

'WHERE IS THE KEY NOW?' asked Dalek X.

'It must still be in that cellar,' said the Doctor carefully. 'Wait here, I'll go and get it.'

He started off but Dalek X stopped him with his sucker arm. 'HALT! YOU ARE NOT PERMITTED TO LEAVE.'

'OK. Why don't we all go?'

'I WILL LEAD THE WAY.'

'Of course. After you. It's that way.' The Doctor pointed. 'The more the merrier – we'll stand a better chance of finding it then.'

Dalek X led, with the Command Dalek and the elite guards behind. The Doctor, Bowman, Koral and Cuttin' Edge brought up the rear with a number of assault Daleks. They filed into the building that housed the Lodestar's computer core. The Doctor recalled his first trip in here, when he had been investigating the dormant computer system and allowing his sense of curiosity to get him into trouble again. There was a metal stairwell leading down deep beneath the surface.

The Doctor turned to Dalek X and pulled an apologetic, slightly embarrassed face. 'Sorry. Stairs.'

'ELEVATE,' commanded Dalek X. He and the other Daleks started to lift off the ground slightly, floating down the steps after the Doctor and his friends. It was an awkward journey in such a confined space, but the Daleks managed the descent with irritating ease. A couple of them ventured out into the space between the stairwells, lowering themselves slowly down while keeping careful watch on the prisoners.

Cuttin' Edge was limping badly, and one of the Daleks watched his painful progress with great attention.

'What you lookin' at?' asked Cuttin' Edge. He had stopped for a rest, flexing his swollen knees and grimacing. Nearby a number of heavy chains rattled and clanked as the others filed slowly past. The chains were still attached to ancient pieces of machinery, left behind by the station's original owners.

'MOVE!' ordered the Dalek.

'When I'm ready,' said Cuttin' Edge. 'My legs are still sore after you lot shot me.' He started to pull himself up using some of the chains, his biceps bulging as he allowed the chain to take his weight. He looked back at the Dalek, which had remained stationary, floating next to the steps.

'Wait a second,' said Cuttin' Edge quietly. Such was the tone of his voice that everyone else on the stairs stopped to look back at him. The Doctor, Bowman and Koral had reached a landing where there were a number of narrow maintenance hatches. Cuttin' Edge glanced down at his companions and smiled at them.

'What is it, Cuttin' Edge?' asked Bowman. 'You're holding us up.'

'I know this guy,' said Cuttin' Edge, pointing at the Dalek. 'I recognise his itty-bitty eyestalk tag.'

The Dalek said nothing.

'You're the one that killed my pal Scrum,' Cuttin' Edge said. His tone was serious, quiet. 'You shot him down in cold blood just to make a point.'

Still the Dalek said nothing.

'Scrum was my best friend,' Cuttin Edge said. 'I ain't never had a friend before him.'

'Hey, kid…' said Bowman. He sounded worried. There was a grim light in Cuttin' Edge's eyes that only he could see.

Cuttin' Edge held up a hand for Bowman to be quiet. His attention was still fully focused on the Dalek. 'I made a promise,' he said. 'I said I'd get you for that. And I meant it.'

'PROCEED,' the Dalek ordered, gesturing with its gunstick for Cuttin' Edge to carry on down the stairs.

Cuttin' Edge had been holding himself up by the chains. Now, with explosive force, he suddenly moved. He wrenched the chains off the wall, looping them around the Dalek's head and yanking it tight with one huge jerk, forcing the eyestalk hard up against its armoured housing. The Dalek squawked and pulled back, its balance shifting slightly.

Bowman started back up the steps to help, but the Doctor caught hold of his arm fiercely. 'No!'

'Cuttin' Edge!'

'HALT!' The Daleks on the stairwell were also starting to turn, but there wasn't much room to manoeuvre.

Cuttin' Edge, his teeth bared in a savage grin, kicked out at the machinery attached to the chains. It flipped over the stair rail and plunged heavily down into the darkness. The chain snapped taut and the Dalek was suddenly pulled downwards after it, tipping over, the blue glow from its underside strobing across the walls. With a terrible clatter, the machinery, the Dalek and the chains tumbled down the stair well. Then the Dalek struck another that had been rising up from below to help, and together they banged and crashed their way down into the shadows.

'EXTERMINATE!' screeched Dalek X. His blaster ray found Cuttin' Edge and lit him up for all to see, bones glowing, head back. He clenched his teeth and refused to scream, his eyes staying wide open in their sockets. Then he reached out, grabbing the nearest Dalek in both arms. The paralysing neutronic flare engulfed the Dalek as well and there was a startled metallic yell from within.

The extermination beam ceased abruptly. The Dalek dropped to the steps with a loud clang as its elevation unit failed and it started to topple down the stairs, threatening to knock the others down like skittles. They were forced to levitate higher, moving clear of their stricken comrade as it bounced and banged down the stairs, dragging Cuttin' Edge's dead body with it.

'This way!' yelled the Doctor, grabbing Bowman and Koral and hauling them across the landing towards the maintenance ducts. He kicked open a hatch and pushed them through. 'Move! Hurry!'

They tumbled into a narrow passage, pitch black and full of dust. They ran through a curtain of sticky cobwebs, dislodging spiders as big as hands.

Bowman crashed into a solid wall and swore. Koral dragged him away, pushing him to the left, along another narrow passage. Bowman's shoulders banged and jarred along the rough walls, his legs scraping against pipes and electrical ducting. Eventually they fell down a step into a small, rectangular bay. The Doctor switched on a pocket torch and checked they were all right.

'What the hell—' began Bowman, coughing up a lungful of dust.

'Service hatches,' said the Doctor, sweeping the torch beam around. They could see old, discarded tools and junction boxes covered in spiders' webs. 'Maintenance ducts. You know the kind of thing. Used by robots to help keep the place running in the old days. Luckily for us the access tunnels are too narrow for Daleks.'

'But Cuttin' Edge…' began Koral. 'Why did he do that…?'

'He saw where we were,' said Bowman. 'Standing right next to the hatches. He made a diversion so we could get away.'

'It cost him his life,' Koral said numbly.

'Then let's not waste it,' said the Doctor.

Bowman looked carefully at him. 'You've got a plan, haven't you?'

The Doctor grinned widely. 'Oh, yes! Do I have a plan!'

Neither Bowman nor Koral could manage a smile in return; they were still in a state of shock after Cuttin' Edge's sacrifice. But they both felt a surge of hope.

'There is one small snag, though,' the Doctor warned them. 'The plan does rely on us staying alive.'

'We're trapped underground with a squad of angry Daleks on our tails,' Bowman noted.

The Doctor winked at him. 'I never said it was going to be easy.'

Chapter
Twenty-Three

Dalek X did not spare a glance at the dead Dalek as it crashed down the stairwell, dragging the human's corpse with it. No Dalek was capable of lamenting a loss or wasting time rueing an error, the Inquisitor General even less so.

He was, however, furious. And anger was something that every Dalek knew.

'THE DOC-TOR HAS ESCAPED!' exclaimed Dalek X. 'INITIATE EMERGENCY TRACKING SCAN!'

Two Daleks approached the maintenance hatches. One of them was an assault Dalek, and it immediately began to cut away a large section of the wall around the nearest hatch. The other extended its sucker arm, scanning the dark recess beyond.

The Command Dalek had descended alongside Dalek X. 'TEMPORAL RESEARCH TEAM ARE STILL UNABLE TO PENETRATE THE TARDIS.'

'WE NEED THE DOC-TOR! HE MUST BE FOUND!'

The Dalek scanning the maintenance tunnel swivelled its head around. 'HUMANOID LIFE FORMS TRACED IN STATION SUPERSTRUCTURE,' it reported. 'THEY ARE FOLLOWING THE MAINTENANCE CONDUITS.'

'ASSEMBLE ALL SEARCH UNITS!' ordered Dalek X. 'SEEK! LOCATE! EXTERMINATE!'

The Doctor, Bowman and Koral moved through the tunnels. They wanted to move quickly, but it was difficult in the darkness. The space was claustrophobically narrow, and they kept snagging clothes and skin on sharp, oily ledges and bundles of wire.

'So what's the plan?' asked Bowman, bringing up the rear. He couldn't see anything apart from the jerky movement of torchlight up ahead as the Doctor and Koral struggled on.

'I brought the Daleks to Hurala for a good reason,' replied the Doctor, his voice echoing dully along the conduit. 'And it wasn't the TARDIS. That was just the lure – Dalek X is so greedy for success I knew he'd come here if I gave him a good enough reason. But this place was a refuelling station, remember. There's a number of immense astronic energy piles buried underground. Chances are there is still a lot of residual energy in them – it's impossible to fully drain the tanks.'

'Astronic fuel is extremely volatile,' Bowman noted. 'So we're effectively sitting on a giant bomb.'

'A *ginormous* bomb,' agreed the Doctor. 'If we can find a way to detonate it, the explosion would not only destroy Dalek X and all his mates, but the Command Saucer and support vessels as well.'

'That would make for quite a dent in the Dalek war machine in this sector of the galaxy,' Bowman realised.

'So hurrah for Hurala,' the Doctor said.

'But it is a suicide mission, surely,' said Koral. 'We will not survive the blast either.'

The Doctor avoided a direct reply, suddenly exclaiming, 'Aha! Here we are…' as he emerged into a wider access area. It was a small chamber, dimly lit by a number of low-level phosphorous strips, and at last they could stand up straight. Bowman stretched, his joints creaking, but he was careful to avoid meeting Koral's gaze.

'If we must lose our own lives to defeat the Daleks,' she said, 'then so be it. We must avenge the deaths of Stella, Scrum and Cuttin' Edge.'

'I'm hoping it won't come to that,' said the Doctor. He took out his sonic screwdriver. 'First things first, though. Let's find the fuel silo controls. They can't be far.'

As the Doctor began to focus the screwdriver and scan for the control systems, Bowman checked some equipment stacked against one of the chamber walls. There were a number of tools lying around, presumably left by the original contractors who had built the Lodestar station. They were old and dirty and forgotten, but some of them still had functioning power packs.

'Listen,' hissed Koral suddenly. She held up her hand for silence and the Doctor snapped off the sonic screwdriver.

They all heard the distant sound of Dalek voices grating out orders. The harsh words reverberated through the metal tunnels. Echoing, far away, but clearly drawing closer, they heard metallic cries of 'SEEK! LOCATE! EXTERMINATE!'

The Doctor looked serious. 'We're gonna have to fight. We can't let them stop us.'

'But we have no guns,' Koral said. 'How can we fight?'

'Guns are not the only weapons,' said Bowman, with the slightest of smiles at the Doctor. He lifted a heavy piece of equipment, blowing a thick layer of dust off its control module. It was shaped like a large, two-handed power drill. 'This is an ion bolter. It uses focused particle streams to propel ion bolts through plate steel. Crude but effective.'

The Doctor searched quickly among some of the other discarded equipment and came up with a device that looked like a heavy steel hubcap. 'And this is a magnetronic condenser.' He tossed the metal disc towards Bowman, who caught it easily. 'Could be useful.'

There was a loud bang and crash from the adjoining tunnel and suddenly part of the wall began to glow a fierce cherry red. 'HUMANOIDS LOCATED!' grated a voice on the other side. 'WALL PENETRATION IN TEN RELS!'

'Move!' said the Doctor, leading the way out of the chamber.

The exit tunnel was much wider than the service ducts, and the Daleks would not have a problem following them. They all heard the wall caving in behind them.

A pair of assault Daleks glided through the burning gap. They scanned the surrounding area and set off in pursuit. 'SEEK! LOCATE!'

The Doctor scrambled out of the tunnel onto a wide metal gantry overlooking a vast, black chasm. Koral and Bowman ran straight into him, and the three of them peered over the edge of an old, rusted railing. They could see nothing but blackness.

'Empty silo,' said the Doctor, his voice echoing madly in the darkness. 'No use. Come on!'

They ran to the left, heading around the curved inside wall of the vast silo, just as the Daleks came into view behind them. 'VISUAL CONTACT ESTABLISHED,' reported the first.

'HALT!' yelled the second Dalek. 'SURRENDER! YOU ARE PRISONERS OF THE DALEKS! SURRENDER OR YOU WILL BE EXTERMINATED!'

'Hurry!' shouted the Doctor as he raced around the perimeter. 'Run!'

The Daleks followed them, trying to manoeuvre for a clear shot. One Dalek rose up from the platform and flew after them, screeching instructions.

Bowman whirled, a look of grim intent on his face. With a heavy grunt, he hurled the magnetron condenser at the flying Dalek like a discus. It whirred through the air and hit the armour casing with a satisfying clang, clamping tight. The Dalek just had time to lower its eyestalk, attempting to locate the device on its body, when the condenser activated and a low whine started to emanate from the disc.

'UNDER ATTACK!' squawked the Dalek. 'LOCALISED MAGNETIC FIELD CONDENSING!'

Suddenly the Dalek imploded, as if crushed by a giant, invisible fist. It was squeezed so hard and so fast that the creature inside was forced through the splits in the metal armour. It squirted away into the darkness in a screaming fountain of slime.

The second Dalek watched the remains of its comrade plummet into the shadows. Then it swivelled its eyestalk back to the fugitives. 'HALT OR YOU WILL BE EXTERMINATED!'

But Bowman was already running again, hurrying after Koral. The Doctor was sprinting with the sonic screwdriver held out in front of him. The tip glowed a brilliant blue and the doorway ahead of them swung open on old, grinding hinges.

They dived through, and the Doctor hit the deck, rolled, came up and fired the sonic screwdriver back at the hatch in one motion. The door rolled shut just as the Dalek reached it.

'Come on!' The Doctor scrambled down a stairwell, Koral close behind.

Bowman followed, a little slower because he was carrying the ion bolter. The muscles of his shoulders and neck stood out like cables, shining with sweat, but his teeth were bared in a savage grin of delight.

The stairwell went down three levels and then they were in a wide, curved corridor. There were several doors set in the walls.

The Doctor slowed to a jog, scanning with the sonic screwdriver. 'Not far now… should be just through here.'

He opened one of the doors and they went through.

'This silo is still in use,' the Doctor said. 'At least, it still contains astronic fuel. The controls system can be accessed from that panel over there.'

He led the way across a wide gantry that stretched towards a large, central dais suspended over what looked like a bottomless pit. The acrid stench of astronic fuel rose up in sickening waves from far below.

'The Daleks will be closing in,' Koral said. 'They'll signal our position and converge on this spot. We'll be trapped.'

'Yes,' said the Doctor. 'I know.'

'Never mind that,' ordered Bowman. 'Let's get to work.'

The Doctor busied himself at the controls, popping open an access panel and delving into the circuitry beneath. 'The Daleks will get here any minute,' he said quickly. His brows furrowed as he concentrated on the work. 'I've got to bypass the override and set up a feedback loop on the fuel containment field. It'll take – ooh, too long probably – so I'd appreciate it if you could buy me just a little time…'

'You've got it,' said Bowman. He grabbed hold of Koral's hand. 'Come with me.'

The Daleks were tearing the Lodestar station apart looking for the Doctor and his friends. The Command Dalek barked out orders to several different search parties as they spread through the refuelling complex.

Dalek X floated in the centre of an empty silo. His

eyestalk revolved slowly, examining his surroundings, analysing, calculating, extrapolating. He scanned the structure using X-ray vision, infra-red, thermal imaging, spectronic diffusion. He compared the information with data absorbed from the sensor apparatus in his sucker arm. Then he downloaded a complete schematic of the Lodestar station from the *Exterminator* for comparison.

Less than a minute later, Dalek X moved across the silo and examined the access door. It had been locked using some kind of sonic recalibration code. Dalek X extended his suction arm and manipulated the locking mechanism, burning through the simple computer it contained using several million potential combinations in less than a second. The door slid slowly open.

Dalek X knew where the Doctor would be. He knew what he would try to do. He realised that he had been tricked into coming here and that the Doctor would attempt to destroy him and the *Exterminator*. This was a desperate ploy and doomed to failure.

But a deep, overriding hatred boiled inside the black and gold armour. Dalek X was determined to stop the Doctor, to destroy him at all costs.

And he would do this alone.

The access gantry was a wide, thick construction with metal floor grilles covering a ditch full of cables and pipes. Bowman prised up one of the lattice panels and jumped into the narrow channel beneath, beckoning Koral to join him. Together they crouched down in the gap and Bowman slid the grille back into place over their heads.

It was cramped and uncomfortable but they could see clearly up through the flooring.

'The Daleks will have to come this way,' whispered

Bowman. 'We stay here and attack when the first one passes overhead. You strike first, disabling it. Then I'll do the rest.'

Koral opened her mouth to ask a question but a grating, metallic voice suddenly echoed across the silo.

'DOC-TOR!' The word was spat across the void with cold purpose.

The Doctor looked up from his work, sonic screwdriver clamped between his teeth. He raised his eyebrows and gave a little wave when he saw Dalek X approaching along the access gantry.

'STAND AWAY FROM THE SILO CONTROL SYSTEM,' ordered Dalek X.

The Doctor removed the sonic screwdriver from his mouth. 'Sorry! Bit busy right now. Why don't you come back a little later?'

'STAND AWAY OR YOU WILL BE EXTERMINATED.'

'I wouldn't open fire in here if I were you,' the Doctor cautioned. 'Astronic fuel vapour – boom!'

'STAND AWAY!'

The Doctor turned his back on the Dalek, working with feverish haste at the controls with the screwdriver. 'I'll be right with you,' he called over his shoulder. 'Just wait there a sec.'

'DOC-TOR!'

The Doctor let out a huge, impatient sigh and turned around. 'Look, what is it? I've already told you, I'm *busy*.' He waggled the sonic screwdriver to show how busy he was.

'YOU HAVE THREE SECONDS TO STAND AWAY FROM THOSE CONTROLS BEFORE I EXTERMINATE YOU!'

'Don't be daft. Exterminate me and you'll never get the TARDIS.'

'WE WILL BREAK INTO THE TIME VORTEX WITHOUT IT!'

'I doubt that.'

'THEN WE WILL FIND A WAY TO PENETRATE THE TARDIS DEFENCE SYSTEMS WITHOUT YOU. DALEKS ARE NEVER DEFEATED!'

The Doctor's eyes widened. 'Wanna bet?'

The grating slid away beneath Dalek X, and Koral lunged upwards, claws extended. She ripped into the antigravity mechanism under the Dalek's base, tearing through the metal and plastic in a shower of angry sparks. There was a flash of energy and the Dalek shuddered, visibly sinking as his power to levitate faded.

'MOBILITY IMPAIRED!' shrieked Dalek X as he crunched down heavily onto the walkway. His gun and sucker arm waved around in sudden panic as he searched for his assailant. 'I CANNOT MOVE!'

Bowman rose up behind the Dalek, clutching the ion bolter. He rested the barrel against the neck grille as the head spun around and Dalek X's eye focused on him.

'HUMAN ASSAILANT!' cried Dalek X, his voice rising in pitch. His shoulder section began to turn, bringing the gun-stick round to bear on Bowman.

Bowman held the Dalek's gaze for a long moment, leaning in so that his face filled the creature's vision. Then, very carefully, he said one word: '*Exterminate.*'

And pulled the trigger on the bolt gun.

The gun was set to automatic. A succession of heavy ion bolts rammed through the barrel and into the Dalek's neck.

'ALERT! ALERT! CASING BREACHED!' yelled Dalek X, shuddering as each bolt shot home. 'FORCE SHIELDS INOPERATIVE!'

Smoke and flames began to spew from the ruptured grille and the living thing inside suddenly let out a piercing yell of agony. Bowman switched position, ramming the bolt gun against a different section of the neck, and squeezed the activator. More ion bolts rattled into the Dalek and the whole machine seemed to shake under the impact. Dalek X's cries rose above the crackle and spit of the fire, and Bowman was forced to step back as the skin on his hands began to burn.

But the ion bolter was empty. Every round had been stamped into the Dalek's neck section, disrupting the electrical controls and skewering the creature inside. With a snarl of disgust, Bowman raised his boot and pushed the blazing Dalek X off the gantry. He tipped and then fell, trailing smoke and a bloodcurdling shriek until he disappeared into the darkness.

'Ex-Dalek,' muttered Bowman, dropping the empty bolt gun after it. Then he sank to his knees, exhausted, blood pouring from his leg.

Koral crawled across and helped him up. 'We're not finished yet,' she told him. 'Come on…'

'Good work,' said the Doctor as they joined him by the controls. 'Clever, too. The underside of a Dalek can't be properly force-shielded because of the gravity repellers. Take those out and you'll short-circuit the rest of the defensive fields. Well done.'

'Never thought I'd be the one to KO Dalek X,' grunted Bowman.

'Well now we've got the chance to KO his Command Ship and every other Dalek here as well. I'm almost done.' The Doctor made a last adjustment to the wiring on the control panel and then snapped the access hatch shut. He clicked off the sonic screwdriver. 'There.'

'Will it be enough?' Bowman asked. 'I mean the *Exterminator* is one big ship, Doctor.'

'You'll be able to see the explosion from the other end of the solar system,' the Doctor promised. 'Believe me, it's more than big enough.' He paused. 'But there is a problem.'

Koral looked up, recognising a grave note in the Doctor's voice. 'What?'

'The detonation relies on the safety override failing to function. I can't do that by remote control, and nor can I set a timer on it.' He looked at them grimly. 'Someone will have to stay and hold the manual override lever down until the silo reaches critical.' He tapped a metal lever on the control panel. 'It's a failsafe measure.'

'We knew this was a suicide mission,' said Bowman.

Koral agreed. 'What are we waiting for? Let's do it.'

Still the Doctor hesitated. 'By my reckoning, the TARDIS is parked directly up there...' The Doctor pointed upwards. 'And... well, we could have made a run for it. Just.'

'You still can,' said Bowman. 'I'll hold the failsafe lever. You can go with Koral.'

'What? No!' said Koral, horrified.

'I'm injured anyway,' Bowman said. 'Get going with the Doctor, and leave me here.'

'No!' Koral argued, stricken. 'I will not leave you! The Doctor can—'

'He already risked his life once for me, Koral. And anyway, only he knows how to fly that ship of his. At least this way you and he both get to survive. Now go on, get going...'

But Koral was having none of it. 'No! You go! I'll stay, I'll hold the lever! I won't let you die, Bowman! *I love you!*'

The last three words were blurted out. Bowman gaped at her but then clamped his mouth shut. The Doctor looked desperately from one to the other.

Then Bowman grasped Koral by the shoulders and kissed her, hard. 'I love you too,' he growled. 'Which is why there is no question of me going while you stay here. What would be the point?'

'Um, excuse me…' said the Doctor.

'No!' Koral choked. She held Bowman's face in her hands and looked up imploringly. 'No, I can't let you go, not now…'

'Running out of time here…' warned the Doctor.

Bowman rubbed a tear from Koral's face with his thumb. 'Don't cry. You'll set the Doctor off – you know what a wimp he is.'

'What?' The Doctor frowned.

'See, he's cryin' already…'

Koral looked at the Doctor, and Bowman quickly shifted his hand to grip her neck and shoulder between his strong fingers. He squeezed on the nerve junction there and Koral stiffened, suddenly losing consciousness. Bowman caught her as she fell, then, hoisting her into his arms, held her limp body out to the Doctor. 'Here – take her and go.'

'Bowman…'

'At least this way she survives!' Bowman's voice was ragged with emotion. 'And so do you. Now go!'

The Doctor took Koral in his arms. 'I'll look after her.'

'You'd better.'

There was a clang from the far side of the silo and a group of Daleks filed through the doorway. The Doctor turned, hesitated for a moment. Looked back at Bowman.

'Give us as long as you can,' he said.

Bowman gripped the failsafe lever. 'Get outta here.'

*

The Doctor hurried across the gantry to the far side of the silo and started up the steps. It was hard going with Koral in his arms but he was determined to escape. He owed Jon Bowman that much at least. Koral was regaining consciousness, murmuring as he pounded up the metal steps, heaving for breath.

At the top he lost his footing and collapsed, crashing to the floor. He held on to Koral but she had suddenly woken up to what was happening. She struggled against him as they got up. 'Let me go! Let me go back to him!' she cried.

'No! Koral! You've got to run! We only have seconds left!'

'Bowman!' screamed Koral.

The Doctor held her back. 'It's too late! We've run out of time! He wants you to live, and that's the least you can do!'

He dragged her along the corridor but she fought him every step. Eventually he turned and grabbed her by the shoulders, shaking her. 'Stop fighting me! Think what Bowman would have wanted! If you go back now we all die. Is that what you want? Is that what you think he'd want?'

She sobbed, then allowed herself to be pulled along after him. The Doctor opened the door at the end of the passage and they burst out into the cold Hurala night. There were stars above them and, directly ahead, the TARDIS, big, bold and blue. The Doctor almost yelled with delight and relief.

The Daleks glided across the gantry. Bowman watched them come, a grim smile on his bloodied lips. They hadn't even seen him yet, leaning over the control panel, one hand gripping the failsafe lever. Indicator lights on the controls were flashing intermittently, lighting his face spasmodically with a hellish red glow.

'ALERT!' screeched the first Dalek. 'HUMAN PRISONER IDENTIFIED!'

The Doctor and Koral staggered towards the TARDIS.

'HALT! EXTERMINATE!'

They heard the Daleks behind them. They heard the shrill whine of the extermination beams and the alleyway flickered with light. The Doctor zigzagged, pushing Koral ahead of him. The air was filled with a sharp, hot tang of ozone.

'Run!' the Doctor bellowed.

'What about the key?'

'What about it?' The Doctor held up his hand and the key flashed as he inserted it into the TARDIS lock. The police box doors snapped open and they both shot straight inside.

The Daleks converged on Bowman.

He stood, unsteady but unbeaten. One hand remained on the lever, sticky with blood. He grinned defiantly at the Daleks as they approached.

'So long, suckers.'

And he pulled the lever.

Instantly the whole world seemed to shake, as if a giant hammer had laid a deathly blow deep inside the planet. There was a distant, heavy reverberation from far below, a growing roar as an unstoppable chain reaction began.

The Daleks were vibrating, jerking around as the entire Lodestar station began to shudder with a terrible finality. Pieces of rusting metal clattered from the ceiling and the gantry gave a loud, ominous crack. Far below, a green light suddenly flared into life.

'EMERGENCY! EMERGENCY!' cried one of the Daleks. 'RETREAT!'

Bowman just laughed.

The Doctor rushed madly around the TARDIS control console. There was no time for Koral to ask any questions – like why there was such a huge chamber contained inside such a small box – and so she was forced to just watch him work. She gripped the railing, looking all around her, numb with the realisation that everything had just changed for her, more than she could ever comprehend.

'No time, no time,' the Doctor muttered, working feverishly at the controls. His teeth were gritted and his eyes wild. The ground was shaking, rattling the metal floor. Suddenly the Doctor let out a huge, 'Ha!' and released the handbrake.

The central column erupted into bright turquoise light and an uncanny groaning noise filled the chamber.

'Oh yeah!' shouted the Doctor. 'Come on!'

The Daleks were rattling and squawking. The bright green light – accompanied by a deep, thunderous roar – suddenly increased in intensity as the chain reaction ignited the astronic fuel below. A huge gust of wind whipped up from the depths of the silo, but Bowman kept his eyes wide open.

He'd never backed down from anything in his life. He wanted to see death coming.

But what he actually saw was a blue box materialising out of thin air, right in front of him. It was difficult to see properly in the emerald glare of the oncoming explosion, but it looked like...

The police box door opened, and there was Koral, standing inside, holding out her hand to him.

The Command Dalek saw what was happening and swivelled its gun around. '⟨EXTERMINATE⟩!'

With a gasp Bowman launched himself through the TARDIS door. It crashed shut behind him and the Dalek blast hit nothing but empty air as the entire station was instantly and catastrophically vaporised.

The explosion ripped the planet open. The Lodestar station itself disappeared in the initial blast – a stone, metal and plastic town one moment, a gaseous mass of atoms the next. The exit wound spewed a glowing, fiery stream of astronic radiation straight up into the atmosphere. Fragments of the deep silos and rock were hurled up like a hundred thousand tonnes of shrapnel, propelled at supersonic speeds. The force fields of the Dalek Command Saucer hovering over the station absorbed the first wave, but they could not withstand the point-blank onslaught of the astronic blast.

The *Exterminator* took the blast amidships, crunching under the impact, flaring with a thousand secondary ignitions as the neutronic power source at its centre overloaded. The ship was ruptured, disembowelled, fire spurting from the rim. And then the vast saucer tipped, slowly at first, and slid into the broiling chasm below.

The crash released final detonations which caught the support ships in a second chain reaction. Each exploded in a bright star of energy, popping like flashbulbs as the *Exterminator* crashed.

The astronic flare would be seen from seven light years away.

CHAPTER
TWENTY-FOUR

It was a glorious day on planet Earth. High above the silver towers and walkways of London, flying cars and distant spacecraft crossed a clear blue sky. The sun glinted on the golden spires of Westminster, just visible inside its protective force bubble.

The Doctor was standing by the TARDIS, waiting for Bowman and Koral. They'd been inside Earth Command Headquarters for the best part of a day, and he had agreed to meet them here. Part of him had wanted to just drop them off and go, dematerialise and disappear, for ever and a day. Pop up some place else, in another era, a million miles and years away. See what happened.

But something compelled him to stay and see this through. Something at the back of his mind that he couldn't quite put his finger on. A lingering sense of comradeship, perhaps. Or maybe the fact that Bowman and Koral had both lost dear friends in this adventure, and the Doctor remained their only link to them now. Shared memories and experiences. Friendship.

The park was busy. The summer sun had brought the locals out. Some things never changed. Men and women strolled along the walkways, warm and relaxed, taking a tiny break from the stresses and strains of their working lives. Children played on the grass. The Doctor was dimly aware of their high, excited voices calling out to each other in pretend battle: cries of 'Exterminate! Exterminate!' and

'You're dead!' followed by the inevitable 'No I'm not. You missed!'

He smiled and shook his head, thinking that the human race would never end its love affair with war.

'I thought you'd be long gone,' said a rough voice behind him.

Bowman was there, standing on crutches, rugged and scarred and old. Koral was with him, one arm linked through his.

'Nah,' the Doctor said. 'There's something about Earth. I just can't seem to stay away.'

'Come on,' Bowman growled. 'What's the real reason? Don't tell us you weren't tempted to just take off in that TARDIS thing. What did you stay for?'

The Doctor shrugged. 'I dunno. Unfinished business, I suppose. How did it go?'

'Pretty good. The Dalek fleet is in complete disarray. The loss of the *Exterminator* has knocked them right back, along with any plans to use time-travel technology. The Supreme Dalek's Temporal Research Team bit the dust along with everything else on Hurala.'

'That's good. And the prison?'

'Earth Command has a squadron of ships on its way to seize Arkheon and liberate the prisoners.'

The Doctor watched the children playing. 'That could be quite a battle.'

'Yeah.'

'They asked Bowman to lead the mission,' said Koral. She pulled him closer. 'But he refused.'

'I'm too old for that kinda thing now.' There was a slightly pained, regretful look on the old soldier's face. 'That's what Koral says, anyway. Besides, I've got better things to be doing with my time.'

'He's taking me to meet his parents,' said Koral.

The Doctor laughed. 'You old dog.'

'Gotta start tying up some loose ends,' Bowman said. 'Earth Command's given me a full pardon. Seems I've pulled their fat out of the fire again. Now it's time to see my folks.'

'I'm glad.'

No one felt the need to mention Stella, Scrum and Cuttin' Edge. Each knew they were in their thoughts and in the quietness behind the smiles.

'Well, talking of loose ends...' began the Doctor, 'I've a few of my own to tie up before I get the TARDIS back on the right time track.' He shook hands with Bowman and kissed Koral goodbye. Then, with a final, ironic salute, he turned and headed towards the TARDIS.

EPILOGUE

It was a forgotten world.

Dusty, torn and left in darkness. Nothing and no one ever came here.

Deep below the surface of Hurala, beneath the vast black crater where the Lodestar station had once stood, all was now quiet. The carnage was silent, and there was not a sign of life.

But deeper even than that, down in the caves, in a crevice beneath the mangled wreckage of the astronic fuel silo, was a clutter of black and gold debris. It was burnt and twisted and split, and it was all that remained of Dalek X. The life-support system was smashed, the containment tank fractured. Wires trailed towards the living creature where it lay on the rocks, twitching feebly in the darkness.

A light pulsed in the shadows. The Dalek's misty eye widened fractionally, disbelievingly. A loud wheezing and groaning noise filled the little cave as an old blue police box materialised in the gloom.

The Doctor stepped out wearing his long coat, the light from the console room spilling out across the writhing remains of the Inquisitor General.

'YOU... LOCATED... MY... TRANSMISSION...' the Dalek croaked.

'Yeah, that was easy.' The Doctor sat down on a rock. 'But there's no one else listening. You're finished. Arkheon is no more. The prisoners have been freed and the Daleks there all wiped out. Thanks to Space Major Bowman, of course. Earth Command is on the offensive. Your lines are in disarray. You're beaten.' He paused. 'Just thought you'd like to know.'

'THE SUPREME DALEK...'

'Oh, he's given you up for dead. Besides, I doubt he'd be in a forgiving mood if you did happen to turn up after all this. You're better off down here to be honest.'

'THE ARKHEON THRESHOLD?'

'Sealed. One of the advantages of being a Time Lord with a TARDIS. It's nice to be able to tie these loose ends up sometimes. The temporal fissure is gone. I put a stitch in time.'

'VERY... THOROUGH. YOUR VICTORY IS... TOTAL.'

'Almost.' The Doctor pursed his lips and frowned. 'There's still you, of course. Still here, still alive. You certainly know how to hang on, I'll give you that.'

'THE ASTRONIC RADIATION WILL KEEP ME ALIVE...'

'Yeah, I thought there was a smell.' The Doctor wrinkled his nose. 'Never mind. It won't do you much good, trapped down here. There's a communications seal around Hurala, part of the radiation quarantine. Five thousand years at least before anyone will hear your cries for help. But neither you nor your batteries will last that long, I'm afraid.'

'I WILL FIND A WAY.' Dalek X glared at the Doctor. 'I WILL SURVIVE! THE DALEKS ARE NEVER DEFEATED!'

The Doctor shook his head. 'You can never see it, can you? You just don't get it. Daleks are *always* defeated. Always. Because you never learn. You never accept the simple truth – that every other life form in the universe is *better* than you.'

'INCORRECT! DALEKS ARE THE SUPREME BEINGS!'

'There's not a life form in the universe that would volunteer to become a Dalek. Doesn't that tell you anything? Well, *doesn't* it?'

Dalek X did not reply.

The Doctor stood up and turned to leave.

'DOC-TOR!' gasped the Dalek. 'YOUR FAILURE TO DESTROY ME... WILL PROVE TO BE YOUR DOWNFALL. I WILL HUNT YOU DOWN...!'

'Yeah, well, good luck with that.' The Doctor paused in the TARDIS doorway, silhouetted in the golden light. His face was stony. 'Cos I'll be waiting.'

The TARDIS door clicked shut behind him and then the police box faded away.

And Dalek X was left to stare, unblinking, into the darkness.

ACKNOWLEDGEMENTS

My family, first and foremost – without whom this book wouldn't have been half so much fun to write, or so worthwhile. And my old mate Pete Stam – who never, ever believes that the book is going to be rubbish, no matter how much I try to warn him.

And, in no particular order – Justin Richards and Steve Tribe, and Russell T Davies, Steven Moffat and Gary Russell and all at Cardiff – for doing what they do, and doing it brilliantly. Thanks for asking me to write this one, and giving me the chance to play with the ultimate *Doctor Who* toy.

And while I'm on the subject of the Daleks, it is only right and proper that I offer my heartfelt thanks to Terry Nation and Raymond P. Cusick, and to all the other writers, designers, actors, artists and technicians who have helped contribute to Dalek mythology over the last forty-five years. Here's to you.

Finally, David Tennant – a *brilliant* Doctor, who will live on in the hearts and minds of kids everywhere for the rest of their lives.

Also available in the Doctor Who Monster Collection:

Touched by an Angel
Jonathan Morris
ISBN 978 1 849 90756 9

'The past is like a foreign country. Nice to visit, but you really wouldn't want to live there.'

In 2003, Rebecca Whitaker died in a road accident. Her husband Mark is still grieving. He receives a battered envelope, posted eight years earlier, containing a set of instructions with a simple message: 'You can save her.'

As Mark is given the chance to save Rebecca, it's up to the Doctor, Amy and Rory to save the whole world. Because this time the Weeping Angels are using history itself as a weapon.

An adventure featuring the Eleventh Doctor, as played by Matt Smith, and his companions Amy and Rory

Also available in the Doctor Who Monster Collection:

ILLEGAL ALIEN

MIKE TUCKER AND ROBERT PERRY

ISBN 978 1 849 90757 6

The Blitz is at its height. As the Luftwaffe bomb London,
Cody McBride, ex-pat American private eye, sees a sinister
silver sphere crash-land. He glimpses something emerging
from within. The military dismiss his account of events –
the sphere must be a new German secret weapon that has
malfunctioned in some way. What else could it be?

Arriving amid the chaos, the Doctor and Ace embark on a
trail that brings them face to face with hidden Nazi agents,
and encounter some very old enemies…

An adventure featuring the Seventh Doctor, as played by
Sylvester McCoy, and his companion Ace

Also available in the Doctor Who Monster Collection:

The Scales of Injustice
Gary Russell

ISBN 978 1 849 90780 4

When a boy goes missing and a policewoman starts drawing cave paintings, the Doctor suspects the Silurians are back. With the Brigadier distracted by questions about UNIT funding and problems at home, the Doctor swears his assistant Liz Shaw to secrecy and investigates alone.

But Liz has enquiries of her own, teaming up with a journalist to track down people who don't exist. What is the mysterious Glasshouse, and why is it so secret?

As the Silurians wake from their ancient slumber, the Doctor, Liz and the Brigadier are caught up in a conspiracy to exploit UNIT's achievements – a conspiracy that reaches deep into the heart of the British Government.

An adventure featuring the Third Doctor, as played by Jon Pertwee, his companion Liz Shaw and UNIT

Also available in the Doctor Who Monster Collection:

CORPSE MARKER
CHRIS BOUCHER
ISBN 978 1 849 90759 0

The Doctor and Leela arrive on the planet Kaldor, where
they find a society dependent on benign and obedient
robots. But they have faced these robots before, on a huge
Sandminer in the Kaldor desert, and know they are not
always harmless servants…

The only other people who know the truth are the three
survivors from that Sandminer – and now they are being
picked off one by one. The twisted genius behind that
massacre is dead, but someone is developing a new, deadlier
breed of robots. This time, unless the Doctor and Leela can
stop them, they really will destroy the world…

*An adventure featuring the Fourth Doctor, as played by Tom Baker,
and his companion Leela*

Also available in the Doctor Who Monster Collection:

THE SANDS OF TIME

JUSTIN RICHARDS

ISBN 978 1 849 90767 5

The Doctor is in Victorian London with Nyssa and Tegan – a city shrouded in mystery. When Nyssa is kidnapped in the British Museum, the Doctor and Tegan have to unlock the answers to a series of ancient questions.

Their quest leads them across continents and time as an ancient Egyptian prophecy threatens future England. To save Nyssa, the Doctor must foil the plans of the mysterious Sadan Rassul. But as mummies stalk the night, an ancient terror stirs in its tomb.

An adventure featuring the Fifth Doctor, as played by Peter Davison, and his companions Nyssa and Tegan